Foul Purity

Foul Purity

Lance Levens

RESOURCE *Publications* · Eugene, Oregon

FOUL PURITY

Resource Publications
An Imprint of Wipf and Stock Publishers
199 W. 8th Ave., Suite 3
Eugene, OR 97401

www.wipfandstock.com

PAPERBACK ISBN: 978-1-6667-3290-0
HARDCOVER ISBN: 978-1-6667-2708-1
EBOOK ISBN: 978-1-6667-2709-8

12/22/21

Chapter One

October, 2018
Ocopeeco, GA.
Pop 3,800

Pain Alpata, full-blooded Creek, squinted at a cluster of rocks on the fast river's far side. Something was snagged. Whatever it was, it swung out in an arch, the current seized it, swept it out even further and brought it back to pound the rocks and recommence the cycle. Back and forth. Seize, sweep and pound. Seize, sweep and pound. Mesmerized, Pain followed it, until he realized what was being pounded.

* * * *

Out of breath, he knocked on the police chief's door. A tall, broad-shouldered man answered, HB Alpata, thirty-eight, a trim reddish-brown beard, tight-fitting, starched jeans with creases showing, and a red and blue checkered, long sleeve shirt.

"Dad!" he said, "just making breakfast . . . "

"You need to come down to the river."

HB cocked his head. "The river?"

Spatula in hand, Rosie eased up behind her husband, followed by their son, Mico, with his cloth newspaper bag hanging on one shoulder. Nate the crow sat on his other.

It was 5:30 AM. Up on the hill, the kaolin plant was already lit up, spewing smoke and rumbling.

"What's the hurry?" Rosie asked.

"The Devil loves to make you hurry," Nate said.

Pain eyed the crow.

"Son, there's something in the river, maybe a body."

"Were you down at the shack?" HB said, lowering his voice.

Pain nodded.

1

Mico eyed Rosie and she slipped her arm around her son. They all knew about granddad's fixation on the shack.

"I'll get the truck," HB said, "Put the eggs in the oven, babe. Spud, get my wading boots from the closet, some rope, three big flashlights and a thermos of coffee. Oh, and the three prong grappling hook. It's in the jail cell."

They rode in HB's big red Ford 250 down the hill from their house, crossed River Street where there were already lights on at Clean Jeans, the wash-a-teria. Up on the hill a stream of cars headed toward the plant above the town, Ocopeeco, pop. 3,800.

HB turned off the road into the grass and headed to the river, glinting in the moonlight.

As he had done once a week for four years, Pain had been searching in and around the shack. On Oct. 25, 2014 Hesegadamassee, the Creek god of breath, summoned him there, as he had other places many times before: The good folk of Ocopeeco loved him for it. Pain Alpata, the Creek healer. But on that October day, he was called to the shack and found nothing. Now, when he inhaled, he breathed in shame. Someone suffered, maybe died, and he failed them.

At the riverbank, HB waded in with the grappling hook, the rope unspooling behind him. In the river in the moonlight, he resembled a Greek god, massive, powerful upper body wading into unknown waters. Mico held the rope's other end on the bank. HB could see the corpse, the shirt rock-snagged. The channel, just beyond, was ripping the cloth away and if it broke free, it would fly down the river and he'd have to go back to the house for his motorboat. He looked back: Pain, Rosie and Mico and Nate, the moon silhouetting them. This would be the first town tragedy since the year the kaolin foreman wrecked his truck on the highway and his brother, a bald, chubby Irish tenor, came down for the funeral from Nashville and sang a show-stopping version of "Abide with Me."

It was a man, face down, thick work boots, the cleats barely worn.

He wrapped the rope around his waist, slipped the hook under the body's belt, and cut the shirt free from the rock.

Ugh!

The rope cinched his gut. The water-logged load pulled deep and hard, yearned to run the river.

He waved to the others to pull, felt their surge, and dug in, but the weight dragged him forward. He weighed two-twenty, could bench press three-fifty, but the body was pulling him towards the channel.

He lost footing and floundered.

Mico dove in, reached the rock quickly and pushed back with his shoulder, but he had no leverage and nothing to stand on. The current whipped him around and was about to drag him away, so he wrapped his arms around the corpse. Only his head was visible.

The truck cranked up.

"We'll head it off at the Neck," Rosie yelled out the window. "Tell Mico to let it go on downstream."

But Mico wouldn't let go.

The body broke free into the channel, Mico clinging to a leg.

HB swam to the opposite bank, crawled out, ripped off his waders and his boots and sprinted into the tall grass. Rosie and Pain sped down River Street and to the bridge. They crossed it and a cloud of dust arose where they turned off the asphalt onto the dirt road towards the Neck.

The Chicken Neck was a bend in the river with a big sand bar. On weekends teenagers picnicked and drank beer and caroused on it.

HB raced through the tall grass, barefooted. Pain brought him here when he was little to learn about the Great Turtle who first emerged from the mud with the Twelve Clans on his back. At the same time his mom, an ex-Sister of Mercy, was driving him twice a week to St. Joseph's in Macon to catechism. At ten, he wasn't sure he was praying to God, the Father of Abraham, Isaac and Jacob or to the Creek version, Ibofanga.

Rosie and Pain got out of the truck and into the water, up to their chest, waiting.

Mico and the body approached, the body in front, two arms forward, two legs behind, a human battering ram.

"It's moving too fast!" Mico shouted.

HB hit the sand just as the body hit Rosie, knocking her towards the bank and shallower water, where she dug in, grabbing one arm. Behind her Pain embraced a leg and Mico swam under the shoulder, driving the body toward the bank. HB pulled the grappling hook from the truck, jumped in and raised it high and drove it hard into the human sponge with a squishy THUNK!

With the rope over his shoulder, he slogged toward the shore. The others pushed from behind until they dragged the dead man onto the sand.

Big Rig Scruggs, 275 lbs. of misogynist muscle, stabbed deep in the gut, his bowels streaming out like a squid's tentacles. He drove a kaolin truck, his huge frog-like head, his eyes, swollen shut.

The river reeked of almost methane and wet grass and exhuded a sigh like a monster exhaling as the group gathered around the great mound of flesh.

As Police Chief of Ocopeeco, HB was also its preacher. He retrieved his Book of Common Prayer from his glove compartment, knelt, crossed himself and read prayers for the dead. Water dripped from his beard onto the thin pages of his old, battered book.

Rosie said a prayer for Big Rig's three sons and his wife, Lurlene, who often wept and sang in the river. The townsfolk called her Weeping Woman.

Wiping her tears away, Rosie whispered: "People will say cruel things."

Still on his knees, shining a flashlight into the body's eyes, HB nodded. "They'll say this is punishment for abusing the boys."

Pain slipped his arm round Rosie's waist, beads round his neck, two eagle feathers in his long hair, one long braid down his shoulder. But it was his face that caught your eye. High cheeks, clear, hairless skin, a red dye circle around his left eye that went up above his forehead. His bundle of sabia, colorful god-invoking stones, tied to his belt.

Still dripping, Mico pulled his paper sack out of the back of the truck. "Dad, I'm late!"

"First, help us get the body in my truck."

HB backed his truck close and they lugged the corpse onto the flat bed. Nate hopped onto Mico's shoulder.

"Go on," HB said. "We've got this."

"Swift current," the crow said.

"Left or right?"

"Mostly left."

Mico shifted the paddle and stroked down the dirt road that would lead them up to the kaolin workers' houses behind the town.

Soon, they were out of sight.

"Come the fifteenth, it's two years," HB said, as he watched them and hauled the gear back into the truck.

Rosie patted her eyes with a kleenex. "I looked out the back door that morning and there was his silhouette paddling up the hill and I thought, well, heck, throwing papers is boring. He's spicing it up."

Pain turned toward them. "Look, he's experimenting. You two so-called adults have forgotten you once did the same thing." He pointed at HB. "If my memory serves me well, you once thought you were Bono. After that, you were obsessed with that flashy guy from Smashmouth."

"Steve Harwell," HB said.

"Smashmouth?" Rosie said, grinning.

Pain nodded. "And his singing was so bad, his mother and I bought ear plugs."

"But those were real people," Rosie said to Pain.

"Yeah, Dad," HB said, "Mico seems to think the town of Ocopeeco is covered with water. That doesn't bother you?"

"Long ago, Ocopeeco WAS covered with water."

Rosie giggled and punched her man. "Dad's right. Hildegard would cheer Mico on. Nobody understood her either."

Rosie kissed her father-in-law's cheek, as he tossed the rope into the truck bed.

HB sighed. "Yeah, I suppose slogging through our higher education system traumatized me. I'm still nursing the scars."

Rosie snuggled and whispered in his ear. "Any of those scars I haven't kissed yet?"

"Hey!" Pain said. "No foreplay in front of the old man."

* * * *

They conscripted several early risers at Clean Jeans to help carry the body into HB's church, a white, clapboard building that fronted River Street, Ocopeeco Methodist in Gothic letters over the shiny oak doors. After they laid the corpse on the front pew, HB phoned the county coroner and then his aunt, his Dad's sister, to prepare it for burial. Ocopeeco was too small for its own mortuary.

Pain waited outside, leaning against the truck. Still wet, he didn't feel cold. The night was unseasonably warm for October. Lately, hachko chapco stalked him, the long eared ogre who makes the ground tremble and punishes anyone who violates tribal code, anybody such as Pain Alpata, who had failed to do his job at the shack. Broken windows, busted faucets, bad brakes—the ogre was not pleased.

HB and the others came out.

Lit up and pouring smoke, the chalk-covered kaolin plant glowed in the dark like some elf-run fantasy from the North Pole.

Pain and the others walked back down hill to Clean Jeans and coffee and Rosie headed to Macon to the university where she taught Medieval Art.

HB trudged home, up through the tall grass. Half way he paused and looked back down at the town, sparkling against the still night sky. His little town was gun rich and slammed with ammo of every gauge; even the grammar school teachers kept a pistol in their purses. And there were five Scruggs cousins working at the plant, a tight knit clan not infrequently mixed up in the Saturday night melees at Roxanne's Bar where skulls split with a pool cue were not uncommon. What was happening? Had ghosts of the Hitchiti nation arisen, the fierce Creeks who fled to Florida when Old Hickory banned them? That Creek connection was one reason his dad had settled there forty years ago in a town that could afford only one twelve unit

Motel Six. But it was his town, where he had been born and had grown up; he would not let this murder destroy it.

* * * *

Two days later, seven AM, time for HB's first of the day's twelve cigarettes, Issachar, the rich, fifth son of Jacob, the one who received for his allotment the valley of the Jezreel, still some of the most fertile land in Palestine. He inhaled its rich, sweet flavor. He liked to start his day with tobacco that symbolized the land's great bounty.

Mico ambled into the study and plopped down on the floor, his long black ponytail tied up in a bundle. These days, he wore an eagle's feather in his hair like his grandfather, who was teaching him the hahagahaga, the Creek laws.

"This morning a customer told me she saw Big Rig and Aubrey arguing."

"Who?"

"Mrs. Downs."

"The Oprah lady?"

"Oprah dolls, Oprah photos, statues, all over the house."

HB laughed. He took a puff of his cigarette. "I was in the hardware store with her one day. Somebody made a wise crack about Oprah and the woman went ballistic. She know what they were arguing about?"

"Nope."

"Where was it?"

"One of Aubrey's painting spots in the woods."

"How did she see this? She lives way up on the hill."

"Binoculars. She spies on everybody."

HB chuckled and shook his head. "Does she pay her bill on time?"

"She's one of the few. I had to make four trips up the hill last week, collecting. Why do folks do me that way?"

"There are lots of single moms up there with three or more kids. It's tough."

"You know, until I started my route I never much thought about that. One poor woman has five kids and it's just her. She works two jobs. Gets home at eight every night. One of the kids is thirteen. She baby sits till her Mom arrives."

HB gave a silent thanks. His boy had a heart for the broken. Partly his doings. Partly Rosie's. She was always bringing home freshmen, bad grades, drinking too much or drugs. She fed them solid food, sat them on the sofa and opened beautiful art books with vistas into the Book of Hours or Hilde-gard's visions and the kids usually perked up.

"That a good tip?" Mico asked.

"That's a great tip. I need to start paying you."

"So . . . Dad . . . can I go with some of the guys from school to a concert in Macon? Two teachers are chaperoning."

HB turned his attention back to his computer screen "So, that tip was just bait."

Mico grinned. "But good bait!"

"I'll ask your mother."

That evening he strolled down River Street to the Clean Jeans. On the way he passed Jim Jeffords's Ocopeeco General Store. Swing blades, Skittles, chicken bitties, shot gun shells and calamine lotion. Jim's inventory was based on what the townsfolk asked for. The street sloped down to the river to the wooden bridge and on the other side, the tattered sign for Big Rig's worm farm: "Red Wigglers, Pinks, and Crickets."

The worm farm prospered because Lake Sinclair was close by, not to mention the Ocopeeco and the Oconee. Some locals swore by Big Rig's wig-glers. Around town trucks, usually rattletraps, bore his logo, a jaunty worm in a top hat waving from a hook.

He crossed the street and stepped into the wash-a-teria. Aubrey sat in the back, smoking, and drinking wine. He frequented the place every evening to find some peace after battling with his muse. Watching under-wear, bras, T-shirts, Under Armor, and Nike, rolling, soapy and bubbly, soothed his battered psyche. A sawed off man with thick horn rims, pro-phetic white hair and a white beard below his belt. The man actually made a good living selling his paintings.

"Duke!" Aubrey yelled.

HB grinned, Aubrey's John Wayne moniker for him.

He plopped down in front of Big Bess, the largest machine in the place, the go-to washer for any woman with more than three kids.

The painter raised his glass. "Now swings the sky to moon and mid-night's dallying mysteries dart to cover. Let us speak amid the dulcet scent of Tide and Dash and cleanse our souls of this sordid saeculum."

HB nodded at the wine. "Is your head clear?"

"Clearer than Euclid on a cloudless day."

"I've got a witness says you and Big Rig had a row last Monday night."

Aubrey nodded. "Your witness is correct. I was happily ensconced in my plein air nook, a little spot about a quarter mile up from the river. I heard whimpering, a boy, eight or nine. He was twisting the little fella's arm — just for the fun of it! When I shouted at him, he back handed me, then dragged the boy towards the truck. I hit him with a pine limb, but it barely stunned him. When I spotted a pistol on his front seat, I got out of there, fast."

"Coroner says he died about ten Monday night. Where were you?"

"Passed out—in the Medici palace."

"That would be your double wide?"

"Correct. Morpheus will not grace me with his somniferous presence without at least one bottle of Chateau du Ocopeeco."

He poured himself another full glass of wine. In front of them, Big Bess's window showed a cluster of tiny socks with delicate frills at the top.

"Duke, tell me something."

"If I can."

"When you pulled that child beating animal out of the river, did you pray for him?"

"I did."

Aubrey shook his head. "Why? Surely such wickedness deserves punishment, not prayer."

HB leaned over and put his elbows on his knees. He looked back at Aubrey. "Do you know the verse from Matthew 'He makes the sun rise on the evil and the good.'"

"Look, don't try to convert me. Just tell me why you pray for such an animal."

HB sat back up. He looked Aubrey in the eye. "Because God loves him."

"Now, you see, that's what I don't get."

"God made Big Rig, Aubrey. He's his child, just like you and me. He will always love him, no matter what Big Rig has done. I will never stop loving my son, Mico, no matter what he does.He could become a serial killer. I would be tormented out of my mind. No telling what would happen to my family. But I would never desert my son. God feels the same way about each of us."

"Yech!" the painter said. "Such evangelical clap trap. I thought you were educated, Duke. Greek and all that. You sound like Billy Graham."

"Thanks. That's quite a compliment."

The painter growled. "I didn't mean it as a compliment! God, let's change the subject" He held up his glass—"Salud to Seurat, cheers to Chagall!"—and took a long drink. "The world, my friend, is nothing if not a labyrinth, and I'm the lost and drunken bug who would discover at its heart the gold of alchemy to transform my leaden mind."

When he set his glass down, he turned to HB. "I should have shot the bastard, but I don't own a gun."

"He was stabbed, multiple times."

The painter glared at him. "I do hope he suffered and continues to suffer in the 9th rung."

"Do you own a knife?"

"A Barlow."

"Where did you hit him with the pine limb?"

"Across the back. But I don't have the strength to knock a sick maggot off a dead beetle."

"When he shoved the boy into the truck, did he climb in on the same side or did he go around to the driver's side?"

"He went around."

"Was he hauling a load of chalk?"

Aubrey stroked his beard. "I don't remember."

"At that time of day, he probably wasn't. How did you hear the whimpering? You must have been painting practically on top of them?"

"He revved the engine way up, destroyed my tranquility. Ticked me off. That's my little private nook. I've been going up there for years and nobody has ever disturbed me until that evening. I sneaked through the woods in their direction. That's when I heard the boy."

New customers arrived, loaded washers and the noise grew so loud they stepped outside to the old pew bench in front. HB set his brown Stetson down. No foot traffic on the sidewalk. The evening sun set kissed the river down at the foot of the street where a few old timers fished off the old rickety bridge.

Aubrey sighed: "Yeah, we need the NEA to fund a William Morris to restructure our world from top to bottom? Nothing but beauty, beauty, beauty."

"I've seen you work. Rotting beef hanging from hooks is not my idea of beauty."

Aubrey threw him a sneering glance. "Duke, duke, I'm like the canary the miners send down into the gas, to warn everybody the place is gonna blow. I look ugliness in the face, that's my hanging beef, and I spit on it. I defy it. Only after we have won the battle with the ugly can we begin to approach that delicate flower, beauty."

The high wail of Weeping Woman wandered up the street from the river. The two men turned their heads. The voice carried on a dialogue with the water, high a while, low a while, no melody, only the moody wandering of a beautiful voice, yearning to find some peace from the chains and folly of its painful life.

They said nothing. Weeping Woman had become as predictable as the sunset itself.

"You didn't go after him?" HB asked, "later that night?"

"Nope."

"Why didn't you report it?"

Aubrey lit a fresh cigarette from his old one. "I mean, it was a domestic dispute. Private, you know?"

HB pulled out his notebook from his back jeans pocket and took down some notes.

Aubrey got a cell call and had to go.

The gossips and rumor mongers would be at it, soon. He'd seen it happen before, when Ann Glynn, a lesbian, was picked as principal. The underground smear knives came out slashing. The good folk of Ocopeeco. Having grown up half Creek, he knew better. The nexus of close-knit ties could be your friend or your foe.

Normally, folks kept their doors unlocked, but after a nasty murder? Families let their little ones walk to school, but after a brutal knifing? And the easy chit-chat in the checkout line at the Good'n Green? Back-handed whispers and cold stares would freeze it.

He told Rosie he always imagined his birthplace and community where he grew up as possessing a certain purity.

Rosie's response: " Maybe, but right now? I think the purity's turning foul."

Chapter Two

Saturday evening, he drove down river to Weeping Woman's favorite singing spot. Following her voice along the dirt road, he found the place and stopped. His headlights shone out over the water into the fog that undulated in and out of his twin beams. He rolled down his window. The sound she made this close up wasn't human, a trapped animal, maybe calling to her mate. He got out, slipped on his waders and picked his way down the bank into the water where he threw down on her with his big flashlight beam.

"Turn that off!" she yelled, her hand up to protect her face.

He did as he was asked and in a few minutes his eyes adjusted. Her straw bottom chair sat in a quiet shallow pool. As he waded towards her, he smelled wild onion and the fog penetrated his skin and dampened his shirt till it stuck to his back.

A small, thin woman, angular features and an intelligent face. The water swirled around her, up to her knees, as if she were a flesh-covered river statue.

"Do you mind getting out," he said, "sit a spell in my truck? I need to ask you some questions."

"I'm not getting out," she answered.

She wouldn't look at him, her eyes were fixed on the horizon, someplace no one could claim.

"He got what was coming to him," she said. "I warned him."

"What exactly did you tell him?"

"Stop hurting our boys!"

He switched his flashlight off.

Grasping her elbows in her palms, she rocked back and forth.

"He believed pain was the way to keep them in line. Hurt them. Do it on a schedule or else one day they'll turn and hurt you. He had this whole big theory about it."

"So, he thought if he hurt the boys while they were young, they would grow up to be well behaved."

"Something like that."

"Where were you between 10 and 12 Monday PM?"

"Watching TV."

"What show?"

"No show. A movie."

A smile broke through her lips. She stole a glance at him, ashamed of her pleasure, but glad life still granted her a little.

"So which movie?" he asked.

"Dirty Dancing."

"Pretty steamy stuff."

"But it's not porn, at least not in my eyes. He didn't want the boys to watch porn."

Big Rig, the keeper of the nation's morals. Did she see any irony?

A clump of beer bottles floated by. She reached out and nabbed them. "Trashy people. The world is full of them."

"Did you see him abuse the boys?"

She sniffed. "At first, but I nagged him, so he took them off into the woods."

"Did you ever try to stop him?"

She glared at him. "Twice. Once, he slashed my arm with a razor blade. Another time he took his belt to me with the buckle end. Some neighbors tried to stop him, but he pulled out his pistol. I wound up in the ER at Coliseum Hospital both times. After that I gave up."

Women scared of their men. He felt guilty for not intervening more. But it was delicate—and sometimes dangerous. Once, he stepped into the middle of a family fight in the kaolin community. He wound up with a nasty knife wound in his thigh and a husband and wife that blamed him for poking his nose in where it didn't belong.

She held up her arm and showed a scar on her shoulder. "He did that."

He jotted a note to check the ER at Coliseum.

"Did you ever get medical advice?"

"What do you mean?"

"Go to a doctor, tell him what was going on?"

"He would have found out and beat me. He didn't believe in doctors. They're all Jews. Jews and the government out to steal your hard earned money."

"Did Big Rig have any kin?"

"A brother up in Atlanta, a loan shark. He looks like Big. He took finance classes in night school, then started wearing a coat and tie, and one day he was calling himself a financial advisor. But I like him. He compliments my drawings."

"I didn't know you drew."

Her grin unveiled a healthy, hopeful woman. "All my life."

"Did he have any run-ins lately?"

"Only half the town."

"He talk about them?"

Grasping her elbows in her palms and turning her face away, she whispered. "We didn't talk."

Her skinny arms. The coroner said the thrusts were deep, a big powerful blade that mangled the bowels. Not some pocketknife.

Finally, he handed her his card. "That's my cell. Call me if you think of anything."

He climbed up the bank, took off his waders and threw them in the back and looked at her, sitting in the river. She could have been a water spirit, a beautiful woman transformed into a hag all because she angered a god.

* * * *

Rosie pounded on Pain's door until he finally opened.

"What's going on?" she said, as she slipped by him with a plate of stollen and a pot of fresh coffee.

"Ambien. Makes me oversleep."

Barefoot and wearing an orange and blue Ocopeeco Panthers football jersey that had belonged to HB, he brought plates and coffee cups from his kitchen.

"How long have you been taking it?" she said as she arranged her cake on his coffee table.

"Couple of weeks."

She pulled the checkered cloth cover off. "Leftovers from church hospitality hour. I saw the stollen and thought of you."

"Uh-huh," he said, setting down cups and saucers. "Sure, you did."

She looked at him. "What?"

"Let's see," he said, "it's four o'clock. In the Rhineland at four o'clock everybody's sitting down for cake and coffee."

She rolled her eyes. "Okay, you got me," she said, as she cut a giant slice for him and a smaller slice for herself. "Could we sit down and eat?"

He kissed her cheek. "I love you, Roswitha Alpata."

She gave him a bear hug and spooned up the rich whipped cream onto the dry cake and watched his eyes and face. Normally, he would salivate at such a dessert. But he hadn't been normal for some time. That's partly why she had come. Once or twice a week she brought him food or a book she thought he'd like. All three of them, she, HB, and Mico were concerned. They thought he would get over the failed call at the shack, but he hadn't. She suggested a therapist, but HB said no. What therapist would comprehend the world of Creek spirituality his dad lived in?

Photos on the wall showed HB getting his doctorate, HB and Rosie's wedding, and Alice Alpata, Pain's deceased wife, the beautiful and holy Alice. A gentle smile, a full rounded face. Brown mysterious eyes.

After a few bites, she stood and examined Alice's picture. "I can never get over those eyes."

Pain grinned as he spooned sugar into his coffee. "She was not made for this world."

"She had to beat the boys off with a stick."

"I said that was the reason she joined the convent. Too many men after her."

Rosie sighed. "I wish I had known her." She returned to the sofa. "So, are you eating well?"

"I get by."

She glanced back at the photo of Alice.

"Do not worry about me. I fast," he said, "but nothing like Ali. I love my beer too much."

She laughed and nibbled the cake with her pinky thrust out.

On the coffee table sat a photo album. She loved to explore it because each time, she learned something about her husband and the rich, but unusual world he came from, so different from her own. The universe of the Creek tribes was deceptive. At first she had thought their beliefs were primitive and simple, but the more she learned, the more she realized their posture towards the natural world was not only profound, but ecologically more sophisticated than any modern model.

"Do you mind?" she asked.

"No, please. You need to learn. I understand. My son is not forthcoming."

"Your son is a closed book!"

She flipped it open to an article from fifteen years before, the Ocopeeco Gazette. "Ocopeeco Woman Dies from Fasting."

There was the holy and beautiful Alice again, only this time, the photo the paper used was taken when she was much younger. With dimpled cheeks, an innocence shone through the old, school days picture.

"Alice always felt responsible for what happened to us in Dahlonega, the accusations and the scandal."

"The woman who accused her of adultery."

"Right. As an ex nun, she knew she had to forgive the woman, but she found it hard. So, she fasted to drive the spirit of hate out."

Rosie flipped to the middle. "Church Roiled over Charges of Impropriety"

"Alice Alpata," the article began, "the choir director of Dahlonega Methodist Church has been relieved of her position, according to the church's board of elders."

"Did you ever learn why the woman accused her?" Rosie asked.

He sipped his black coffee he held with two hands.

"Not really. Ali said the woman was emotionally disturbed. Eventually, she had a break down."

"After Ali died."

"Right. Ali had actually counseled her at the church's outreach center."

He got dressed while Rosie continued to peruse the album. He returned in jeans and a T shirt.

"HB told me he's meeting Al at the college," he said, sitting back down on the sofa.

"He is. You know, I suspect he goes just to show off his Greek with Al."

"He does love his Greek. He told me that was one thing that got him through Afghanistan, reading Pindar and Euripides aloud."

"He may look like a thick headed cowboy, but I once saw him spout off thirty lies of Homer, the bard's depiction of Athena. One of my hot shot Ivy League art colleagues had just written a book on the Elgin Marbles. The man had misquoted Homer. HB left the man jaw dropped."

She spread a fat dollop of whipped cream over a slice of cake. "And they'll probably talk about the Woman taken in Adultery in the Gospel of John."

"They will," he said. "Al's really the only one who understands."

Rosie nodded with her mouth full.

Pain scowled. "Adultery."

He took dishes back to the kitchen.

She marveled at how different they were: the son a big, bearded lumberjack, logical, rational, the father, short, stumpy, all muscle, moved like a cat, an empath who felt the pain of others.

When he returned, she asked him to tell her about all the times Hesegadamasse summoned him and guided him to people in pain or danger. "I wasn't present for most of those," Rosie said, "but I remember the asthmatic boy well, because he was in Mico's class. You found him in a tree house."

"He climbed up," Pain said, "had an attack, no inhaler, and couldn't get down. The tree was way away from his house, so his parents didn't hear him calling. Plus, he was weak and couldn't scream too loud."

"That was a wonderful rescue."

"Now I feel like a failure. I pray to Loca, the turtle, who brought all the creatures out of the mud into the light, but I feel trapped in the same mud."

Rosie hugged him. "Were there people who actually threatened Alice?"

"They spray painted her car. Wrote vicious articles in the paper. We couldn't go to the grocery store without some jackass giving us a nasty look or a wisecrack."

"And she knew she had to forgive the woman, once it came out that she was mentally ill?"

"Ali already felt guilty for leaving her order to take up with a bum like me. And then this false charge. She felt there were wicked spirits that had taken up residence inside her. The only way to get rid of them was fasting."

Pain rose and stood in front of his dead wife's photo.

"Adultery" he whispered. "It's like a shadow that follows him, all of that boy's life."

* * * *

When HB visited the university, a barrage of what-if's always hit him like a sudden rainstorm. The brisk December air, football season, undergrads bouncing down the sidewalk energized, and reeking of hope—they nudged his imagination into shaping all manner of roads not taken. But the ivory tower? HB Alpata? That would mean two academics under the same roof. He preferred the interplay, the bob and weave between Rosie's world and his. Weren't a chief and a scholar the perfect recipe for a savory marriage meal?

The religion department was in the nineteenth century building, so five stories, Victorian spires, creaky spiraling stairs and long windows.

He passed by bearded, sleep-deprived males, puffing pipes, serious. And women, also half asleep, sitting on the floor outside their professor's office, a Hebrew Bible open or a Greek grammar.

Just after he and Rosie married he and Al spent three years together in grad school. They formed a strong bond which they kept up, even though their working lives played out on different planets.

The door was open, Al leaning back in his chair, puffing a tobacco-less pipe and reading. Behind him a window opened onto leaf less sycamores.

"HB!" he yelled, leaping out of his chair.

Black beard, black hair, horn rims, always cheerful. No signs of wear and tear, HB thought, whereas eight years as the chief had put some wrinkles in his face and scars on his body. Maybe Al just concealed his better.

They hugged.

"Still catching the bad guys?"

"I notch 'em in my Bible."

"Saw the murder story, the kaolin trucker."

"You big city folks so bored you're checking up on country crime?"

"No. Listen, the crime rate has shot up here. Assaults on campus. Drugs. Makes me nostalgic for a panty raid."

"Al, you never once went on a panty raid.

Al laughed.

"You were too busy learning a new Semitic language every summer. Akkadian, Sumerian, Coptic."

"True. The Sumerians would have cut off every panty raider's hands. Sounds like this trucker's murder was pretty messy."

"Even grossed Mico out."

"Thirteen year olds like digital gross out, not the real thing."

HB rolled his head back. He removed his Stetson and set it in his lap.

"So, what about the book?" Al said.

HB's decades long itch to rescue John7:52-8:11 from the non-canonical dust bin. Most New Testament scholars labeled it a late addition to the canon. In seminary, he and Al talked about someday proving that the woman taken in adultery was central to our understanding of Jesus: merciful, even with an adulteress. HB had notes, even an outline. But even today as they discussed it, he had that old feeling that his interest had as much to do with his mother as anything.

A student popped in with some xerox copies.

"Doc, here are the Dead Sea scrolls you asked for."

He laid them on Al's desk.

"An article for Biblical Archaeology Review," he said.

"Still working on the Essenes?"

"I am. How's your dad?"

HB told him the whole story.

"You worry he's going to die the way your mom did?"

HB nodded, his big brown Stetson so out of place in Al's book lined office.

"Will he consent to see somebody?" Al said.

"Pain Alpata? Talking about his conversations with Ibofanga or his tête-à-tête's with Sequoya drinking sassafras tea."

"The FDA labels sassafras tea poisonous."

"Figures. Dad says Sequoya loves it."

"You know, I've heard these stories from you for so long, I don't think twice about them. But your dad is so calm and rational. We've had a few of his high school English students here at the college. They rave about the guy."

"Dad was a great teacher. But, well, you know . . . he brought me up to be a white stick Creek, a seer and counsel giver, not a warrior and chief. So . . ."

"You were torn between two worlds."

"In the old days when the Creeks wanted to get the truth out of a man, they tied him between two horses, heading in opposite directions. They tried not to split him in two."

* * * *

He pulled into the dirt yard of the Enron station, the last stop before the next town, some twenty miles away. Nestled in a grove of tall pines, the flat roof was covered with pine needles. Six pumps, a shower, three beds in back. The kaolin drivers stopped here to stock up on smokes and jerky and Red Bull.

The temperature had dropped so he wore his thick, fur-lined hunting jacket. He didn't get up on the highway much, but judging from what he overheard at Roxanne's bar, the owner might be peddling Hillbilly heroin to the truckers. The ones heading on to Savannah could sell the product on the docks, make a little profit, hit River Street, and blow their profit.

He entered with a cheesy grin. "Mr. Little, I need to purchase some of your finest beef jerky."

Lizard Little stood behind his register, a freshly lit cigarette dangling from his mouth. Short and sweaty, even in the cold, he wore horn rim glasses with scotch tape thick at the nose bridge.

Little sneered at him and nodded towards the jerky.

The man hated him. He'd tagged him with a DUI last year. Had to turn over his car keys to his church- going grandmother to drive him around. Every afternoon the two crept through town, Lizard slunk down so nobody would see him, his granny inching along at ten miles an hour and smiling like an angel.

In the process he'd taken a look at Lizard's finances. The sweaty little man had a hefty bank account. And probably not from selling beef jerky. And to play the good old boy role down to the last can of Skoal, he lived in a double wide.

HB plucked up two packs of jerky, dropped them on the counter and pulled out his wallet. There was a revolver with a duct taped grip on the shelf under the counter.

"Coming to Big Rig's funeral?" he asked.

Lizard tilted his head back and smoke streamed up into his eyes.

"Maybe. You gon' preach?"

"I think Lurlene's got somebody coming from Milledgeville."

"Guess she don't want no lawman preachin' over her dead husband."

HB told himself to stay calm. The madder Lizard got, the more likely he was to blurt out something he would regret later on.

"You ain't got no right," Little went on, "preachin' and wearin' a badge."

"How do you figure that?"

"Separation of church and state. Chief, I figured you'd know that—you bein' so smart and all. It's in the constitution." He hammered his point home by pounding the counter with his index finger.

HB pulled out a small gray book from his inside vest pocket. Embossed in gold on the front: The Constitution of the United States of America.

"You wanna show me where that's found?"

Sniffing, Little removed his cigarette, set it on the edge of the counter. His eyes fell on the book, then went back up to HB. "How I know that's the real thing?" he said, slowly.

HB grinned. "Lizard, ease up, son. I'm not here to bust your chops. I'm investigatin' Big Rig's murder, that's all."

Lizard made a face. "Do we hafta talk about that?"

"Hey, I'm a cop. This is what I do."

"Thought you was the preacher."

"He stop here often."

"'bout every third day. Usually got a couple of packs of peanuts, candy bars, wienies, a gallon of milk, a carton of Red Man and every now and then some Pepto. Used to get magazines, Hustler, Playboy, but he decided he didn't want them boys o' his to find his dirty mags. Said he wanted to be a good daddy."

HB chuckled. "That's enough food for a boy scout wienie roast."

"Boy could eat. Had to disinfect the bathroom after he left."

HB stepped away from the cash register, fingered the candy bars, picked up one and read its nutritional value.

"He always fill up?"

"Not always."

"He ever shower here?"

"Big Rig? Not with him livin' just a mile away in Ocopeeco."

"You have a shed out back, don't you?"

"Maybe."

"Mind if I take a look at it?"

"Hell, yeah, I mind! You can't come in here snoopin' around without a warrant."

"What are you hiding?"

"I ain't hidin' a thing!" He stepped out from behind the register and pointed to the front door.

"I think you'd better leave."

"Nope. I think I'll take a look in your shed."

He stepped into the yard. Lizard dashed out back. By the time he made it to the shed Lizard had flattened himself against the shed door, arms wide, like the crucified Christ.

"You can't do this, now . . . this ain't right . . . "

HB shone his big flashlight through the wide cracks between the shed boards: a tractor, cardboard boxes of canned goods. He switched his flashlight off.

"Looks okay to me," he said, "Don't know what you got all worked up about."

Blinking and shoving his glasses up, Lizard wiped his sweaty face on his short sleeved shirt.

"I just . . . I just get real protective 'bout my stuff. I mean it's hard bein' a small business owner."

"I'll bet it is," HB said over his shoulder as he walked to his truck.

Inside his F-250 he waited and watched.

Now he suspected what he'd heard at the bar was true. Lizard was hiding something.

* * * *

"My grandfather was a sniper in World War Two," Rosie said, as she knocked a long neck off the fence post with her .22 automatic rifle, "three hundred forty-five kills. A German record."

"Don't cross Mico's mom," Nate said to Davy, Mico's friend.

Trying to smile, Davy said: "I won't."

The weekly Alpata bottle shoot. Across the river at the dump, a one-time bootlegger's trash pile, now, still a pile but lots of bottles, mostly from Roxanne's bar. Nate perched on the tail gate; HB was in a fold up chair, nursing a beer; Mico and Davy slouched in the truck bed and Rosie stood out front with her rifle. The day was overcast, smoke in the chilly air. Around them a grove of towering pines.

"Spud," HB said, "see what your Mom can do with a couple of rollers."

Mico hopped down, plucked out a half dozen bottles from a paper sack.

Rosie put down her rifle and unholstered her Glock.

"Ready?" Mico said.

"Ready."

He threw a bottle. It bounced on the dirt and as it arced up, she blasted it. She did the same with a second, a third, a fourth and a fifth.

The boy offered a bottle towards his Dad.

"Your turn!"

"You wanna show me up in front of young Davy here?"

"Kinda, yeah . . . "

Davy looked back and forth, trying to figure out when he was supposed to laugh. This was his third outing with his friend's family, which was very tight.

Rosie moved to the truck bed and climbed in while her husband stood, reached over and took her Glock.

She whispered to Davy: "He likes to bad mouth himself. Thinks it makes him look humble."

The teen grinned, although it was obvious he didn't get it.

Of the rolled bottles HB hit three of five. Rosie hopped down out of the truck to examine the two he missed.

"These bottles are defective," she announced.

Then she approached her husband, grinned, slipped her arms around him and kissed him, passionately.

"E-e-e-eu-u-u!" Nate screeched, "Not in front of the children!"

Mico ducked his head, Davy stared, mouth open.

They ran the sixes, six bottles on six fence posts. At the signal, the shooter had to fire the Glock as fast as possible. Only one shot per bottle. Davy hit one, Mico two, HB four, and Rosie six.

A second round. Sixes from the hip. Davy and Mico zero, HB three, Rosie six.

And last, Flyers. HB threw the bottles high for everybody else and Mico threw for him. Mico hit one, HB hit two, Rosie popped five.

They built a fire while Rosie unpacked the hot dogs and coat hangers. After the flames were high and everyone had a dog in the fire, Mico looked at his Dad: "So, who do we like for the murder?"

"Who do we 'like'"?

"You know, that's what they say on TV. Davy gets his papers dropped at Lizard's, so we were up there the other day. Some bad lookin' dudes comin' in and out."

"Inspector Alpata," HB said, "based on your observation that Mr. Little has some unsavory customers, you have concluded that he committed the crime?"

"Fallacious reasoning," Nate said, "Guilt by association."

"Exactly," HB said. His dog was burnt and crisp, dripping juice.

The others made disgusted faces at the burnt meat.

He slipped it between a bun he had already lathered with mustard and ketchup. "M-m-m-m!" he said, running it under his nose.

Rosie sliced her wiener with a knife and fork. She noticed Davy was puzzled by her etiquette.

"This is how we eat wieners in Germany. We call them wurst, pronounced with a "v". You say it."

"Vurst,"

"Sehr gut. And normally we don't put them between a bun."

HB threw Nate a bit of meat. The crow snapped and snapped until he got it down.

"N-a-a-a. Not so much," he said.

The chief raised his eyebrows. "Really?"

Rosie drug a pine limb onto the fire. "It doesn't taste like death."

Nate nodded. "What she said."

"I like Weeping Woman," Rosie offered, as she snapped twigs from the trunk. "A mother's protective instinct is a powerful force. It could easily drive her to kill."

Her husband nodded. "The woman's got enough pent up anger to launch an ICBM."

"What's that?" Mico asked.

"An Intercontinental Ballistic Missile," his Dad said. "Back during the Cold War, they were a hot topic."

Mico squinted at HB. "But I don't get it. Why would a wife want to kill her husband? They're supposed to love, honor, and cherish, aren't they?"

Rosie kissed her son on the top of his head.

"For that blessed comment," HB said, "I'm going to make you one of my super-duper Holy Boy specials." He reached for a coat hanger.

"No!" Rosie said, "Mico!"

"Dad, really, I'm stuffed. "

HB paused and gave them both a Cheshire cat smile. All eyes were focused on him. "If I didn't know better, I'd say you all don't appreciate the succulent taste of my burnt to a crisp, gourmet dogs. As to Weeping Woman as the killer," he said, standing and knocking the dirt off his pants, "her arms are toothpicks. Coroner says there were six or seven power thrusts made deep into the victim's gut. You know how big he was. It was a slick and slippery gut-o-rama."

"E-e-e-u-u-u!" Rosie said.

"Cool!" Mico said

"She didn't have the strength," Davy said.

"Exactly."

Nate took off up through the smoke and the pines. In a few minutes he returned to the ground in front of HB who was already loading the truck.

"Aubrey's the man," the crow pronounced. "He didn't just prevent the savage from savaging the boy. When he saw Big Rig hurting his own son, the painter glimpsed the beast that lurks in his own heart and it enraged him. Normally, his art sublimates the creature, the pain-making, shadowy monster he confronts in every painting, but for this one blinding moment, he attacked the beast itself, the one standing in front of him. That explains the violence of the blows. In effect, he was killing that part of himself he both feeds off and hates."

Silence.

"Deep," Rosie said.

"Where'd you get that?" HB asked.

"Marx."

"Marx?" HB said, "That doesn't sound like Karl Marx."

"Who said anything about Karl?" the crow answered.

HB cocked his head. "Na-a-a-te. . ."

"That's from the Marx who said there ain't no such thing as a sanity clause."

"Groucho? You're pulling our leg!" Rosie's face contorted between and a guffaw and a scream.

"I'm pulling your leg, your arm, any member I can to get you out of all this talk of murder and mayhem."

"He's right," Rosie said, "once again, we have turned a Norman Rockwell family picnic into a seminar on violence and mayhem. Davy, we have probably scarred you for life."

Young Davy giggled.

"But I love violence and mayhem!" Mico said.

＊ ＊ ＊ ＊

The river flowed by the graves and stones like a mother checking on her sleeping children. Green grass sloped up to a dirt road where the mourners parked and treaded carefully down the incline to the tent. When the Rev.

Bobby Babbitt arrived in his black Mercedes, the mourners below were forced to turn their heads and look up to him. After he stepped out, he put on his sunglasses and surveyed the crowd: a broad-chested man, an obsequious smile. Brown, moussed hair, tan and oily skin. As he made his way down the bank, his two assistants sped ahead. At the wooden lectern in front of the family, they sprayed Babbit's throat and spritzed him with hand sanitizer. Then he greeted the family, Weeping Woman, the three boys, Darren, Darrel and Darnell, and the loan shark brother from Atlanta. He mingled, shaking hands with friends and acquaintances, slapping backs and bowing to the older ladies.

HB observed, recalling the other funerals where Babbit preached. The man could transform himself into a Methodist or a Baptist or a Presbyterian. He knew the buzzwords and lingo of each. Did he believe anything himself? Probably not. He lived in a palazzo on Lake Sinclair that grew by a wing or a dock or a new boat every year.

The assistants distributed brochures for his Milledgeville Mega Church: "The Whispering Pines, where the spirit of the wind meets the spirit of the Lord."

Finally, he prayed, and began: "Big Rig Scruggs" he said, (a man he had never met), "devoted his life to caring for this blessed earth, the only earth, good people of God, that you and I will ever have. Yes, he tended that chalky white gold that puts corn bread and butter beans on our table every Sunday dinner."

HB whispered to Rosie: "He also reduced his carbon footprint by selling black market gas."

"That just made him money. It didn't reduce the amount of gas used."

"C'mon," he whispered, "I'm trying to get into the whole Big Rig the environmental saint thing."

She punched him in the ribs.

"And what sacrifices he made for those precious boys," the preacher continued. "He refused to do for himself, but he always did for them. Duty, responsibility, honor—that's what makes a good parent and that was Big Rig Scruggs."

Rosie glanced back at a deep phlegm-clogged cough. Aubrey wore a blue velvet jacket with a green silk ascot. Leaning on a cane, he had trimmed his beard, dyed a gray streak in his hair, which he wore in a ponytail.

She punched her husband just as the painter stormed off, stabbing the earth with his cane.

"Degas has no gout for irony," she whispered.

"Why don't I enlist his services for your portrait? I can see it now," he made a frame with his hands, "Dr. Roswitha Alpata, posed on the wrap around porch of the old manse."

She squinted at him with that wicked gleam he adored: "Do that and I'll sic Nate on you with another machine gun barrage of Freudian frick a frack like the sample we got at the last bottle shoot."

"Yeah, I've been meaning to ask you: why do you let him read that stuff?"

"I don't let him, he does it on his own."

"But I thought you were supervising him."

"Look, when I found him in the woods, broken wings and half starved, I nursed him to health and played CD's of simple fairy tales and Bible stories. He graduated to C S Lewis and Tolkien and Chesterton. His first words were: 'Sal-va-tion is from the Jews,' followed a few days later by 'Aslan is our king.'"

"So-o-o, why Freud?"

"He says if he's going to be a first rate theologian he has to know how the enemy thinks."

Pain joined them after chatting with some of his former students at Ocopeeco High. His coat and tie immaculate, his hair glistening (Rosie suspected a feminine hair product) and tucked into a tasteful bun. The look was impressive, even the red dyed circle about his eye.

"That group was in my last class," he said, "before I retired."

"They still harbor bitter grammatical memories?" HB said.

Wagging a finger at his son, the old teacher grinned. "Now, you know that is not true! My students loved me."

"Mr. Punctuation," Rosie said, "Eats Shoots and Leaves."

"Grammar's important," Pain said.

"I wonder if Lizard agrees with that reading," HB said, nodding back to the gas station attendant.

Lizard was jittery, smoking, texting.

"He may prefer Eats, comma, Shoots, comma, and Leaves."

Rosie hugged Pain. "I'm so glad you came. This is your first day out of that cabin in . . . how long?

"It's been a while."

It broke his heart to shut his children out of his life, but the battle he was fighting was beyond them. He wished they DID understand, especially HB. It grieved him, watching his son, as a teen and then, as a college student, year after year, abandon the dying ways of the Creek.

"I'm feeling a little better," he said to her, but even as he hugged her, she eyed her husband and they both knew he was lying. He was fasting. She recognized the signs. It was so frustrating. Alice died the same way, and yet, here he was walking down that same deadly road.

HB knew if he let himself start worrying about his Dad and the way he was atoning for that missed call from Hesegadamasse, he would work himself into a state. What else could he do? He had talked till he ran out of words.

As if a dark angel overheard his thoughts, a heavily perfumed and boozed up Roxanne slipped her arm around him. Dressed for a night on the town. Thick blond hair, an hourglass figure, powerful shoulders from flinging cases of Bud and PBR at the bar. And wide, tanned cheeks, one gold tooth, her arm around the chief and the man's wife not two feet way.

"I don't like funerals," she said.

He removed her arm.

"I mean, does anybody like funerals?"

"No," Rosie said, arms crossed, glaring at the intruder, "but they serve an important purpose."

Blinking and trying to steady herself, Roxanne said: "They do?"

"They help the community accept the inevitability of death without each one of us succumbing to fear and despair."

"Memento mori," HB said.

Roxanne's eyes opened wide: "Well, my goodness! You all sound so pro-found."

In the embarrassing silence, she took a deep breath and tapped HB on his chest with her bright red fingernail, rolling her eyes as a daring thought made its way to her lips.

HB glared at her, hoping he could stare her off.

"Son, if you and me was to have hot, steamy, jungle sex, and then a fine little male stud, that boy would be a first round NFL draft pick, four years at fifteen mill," she said, tapping his chest with her finger.

Pain made a tragic/comic face at his son.

The silence around Rosie rumbled.

"Mrs. Sapp," the chief regained his composure and squinted at her "As you very well know, I am happily married, and my beautiful wife is standing right here."

A clownish, sad face came over Roxanne.

"Aw-w-w-w-w, that's so sweet!" She turned to Rosie and for a second, her mind seemed menacingly clear. "Honey, you keep you a tight rein on this hunk o' burnin' love."

She signaled tootle-loo with a jaunty wiggle of her pinky.

As they watched her sashay off, bold and brassy, they breathed again.

"What the hell was that?" Pain whispered.

"That, Dad, was the snake in the Garden."

Bobby Babbit was finished and was stooping over, shaking the boys' hands.

When he came to Weeping Woman, she stood up, put down her purse, ran her fingers quickly through her hair and flung her arms around him. His relaxed smile told the onlookers he had this. He returned the gesture, "Now, now, I know how hard it has been . . . ", but she tarried too long. After she ran her fingers through his hair, his smile sagged. He tried to unglue her arms, but she clung, squeezing, refusing, shaking her head.

"No. No. No-o-o-o."

Everybody gawked. Mindful of his image, he patted her on the back, and consented to a minute more of consolation. The second time he tried to free himself, she moaned and that quickly turned into a wail that carried above the tent and everyone recognized it as the unearthly plaintive cry they heard every night rising from the foggy river, aural waves bearing the soul of her woe, but also knowing the community's pain, their shattered dreams and their silent tragedies. She shrieked, long, tortured, and accusatory; the preacher's grin vanished. He was trapped; he was making a scene, like the lover of a spurned woman. This could wind up on Facebook: "Rev Bobby Babbit 'Consoling' a bit too long." He was sweating. The salt stung his eyes. His heart pounded, and his freshly starched shirt was soaking wet against his skin.

Several local men stepped up to hoist the screamer off the ground and into the arms of some waiting women.

The preacher righted himself, jerked at his coat and cuffs, and straightened his tie. One of his assistants held up a mirror as the great man swirled his curls and his smile snaked back across his face.

Without his usual goodbye fanfare, Rev. Bobby Babbit climbed the slope and sped away, thoroughly shaken.

"His sermon must have really touched her heart," Rosie said.

"It touched something," HB replied.

Chapter Three

In his convertible, Jerry Lee Lewis, aka Happy Damon, paused on the hill to inspect the little town down below. Ocopeeco. Sleepy, creepy little burg. Through his binoculars he watched the police chief and a hot blond putting up a wreathe on a church front door. Police Chief and preacher. He wondered who had his way with the blond, the lawman or the holy man. Weird. A badge and a Bible. The chief popped the blond on the butt! She squealed and threw a pine cone at him. A killer bod in jeans.

Out in the free world, you could get away with anything. Locked up, where he'd been for two years, you could do nothing.

The chief put up a ladder and the blond climbed up to hang a string of cedar boughs. Damon chuckled and gave his package a squeeze. The blond reached high, showed the whole town her fruit. Then she stepped down, slow, swinging that thing, eased into the lawman's arms and planted a kiss on him. The lawman was a big boy. The old TV Rifleman with fuzz. But the big ones were slow and stupid. Probably ate bacon every day.

An Indian-looking kid appeared with a feather in his hair. The chief and the kid tussle. Family fun. Yeah, he'd like to have some family fun with the blond.

His boss, Mr. Jabba the Hutt Handy, in Atlanta, was hot to get back his money, the half million Big Rig and Lizard Little stole. He imagined the man biting his nails on his fat fingers, Mr. Harvard Grad, chicks surrounding him, feeding him grapes. Or him walking his mangy white poodle around his West Paces neighborhood, trying to look respectable. He gritted his teeth. Why is it, he thought, us smooth operators wind up working for the pizza-covered money moguls?

He put the red nose on, slapped white paint over his face and turned on the music. Revved up his engine, thinking about the blond and how he was a free man again. This was gonna be fun.

* * * *

28

"GREAT BALLS OF FIRE" was blazed in red letters across the side of the '55 white Cadillac convertible. While the song blasted the citizens of Ocopeeco, the mobile ad rolled slowly up and down River Street. The driver steered with one hand, waved with the other. He wore a gold short sleeve shirt, his head shaved bald, except for a scalp lock. On his nose a red clown ball. His long face was chalk white.

At the Clean Jeans, several young moms stepped out; they waved and squealed "Jerry Lee!" Easy Jim Jeffords, septuagenarian, sidled out of his hardware store in his overalls and lit his pipe. When the car passed the post office, the two black female workers, in their early thirties, peeked out the door in their wool gray pants and spiffy blue shirts and Jerry Lee blew them a kiss.

The car cavalcade unrolled for thirty minutes.

HB and Rosie stood outside the church as the Cadillac pulled right up to the curb, just a few feet from their steps.

"Do I have the pleasure of addressing the Doctors Alpata?"

HB approached the car. "I'm HB Alpata and this is my wife, Rosie."

Damon thinking "the Doctors Alpata" was a classy touch. Heard it on NCIS. Needed a whole list of phrases like that. Tape 'em under the dash.

His all leather interior was studded with gold silver dollars. A set of Texas long horns served as a steering wheel.

"Happy Damon," he said, leaping out without opening the door. He came around and hopped onto the fender, swinging his legs like a kid. "That's Damon with an umlaut." He punched the air with rabbit's ears..

"Why an umlaut?" Rosie asked.

"Don't want folks to think I'm kin to that faggot actor."

"Matt Damon," HB said.

Damon sneered.

With his long, five o'clock shadow he could have been twenty-five or fifty. He buttered them up with how he loved the feel of Ocopeeco. It was just the right size for his style of entertainment, the kind of place where he would be inspired to put on a spectacular show.

"And that would be a Jerry Lee Lewis cover show?" HB said

"You are correct, chief. The best and maybe the only."

That morning HB got an email from the sheriff in Columbus. The previous weekend the weird showman had an entire gym of septuagenarians swinging and sweating like teens. At the farmer's market in Atlanta his show ran back to back with a watermelon festival and ended with a melon fight to "Whole Lotta Shakin' Goin' On." The cops were called in, which only enhanced his reputation as a showman.

As he machine gunned words, he sucked cigarettes, as if the smoke was air itself and he was on his last, dying gasp.

Only addicts and recovering AA's smoke that way, HB thought. Was this bird coming up or going down?

"I guess you need to know which regulatory hoops to jump through?" he said.

"Indeed. I hope not too many."

HB scribbled down the name and cell of the high school principal. "Miss Ann Glynn. The high school gym is where you'll put on your show. She'll get you set up."

He noticed a pistol on the seat.

Happy reached down and showed it to him.

"An S & W 29?" HB said, pulling the weapon out of its holster. "Look at this monster," he motioned to Rosie who stepped down to see.

Happy nodded. "I'm a kind of a gun freak."

Rosie pulled out her pistol.

"A Glock 42. Nice," Happy said. "Mind?"

He sighted with it while the couple examined the Dirty Harry special.

"What are you shooting?" he asked Rosie.

".380 ACP cartridges."

HB shared his Beretta M92FS and pistols were swapped, sighted, and polished after Happy whipped out a chamois cloth and the three enjoyed a moment of pistol hygiene bonding.

"Okay, we've shared guns," Happy said, "Now I'll share a secret." He held the Beretta up to the sun.

"What?" Rosie asked.

"I celebrate mine's birthday."

HB chuckled, winked at his wife.

"Why the wink?" Happy asked.

Rosie shook her head and wagged her finger at her husband. "I have a family Bible from Austria. In it my maternal grandfather, a WW II sniper, recorded the date he purchased his Karabiner 98k sniper rifle, 6x telescopic sight. Beside the entry he drew a heart and the words: 'Meine einzige wahre Liebe.' (My only true love.)"

"God and guns," HB said.

"Yeah, the Germans had some bad ass snipers. Like Matthäus Hetzenauer."

"How do you know that name?" Rosie said.

"Told you, I'm a gun freak, history, mechanics, metallurgy."

"My grandfather WAS Matthäus Hetzenauer."

"Whoa! Your granddaddy was the most decorated German sniper of World War Two?"

"It's not something I'm particularly proud of."

"You should be!" His face muscles rippled. "The hand to eye skill, the athletic prowess, the cunning . . . "

"The dead," she said, "the husbandless wives, the sons and daughters who needed a dad."

"Ah-h-h. Bleedin' heart talk. Hetzenauer was good, but he didn't hold a candle to Simo Häyhä. Five hundred and five kills! That's a shooter!"

"That's a cold blooded killer," Rosie said.

Shaking his head, the showman stamped out his cigarette. "Chief, better watch yourself, son. This woman's gonna make you soft. Slow down your step, one dark night when you're chasing after the bad guys . . . " He formed a pistol with his right hand, pointed it at HB and pulled the trigger with his thumb.

"You still keep in touch with your posse Comitatus buddies?" HB said. He distanced himself from the car, folded his big arms and glared at the showman.

Damon clucked his tongue, snapped his head away.

"That was twenty years ago."

"Water under the bridge, then? Except maybe that stint with the Omni Christian Book Club."

The man's face soured as he ripped the keys in the ignition and revved the engine so loud no one could speak and be heard.

He let it die slowly down.

"Damn," he said, cheerfully, "Didn't know they had com-pu-ters in these little mud hole burgs."

He revved again; up and down the street people turned to gawk. Smoke blew out of his tailpipe till it engulfed the Alpatas.

Damon peeled away, pumping a fist.

Holy Saint Maximus!

* * * *

Mico lay on his side as Pain stirred the fire with his old iron poker. Every Saturday evening, he spent with his grandfather learning the ways of the Muscogee. Pain's cabin smelled of wood smoke and the burning of scented candles in the windows. The floor covered with rugs woven by Pain's grandmother, eagle patterns, patterns of flowers and deer, hawks and snakes.

Pain sat down in his rocker and began.

"You asked me about Big Rig and why he was mean to his own children. It was Twisted Horn. One day many people gathered to have a Corn Dance. There was great excitement. But as they moved around and gathered and worked, they found a man in their midst who was asleep. They tried to wake him, but he would not wake up. He wasn't dead because he was breathing. They puzzled and puzzled because they had never seen a man who would not wake up. Finally, they said: Someone must find out why he cannot wake up. They selected frog. Frog said: I will do it, but you must give me two days. So, on the first day frog lay face down. He listened to the earth, all its rumbling and rivers and roots growing and water crashing through rocks. He rolled over and said to them: No. The next day he lay face up. He searched the skies with his eyes, watching the flights of the hawk and the eagle, the squabbling jays and the sweet nightingale song. Then he said: His heart has been stolen by the Twisted Horn. If someone can climb up to the Twisted Horn and retrieve his heart and bring it back, he will live. Otherwise, he will die. They knew a little one had to go. Only the little ones were light and fast. A mouse spoke up and said: I will go. Spider wove him a web to the top and the little mouse climbed it. When he reached the place where Twisted Horn stayed, he hid in a corner. Twisted Horn had a box where he hid the hearts he stole. The mouse went to work gnawing. Soon old wicked Twisted Heart heard him and said, "Ah, a mouse. Nothing." Mouse gnawed the box open and found many hearts. Some from people already dead, but a few were fresh and the people still alive. He found sleeping man's heart and returned down the web. They put the heart into sleeping man and he awoke feeling refreshed and thankful. Big Rig's heart was stolen and there was no one to retrieve it."

Mico considered this. "But Big Rig wasn't found asleep. He was found dead."

"Hm-m-m," Pain chuckled. "Your mom told me how sharp you are."

He brought hot chocolate for Mico and coffee for himself.

Mico looked down. "I worry about you, grandad."

Pain slipped over and put his arm around his gangly grandson. Mico laid his head on Pain's shoulder. Tears came into the boy's eyes.

"Is it possible that Hesegadamasse just dialed a wrong number?"

Pain chuckled "No, it's not. And it doesn't work that way. It's not possible because I felt a deep hurt and a grief, as I always do, and I knew someone needed help."

"But how do you know?"

"I can't explain it. Words only say so much. Most of what's important words can't convey."

"Yeah, Mom says that, too. When she goes off on Hildegard."

"Hildegard of Bingen was a great scholar and a saint. She should have been a Creek."

"Dad says we have to be able to forgive others when they hurt us, but we also have to forgive ourselves."

"Your Dad is wise. But sometimes the head and the heart aren't on the same page."

"What does that mean?"

"It means I know what I'm supposed to do, I just can't do it."

* * * *

The night before the Jerry Lee Show, HB was on the phone for hours lining up security from Sandersville, cleanup crews from Milledgeville, concession booths from Macon. Just before he crawled dead tired into bed, he got a call from Lizard Little, talking fast, whispering. Said they had to meet. HB balked but gave in. The man's voice was soaked in fear.

He told Rosie and pulled his truck out of the yard about 1:15 AM

Lizard greeted him at the trailer door in his open bathrobe, hair down his face, his glasses at the tip of his nose. He was wearing a child's pair of Mickey Mouse slip ons.

After he fetched two PBR's from his fridge, Lizard punched off Maury Povich and HB slipped into a Barcalounger. The room was choked with smoke and the smell of bacon and eggs.

"So, what's got you so worked up?" HB asked.

"Happy Damon."

A cold chill went through HB. This is just what he had feared.

"You know him?"

"I know his work." The watery eyes behind scotch taped glasses.

"And what's that?"

"He's a hit man. Works for Mr. Handy."

HB thinking he does not like to hear those two words, "hit man," uttered outside a TV cop show. Not here, not in his innocent little town.

"Handy?"

"Mansion out on West Paces Rd."

"So, this Handy, has sent Happy down here to take you out—for what?"

"I ain't done nothin' wrong! I swear, Chief. Look, I'm spillin' the beans and then some. It was all Big Rig's doin's. The dumb ox. Told him it was a stupid idea. Now he's got himself killed and he's gon' get me killed, too.

"Sometimes kaolin is shipped in big bags. The amount in each one is measured exactly, and they come in different sizes. So, if you make toilets, you need one size; if you make Playboys and Hustlers, you need another. The bags are weather resistant."

"Big Rig bought empty bags at the plant. Told the guy he needed them for his worm farm. Handy sent me the fentanyl. I stored it in those bags in my shed. When Big Rig pulled in, we swapped the kaolin and the product and before long, Big Rig Scruggs is hauling a load of Chinese Happy through the heart of sleepy south Georgia."

"What happened to the kaolin you emptied out?"

"We put it back in the bags it come in, then Big Rig hauled it to an old bootlegger's dump in the woods."

"Who killed him?"

"That maniac Damon. Chief, I'm telling you, he ain't human. I need protection. I'll pay you. I got money."

"What did y'all do to make Mr. Handy so mad?"

"Big Rig started selling for himself and keeping the money."

"That was stupid. Didn't he realize Handy would find out?"

"Yeah, he did, and he didn't. He's got a dozen stops where folks know him, so for a while there he was making a pile of money. Went to his head. Figured he'd get away with it a while and then stop. Stomping around, thumping his chest. Mr. Big Shot. Even talking about buyin' him a big house over in Sandersville. But I knew that wouldn't last. Every morning I was getting up thinking this is the day some dudes walk into the station, black suits, coats and ties, shades, New Jersey plates, or maybe hairy naked arms with tats up to their eyebrows and fat lips studded out like the Millennium Falcon."

"So—were you in on the scam?"

"No! I ain't stupid!"

"But you know where Big Rig's money is."

He folded his arms and turned his head to the side.

"Lizard. . ."

"But chief, I'm fessing up. Don't that count for something?"

HB took off his Stetson. "Maybe."

"But what about now. Chief, I don't wanna die!"

* * * *

The Ocopeeco High School gym throbbed with the piano pounding of Jerry Lee Lewis, aka Happy Damon with an Umlaut. Against the projected backdrop of *Great Balls of Fire*, the Dennis Quaid movie, Damon stooped in silhouette over his instrument, tearing at the keys, a dog digging for a bone.

White bucks, sunglasses, red-striped short sleeve shirt. He threw a long leg onto the piano, played backwards, upside down, sideways, one hand, two hands, two hands and a foot. Out of options, he jumped onto the top where he shook his booty and lip synched.

HB clocked his opening number at twenty minutes. He and Rosie sat in the bleachers, high above the fray.

"Boy's in better shape than I am," he said.

"He just lost five pounds."

Below, the old folks from three counties sweated, cackled, and squealed as a steady stream of liquor moved in and out of the building from the parking lot. Many dancers had actually seen the star in his heyday.

HB grinned at his wife. Her eyes were lit up and the medieval art scholar was jumping and jiving in her seat.

"What?" she asked.

"Just glad you find this so interesting."

"I love this! In Germany, the fifties were the era we fought our way out of rubble. We missed rock and roll."

"Yeah, I kinda like it, too."

"But there's still one thing I don't get," she said.

"What?"

"How your staid, southern protestant culture suddenly burst out with all this orgiastic music and booty shaking."

"Look," he said, "millions of young men were arriving home from war to millions of girlfriends and wives. All that pent of energy—the stage was set for a giant party. And Protestant southern culture was never that staid. Square dances, moon shine, wild flings deep in the pines—maybe folks didn't want to talk about it much, especially grandma and her knitting circle, but it was there."

Rosie nodded to the stage. "But why'd this character pick little Ocopeeco? In Madison, or Sandersville or Cochran, not to mention Macon and Columbus, he'd make a much bigger haul in any of those places."

"Maybe he's just a small town boy at heart," he whispered with his southern drawl. He squeezed her knee, which she hated because she knew it meant something deeper was going on and he didn't want to let her in on it.

She growled. "That man may not have a heart. Did you look into his eyes?"

"The Heart of Darkness."

"'Mr. Kurtz, he dead,'" she whispered, snuggling up.

"Hey—my little redneck."

"I'm getting there."

As they observed the dancing, Rosie drew close. Her man was putting on a happy face for her benefit. Beneath it lay a world of fears. She laid her head on his shoulder.

"Worried about Dad?"

He slipped his hand over hers. "I am."

"But it's more than that."

"What do you mean?"

"It's that old guilt, betraying your Dad and his Creek world."

He sighed. Silent, he nodded.

She could see that her words touched him.

"You are such a strong, loving man."

She turned her soft lips up to him and he kissed her. When he pulled away, he looked into her eyes. She put her finger over his lips. They embraced, quietly and held each other.

Peace came over him that allowed him to turn his thoughts to the talk with Lizard. One murder and his sweet little home is suddenly visited by the Joker.

How did that brutal trucker plunge his little town into such a mess?

Tonight, he'd have to do an old-fashioned all night stake out. At Lizard's trailer. He hadn't told Rosie.

What if Lizard was lying? The little man's notion of truth shifted with the wind. But maybe this time he was right. He was shaking so in his trailer, he could barely light his own smokes.

That afternoon he had discovered Lizard spent some time in the Fulton county jail for black market gas. Maybe that's where he contacted Handy. Maybe even visited Handy's home, got high together.

Back in Ocopeeco, Lizard or Big Rig notices that powdered kaolin looks like fentanyl. They decide it's the perfect fit, switching the drug and the kaolin. He gets in touch with his high-rolling friend. "Hey Mr. Handy, remember me, Lizard Little, the guy dumb enough to get caught for peddling black market gas?"

The rafters roared again as a new number started up.

Avoiding the dancers, who were flinging their arms, on the verge of losing control of their arthritic bodies, Mico and Davy stepped carefully across the dance floor.

"Mico!" a woman shouted.

He waved, wincing.

"Who's that?" Davy asked.

"Mrs. Beasley, remember? Second grade?"

"Ye-e-e-ch, that her husband? He looks a little young."

"Her first old man died from Old Timers. Mom says Mrs. B's either having a late mid-life crisis or else she's making up for years of her husband's party pooping."

Their second grade teacher and her beau twirled around and launched a visible line of sweat onto a pair of bespectacled octogenarians.

"Hey, sex machine!" the old man cracked, "watch it with the rain showers!"

Mrs. Beasley giggled.

The boys had to pass through the center of the dancers to get to the drink stand.

The music stopped.

The boys were trapped!

With the crowd of oldsters surrounding them, panting, fanning, wiping themselves with handkerchiefs, the lights dimmed, an oldies ballad came on and the dancers transformed into lovers, clinging to one another like drowning sailors as the whole crowd drifted into an amorous moment.

The teenagers could handle the wild dancing and jitterbugging, but a half a hundred old couples in the throes of body-grappling love was too much. Mico felt his stomach twist and the hairs on his neck stood stiff.

A woman took him in hand, a lovely young blond, gentle and grinning. She could have been his mom, moving her body to his around the floor to the soft strains of the lovers' melody.

Davy disappeared.

"Good evening, Mr. Alpata," the blond whispered in his ear.

"Hel . . . hello, Miss Daniels."

His seventh grade PE instructor and his first fantasy goddess.

His eyes found Davy by the drinks booth. His friend waved and made kissy kissy with his lips.

A year's growth had brought his height to hers, so when he regarded her eye to eye, it rattled him. The year before he was shorter, had to look up, as a boy should to a beautiful young teacher.

"My, you have grown," she said. "Soon, you'll be as tall and handsome as your dad."

"Yes, ma'am."

"Do you still have your paper route?"

"Yes, ma'am."

"Are your customers still remiss in their monthly payments?"

"Yes, ma'am," he said, grinning.

"You're learning a lot about human nature on that job. We are, all of us, flawed creatures, and that includes handsome young paper boys."

He nodded, too vigorously.

The song was interminable, and Mrs. Daniels chatted on and on about everything, while her leg brushed up against his leg each time she moved. The steady brush and swish of her skirt, the heat rising from the dance floor, the saxophone's notes entwining around them—it all conspired to do what nature usually does.

"Why are you backing away, Mico?" she whispered. "A woman wants to be held firmly by her partner. It makes her feel safe."

Miraculously, he managed to do both, thrust his pelvis back while grasping her close from the waist up. Over at the drink stand Davy was bent over, laughing.

The end of the song brought Happy Damon out of his role into the real world. He set his eye on the blond dancing with a kid. Long, tan legs, hair back in a French twist. Pouty, moist lips.

"Woo-wee!" he said, as he hopped down from the stage. "Y'all gimme some of that good Co-Cola. My engine's runnin' on empty!"

The PTA mom at the stand smiled stiffly and handed him a big cup of Coke with ice.

After guzzling, he wiped his mouth on the back of his hand.

By now Mico and Ms. Daniels had made their way to the same drink table. Spotting Damon, she slipped behind Mico as he ordered.

Happy grinned at her, but she turned her head away.

"Mico," she whispered. "Walk with me outside to get some air."

But Happy was quick. He leapt in the way of their leaving.

"I don't believe we've met," he said, smiling, toothpick in the corner of his mouth.

Lips tight, she responded. "We haven't. My name is Grace. I've enjoyed your show, but now, if you'll excuse me, young Mr. Alpata and I are about to step outside to get some fresh air."

"I'll join you," he said.

She pulled Mico toward the door. "If you wish," she said under her breath.

Outside, Happy lit up, blew a long stream of smoke into the chilly night air. Clutching the little warrior like a momma would her baby. Never been with a big bad man. Telling herself: bet he's . . . what, depraved? Yeah, that would be her word. Hold on little sister and Happy will show you depraved.

Mico glanced at Jerry Lee and then back to Ms. Daniels.

"So, Grace, what does a fine looking filly such as yourself do for entertainment in this Sahara of the Beaux Art?"

Grace put on a tight, fake smile. "I think as a small community we manage to entertain ourselves quite well, thank you."

"Me, I like hot music on Saturday nights, a dozen or more restaurants where you can get any dish under the sun and," he grinned towards her, "a fine lookin' lady on my arm. A blond, usually. Smooth, tan legs. School teachers. Hey, I bet you're a schoolteacher!"

Grace grabbed Mico and moved towards the parking lot. Mico looked behind him to see Damon leaned against the gym wall, grinning.

"Now, that's unneighborly, Miss Grace," he yelled. "I'll have to call my therapist Monday, tell him I was traumatized by a heartless schoolteacher."

When they reached her car, which was close by, they could still see him, leaning, grinning.

As Mico opened her door, she whispered, "Thank you!"

"Yes, ma'am" he said.

She kissed him on the cheek, started her white Toyota and drove away.

As he returned to the dance, he passed by Jerry Lee Lewis. As he drew close, the showman whipped out a knife.

Mico jumped back

"What's the matter boy? Guilty conscious?"

He sneered and pared his nails with the long, shiny blade.

Chapter Four

The steam off the coffee thermos gave his cab that smell he associated with long stakeouts, along with Rosie's delicious sandwiches. She bought real tuna in Macon, chopped it with onion, cilantro, and olives. He took a bite, savored the flavor. Letting his mind wander to her at the counter, chopping, those elegant long legs, that warm come hither look she gave him, food and making love.

He opened his Bible to the Psalms and prayed the ninety-first. "You will not fear the terror of night, nor the arrow that flies by day, nor the pestilence that stalks in the darkness, nor the plague that destroys at midday."

He also prayed for Lizard's safety, and, yes, for Happy Damon, a lost man God loved as much as anyone. How many times had he prayed for men who hated him or wanted to kill him? The town council thought his praying for the bad guys made him soft.

A light went on in the trailer!

Lizard going to the head. The toilet flush, the door slam, the light off. Man peed every hour. Prostate issues.

He'd gone to Macon and put together a file on Damon. His real name: Iraneus Loadholt. Raised in Alabama orphanages. Involved with the Gordon Kahl group, the white supremacist who gunned down two federal marshals come to arrest him. In 1967, Kahl wrote a letter to the IRS saying he would no longer pay taxes to the "Synagogue of Satan under the 2nd plank of the Communist Manifesto." Loadholt joined in the late nineties. Later, he dropped off the radar. So, now, he's Jerry Lee Lewis employed by Mr. Handy, a wannabee drug commissar in Atlanta. Thinking this kaolin-fentanyl similarity promising, Handy turned his greedy eye on tranquil Ocopeeco, a lamb to be led to the slaughter.

Damon would try to flush Lizard out.

Earlier, he'd spent nearly an hour trying to convince Lizard to stay put, no matter what. Jerking his head, twitching, yapping fast, the little man had too much speed in his tank.

HB explained Handy needed to keep him alive.

"So, why'd he send a maniac killer," Lizard asked. "If he wants to keep me alive?"

"He's trying to scare you into giving up his cash."

Lizard sniffed, would not look him in the eyes.

* * * *

Camouflaged and on foot, Damon watched through his binoculars as the chief pulled his Ford 250 behind Lizard's trailer. It was 12: 30. He was glad the little queer bait hired the chief. Handy said he'd call in somebody from the outside, but the little snake turned out to be a support your local lawman guy. He took a bite off his power bar. 35 gms. of protein, 15 of fiber. Lately, he'd eaten too many McDonald's garbage burgers. Always on the road. Interstates and motels. One week in Fat Butt, Ohio, the next in Retard, Georgia. His biome was suffering. He'd been doing well ever since he started eating veggies and fruit and cut out all the processed garbage.

He wondered if Marshall Dillon had just come from nibbling his blond's toes. The granddaughter of Matthäus Hetzenauer. The hot granddaughter. Her pout whining about the war dead. Wanted to say: Baby, I don't care. Ten dead, ten million dead. It's all the same. Then pull her trigger. Feel her go off under him.

He relocated and with his binoculars watched the chief chowing down on a sandwich. Not even trying to hide his big Ford 250. The bearded Rifleman was too big and too clumsy. Not paying any attention to his microbiome.

Two hours later, the Chief hadn't budged. He was probably snoozing by now.

Damon hummed and doused his cross bow arrow in oil and reached for the lighter.

* * * *

"Chief! Chief!" Lizard shouted from his doorway.

His trailer, on the other end, was in flames.

HB had seen the arrow speeding through the night. He slipped out, crawling toward the blaze on his belly, eyeing the woods, waiting for a glint, a flash.

"Stay put!" he shouted at Lizard. "Don't come out!"

"But it's burnin' down around me!"

"Stay in the trailer!"

He fired a half dozen rounds into the pines with his Sig Sauer. In the moonlight pine bark exploded.

Another cross bow arrow thunked within inches of Lizard's face.

"Wa-a-a-a!"

The flames were dying, but Lizard was too excited and didn't notice it.

"Close the door and get inside."

"Hell, no, this thing's burning down! I'm coming out!"

"No! No! Stay put!"

Another arrow pinned his bathrobe. He yanked and it ripped away, leaving him in his underwear and his pale toothpick legs.

The next arrow pierced his thigh.

"Wa-a-a-a-! I'm hit!"

HB opened up his Sig Sauer at the pines where the arrows were fired. He emptied the load.

A car cranked up.

He reached Lizard, writhing in pain, ripping out the indoor outdoor carpet. Dialed EMS, left the cell and took off in the direction of the engine sounds.

By the time he reached the highway, the vehicle was way ahead, a sports car, the whine of the gears, the pop and shift. He whipped off road, through a field of corn stubble. His truck bounced and rocked and slid. When he came back onto the asphalt, he had gained ground. Ahead, the car was on a long stretch. Must be doing one-fifty, he thought. His Ford was no match.

After the long stretch, he turned a sharp curve, and as he pulled out, there it sat, a red XKE. He braked hard, tires squealing, slinging up rock, then swerved over to the side of the road where he switched off the ignition and hit the seat, prone, expecting gun shots. Nothing. Reached for his .30-30 loaded and mounted in the back window. He kicked open the shotgun side door and eased out backwards until he sat on his knees. With his binoculars he scanned the field behind him: soybeans, bare furrows in winter. No rocks or trees or gullies to hide in. Damon was on the other side, waiting.

Why did he stop? With the XKE he could have gotten away. No. That would be too easy. He sensed it at the church that first day; Damon was all about a showdown. Had to face down the chief. That whole gushing on about Rosie's grandfather. Had to test his skill. Some kind of perverse honor code.

On his belly he crawled around to his front tires and peeked out. A shot popped rock inches away with a screaming ricochet. He crawled back, reached inside for his knapsack and pulled out a grenade. Never know when you need the cavalry. His old mentor, Bang 'Em Up Brown, Bibb County

Sheriff emeritus, advised him to keep a stash in his truck. "Sometimes, boy, you get in a tight spot, no way out but a load of hot flying metal."

He paused a moment to pray Psalm 144: "Praise be to the LORD my Rock, who trains my hands for war, my fingers for battle."

He lobbed it over the road. After the blast, he sprinted across the asphalt through the acrid stink and smoke into the tall pine grove and found a fat trunk to hunker down. Once the smoke cleared away, Damon unloaded a long round of automatic fire into the tree, nearly cutting it down. When it stopped, HB sprinted again toward the sound of the shots, moving uphill between boulders and pines until he found a head high rock.

Not once had he laid eyes on the man. He hunkered behind the rock, waiting for another lead storm. Three minutes. Five minutes. Eased out. Wood smoke. Saw and smelled it at the same time. Crouched low, he raced up the hill until he reached the top and a plateau covered in pines. Fifty yards ahead trees were burning. Then he heard singing:

"I fell into a ring of fire. I fell into a burning ring of fire. I went down, down, down, the flames went higher. And it burns, burns, burns, the ring of fire, the ring of fire."

A flame thrower spewed out a stream that torched trees around him. Damon moved in a circle, himself in the center, raging in some conflagration fantasy, his face painted white again as on that first day and the scalp top dyed red. He was naked, his body a swirl of red, yellow, and blue concentric circles that spelled HB until he had to look away.

Another burst of Damon's flame arcing and spilling like a fireman's giant hose searing the trees jolted him into a flashback. He was in country, on his back, helpless because a Taliban choked him with his rifle, squeezing his throat till he couldn't breathe, fierce eyes and thick black brows and lashes, the man bellowing like a pig, his coffee-brown teeth bared. HB sucked in for breath, but each time less air, less air, the bearded face growing hazy, his strength waning until his fingers found the enemy's knife. At the first thrust the Taliban's eyes jerked open; he twisted the blade in the man's gut, over and over, the body trembled, then went spastic, then limp until the man rolled off. He fell on him stabbing his arms, his neck, his face, the eyes, destroy those burning eyes! He collapsed.

When he awoke, he stabbed the corpse again until they found him, still thrusting the knife into the lifeless body. They pulled him off and sent him to sick bay.

"Down, down, down, into a burning ring a fire!"

He shook his head until the image cleared, and punched in the Tri County fire station in Gordon, the station in Sandersville, and the one in Milledgeville, where some sassy teenager kept him on hold! The fire was destroying somebody's timber and livelihood, he screamed. They needed fire trucks out there pronto. When he finished and looked up, Damon was gone! He sprinted back to the highway. When he reached the road, the XKE was gone, too.

In a half hour he pulled into an all-night 7/11 on an entrance onto I 16. By now it was bright and a warmish December day. Still shaking from the flashback, but energized, he raced through the glass door, a big, bearded, ex-linebacker, he knocked over a cardboard Santa Claus.

"Whoa Mr. Comasterbator, where's the fire?"

Behind the counter, chuckling, sat a cadaverous black with dreads. The man was reading a paperback. Put his book down, took a half-smoked cheroot from a burned smudge on the counter, took a drag and let the smoke trickle out his nose over his eyes as he grinned, showing a large gold tooth.

"Lookin' for a sports car, red, an XKE. Came through about a half hour ago."

The man nodded. "Oh, yeah. The Ringmaster. Cra-a-azy dude. Helicopter picked him up on the highway." He thumbed toward the entrance ramp to I 16 as if a helicopter pick up was a daily occurrence. "Gimme a gift, if'n I wouldn't call the law."

"What kind of a gift?"

He pulled out five fifty-dollar bills and cackled.

"Why did you call him the Ring Master?"

"On account of his talk, and bowing and hand jivin'. Oh, lest I forget, I do believe there were some illicit substances flowin' fre-e-e-ly through his veins."

"You got that right."

He walked back to the glass doors. Red and yellow streaks peaking over the pines. A helicopter pick up in the middle of I 16.

Handy had a long reach.

"You gon' lock me up? Aidin' and abettin?" the clerk asked.

"No sir. And you can keep your gift."

* * * *

The EMS techs had removed and bagged the arrow bits in plastic bags when HB pulled up. The sun was shaping the trees with reddish light. Strapped in his gurney, Lizard lay glassy-eyed, staring at nothing.

"When the morphine locked horns with the speed," the tech said, "that pretty much x-ed out his cognitive functions.".

She was a perky tan blond, about thirty, hair cut short. She handed him the arrow pieces.

"Don't get many calls for cross bow arrow removals," she said, shielding her eyes from the sun.

"The shot came from forty yards away, direct hit in Lizard's thigh."

Impressed, she nodded.

"You're the preaching chief of Ocopeeco," as she took Lizard's blood pressure, pumping the cuff.

"Guilty as charged. HB Alpata." He stuck out his hand.

"Nancy Klein," she said, and they shook.

She ripped the Velcro off. "You're the reason all the unattached techies wanna get a call from Ocopeeco."

"Well . . . " he said, grinning.

The two women lifted Lizard up into their bus.

"Y'all working out of Macon?" he said, following.

"Coliseum," Nancy said. She nodded at the victim, "I was gonna say your friend here was real lucky, but if somebody is that good with a cross bow and didn't kill him, I'd say the shooter's not done."

"Yup. Wing and not waste."

She turned her full attention to him, smiling. "A pistol packin' keeper of the peace, a preacher and a poet."

"Steady on there, Nancy."

They closed the back bus doors.

As she climbed into the driver's side, she handed him a card. "My cell's on the back. Gimme a call sometime."

He took the card and flapped it against the tips of his fingers. "Nancy, you're parents are to be commended for the lovely, intelligent daughter they raised. But I am happily married."

She held up her own wedding ring.

"Home of the brave, Chief, land of the free."

Holy Saint Maximus!

* * * *

He searched the pines beyond Lizard's trailer and found three spots where Damon waited. Cigarettes at each, and a power bar wrapper. But the spots were even farther way from the trailer than he'd guessed, at least forty yards. The guy was some kind of long range super star.

Back home he found post-it notes on his monitor. Roxanne had called their land line. Rosie drew pitchforks above the name and burning flames that were supposed to represent the fires of Hell.

For Roxanne.

He shook his head.

She also reminded him he was preaching Sunday. Because their congregation was so small and he was so busy, he only preached once a month. He looked forward to it.

He headed into Macon and Coliseum Hospital. Traffic was thick on I 16, the eight o'clock going to work crowd. As he passed the Ocmulgee temple mound, the cars ground to a halt. Glad to be in his truck since it was cold, the engine putting out thick smoke. He recalled the evening his dad took him to the mound, thanks to the park ranger, an old friend, who let them in after hours. On top they could see across the Ocmulgee to the twinkling lights of Macon. It was twilight and bats criss crossed above them. Even at age eleven he knew he had one foot in the present and one in the past. But if it made his dad happy, he was willing to do it. Pain taught him a chant which he enjoyed and sang well. It made his Father glow to hear his singing in the moonlight on the ancient burial site at the top of his lungs words he didn't understand, a sad Creek funeral lament, as it wrapped them both in its arms, arms that had known centuries of abuse and desperation. His Dad joined in harmony. He was already growing taller than his father and he recalled ordering his body to stop so his growth wouldn't leave his dad behind. It was wrong for a son to be taller than his father; but that was only a symbol of all the other ways they were moving apart. His mom, Alice, was already taking him for catechesis at St. Joseph's where he learned the Holy Spirit needed to nudge Hesagedamesse out of the frame.

Lizard was on the sixth floor. HB removed his Stetson before entering the room where the victim lay, sassy, propped up, flipping channels.

Lizard threw up his hands. "Well, Chief, here I am, a sittin' duck. Figure that maniac'll poison my jello or disguise hisself as a brain surgeon and cut out what good sense I got left."

"I contacted the Bibb County chief. Soon as I leave there'll be a man at your door."

"Not some doughnut belly. Gimme one of them mean Terminator types with steel teeth and massive bi-ceps. I mean, Chief, they's been a half dozen of these medical dudes traipsin' through here, takin' notes and photos. Never seen an arrow wound, they say. Act like I'm some kinda two-legged guinea pig. And the local law? They all doughnut bellies and pudgy faced. Man, the crooks must be sproutin' like weeds in this county."

"Got any body in mind you want to stand guard?"

"You."

"Me?"

"Yeah, you the only one big enough and smart enough to take down this monster. Rest o' these goobers can't tie their shoes."

The little conniver was in good spirits, at least. But he didn't seem to get it. Handy was waiting now to see if Damon had scared Lizard enough to give back the money he stole. He wondered if Lizard really didn't get it or was he acting dumb.

"Well, we proved one thing for sure," he said.

"What?"

"You weren't lying."

"Lying! Chief . . . "

"Look, Lizard, Up to this very day you and I have had a relationship based mostly on me trying to figure out how much and why you were lying. Hell, how many honest-to-gosh truthful statements have you ever uttered in my presence."

"Well, if you're gonna get picky . . . "

"Picky! Up until the moment I saw that arrow sailing into your trailer, I still wasn't certain you were telling the truth. Fentanyl? An Atlanta drug king? In Ocopeeco?"

"Hell, Chief, since you don't believe a word I say, how you know I ain't hired somebody to Geronimo my trailer?"

"Does Geronimo smoke Gauloises?"

"Huh?"

"Cause if he doesn't, he's out of the frame. Happy Damon, on the other hand, does. I recognized their stench the day he pulled up in front of our church."

"So, I'm off your list, but still on his."

"Something like that. Handy sent a copter to pick Damon up on I 16."

"Fat showoff."

"How far does Handy reach?"

Closing his eyes and rubbing his face, he said: "He claims he owns the Savannah ports. But that's a crock. All south and central America come into that port. I do know he's got men in the longshoremen and a few in the Atlanta PD."

A perky black nurse came in to check his blood pressure which had been high.

"Mr. Lizard, you been smoking again?" she said as she wrapped the cuff around his pale, skinny arm. She had short hair and long curly lashes. Popping gum, she moved and talked with the insouciance of a teen age pom pom girl.

"I swear I ain't broke no rules, Crystal. 'Cept may be the one says don't hit on the sexy black nurses."

She rolled her eyes and patted her foot as she squeezed the pressure ball, listening.

"175 over 95," she announced, as she frowned. "Smoking makes your pressure go up. You know that don't you?"

"Do now," he said, grinning at her. "Why don't you drop in later and gimme some pointers how to get my numbers down?"

"Pointers? Son, you don't need pointers. You need a good kick in the butt. Make you give up that nasty habit."

After she left, he slipped a pack of Marlboros and a lighter from under his pillow and lit up, dragging tight and close to his mouth, then leaning over and blowing the smoke under the bed.

Misguided thinking, HB thought. Thinks he can get away with smoking; still thinks he can get away with Handy's cash.

"So, what are you going to do?" he asked.

"Do?" Lizard said. "Hell, get outta here and maybe relocate."

"Not a good idea."

"Why not? What do you know I don't?"

"I know Handy's waiting to see if you're going to cough up his money. I also know Damon was just playing with you. Next time, he won't wing you."

The little man shifted his eyes away and twitched his mouth. Either he hadn't thought about this, which HB found hard to believe, or having somebody else say it aloud had a sobering effect on the man.

He lowered his voice. "That's what you think, huh?"

"That's what I know."

He made his way over to the Bibb County chief's department where he used their nation-wide data base to look Handy up. Real name: George Washington du Bois Handy. A Waffle House chef whose fries and grilled cheese sandwiches impressed an Atlanta wise guy so much he hired Handy and the short order chef never looked back. Only one speeding ticket. A model citizen.

Lizard was convinced Damon killed Big Rig, but something didn't fit. For one, Damon was a long range killer. Plus, he was a firearms fanatic. How many people would have known about Rosie's grandfather? He saw it that first day, the way the guy fondled his pistol like a precious pet. Plus, Big Rig would never have let a psycho creep like Damon get close enough to him to lay a knife on him. If his throat had been cut from behind, maybe, but a gut grinding head on? The trucker would have kept Damon at a distance. The person who killed Big Rig had to be someone he was willing to get close to, or maybe someone he was trying to get close to and they resisted.

Chapter Five

The plant manager shouted on his cell: "You better get up here right now, chief, before somebody gets killed!"

The manager met him at the Rio Grande gate, a lanky pelican-like galoot named Dixon, captain of the softball team. HB recalled his long skinny right arm fired a blazing underhand when he pitched for the Planters versus the Towners.

They walked fast, Dixon talking faster.

"I got 'em separated for now. We got five Scruggs cousins at the plant. After the killing, they all got hair triggers. And there's troublemakers like to egg 'em on, saying Big Rig ran drugs."

At night, the kaolin plant took on an other worldly aura. Caked in lumpy white like a Nordic god's candy cane castle, belching smoke and chugging away 24/7, it gleaned prosperity out of the trillions of tiny cretaceous organisms it processed. As a boy, more than once he woke up from a bad dream to stare sleepily out his window and there it stood like the very engine of his nocturnal fantasies.

They climbed a steel stairway, passed between massive rumbling boilers and wound up in a wire pen, ten by ten by ten.

Two men sat on a wooden bench, bent over, elbows on their knees. One held a rag over his bleeding ear; the other daubed his nose with paper towels.

A guard nearby stood over them with a .20 gauge shotgun.

Dixon approached them, hands on his hips and his teeth bared. "I am not gonna let you two idiots mess up my safety record! We going on 5 years without a single lost time accident."

He looked at the heavy set man. "Scruggs, I swear, I think you woulda used that wrench. You coulda killed Poteet!"

Scruggs looked up from daubing his ear, the clump of knotted hair sprouting out of it clotted with dried blood. Knots of muscle across his chest and upper arms. He gave off a strong smell of onion as he turned his head towards Poteet.

"I ain't killed him, but I will, he keeps mouthin' off 'bout Big Rig."

Dixon turned to HB. "See what I'm dealin' with here?"

Poteet jiggled his leg, gripping the bench as if it were about to blast off. He raced his hand through a shock of greasy brown hair, the V line in front. He flashed a quick grin up at the manager.

"I ain't gon' say nothin' else, Mr. Dixon. I swear . . . ."

The man was not exactly lying, but picking on his slow-witted co-worker was obviously too much fun. Like gasoline and matches, these two. HB reckoned the man would do it again and Scruggs would kill him or maim him for life.

He took Dixon aside. "Scruggs ought to have a doc look at his head. Could be a concussion."

Dixon grimaced. "I ain't taking him to no doc and that's final."

"Okay. You're the boss. Maybe I can lock 'em up and let 'em cool off, but then you'll have to report it, and I'll have to report it, and it'll begin to look a lot like a lost time accident."

Dixon pulled his nose and popped in a stick of gum.

They were standing on a steel floor, see through, revealing below them a conveyor belt slowly moving chunks of just-mined kaolin.

"Hell, we can't do that. Look, give Poteet a talkin' to. He's already on thin ice. He's been clean for six months, but this Big Rig thing's set him off. Now he's back usin' again. Got a fine wife and three kids at home, one in Middle School. Talk to him. He's gotta straighten up."

HB took him to his truck where he opened up Rosie's coffee mug. Soon the man was sipping and talking.

After chatting a few minutes, HB realized the man was faking contrition.

Poteet eyed the cigarettes on the console.

"You mind?"

"Sure."

He lit up, hands shaking.

"Nervous?" HB asked.

"A little. That fat-head booger woulda clicked my ticket. Hell, he still might."

HB took off his Stetson and ran his hand through his hair.

A fat, gibbous moon loomed above the plant, speckled gray.

"You ain't gon' find him, are you?" Poteet said, smirking, flipping his cigarette with his thumb.

"What makes you say that?"

With smoke clouding his head, the man chuckled. "Hell, chief, you ain't even got a fingerprint scanner."

He did not, but when he needed one, he hopped over to Jeffersonville and the sheriff always obliged.

"You better be worried about yourself," he said. "Your boss says you got a family, responsibilities. You want to lose all that?"

"I ain't losing nothing. I got it figured out."

"Next time I see you, you'll be lying on the side of the road in a ditch with a bullet or two in your brain or your throat'll be slashed open like a fat October sow."

"Why you son-of-a-bitch. . .!" Poteet leapt for him, but HB chopped him hard in the throat and the man doubled over, gagging and cussing.

Dixon appeared at his open window.

"What happened?"

"Mr. Poteet doesn't agree with my assessment of his prospects."

Dixon walked around to the other side and opened the door. He grabbed the man and dragged him out on the ground. "Get on back in the plant," he said.

HB and the manager watched as the man staggered, fumbled around on the gravel for his smoke, took a few puffs and sashayed down the concrete walk.

"I got a brother-in-law just like him," Dixon said. "Talks a mile a minute, can't keep it zipped and high on something every week-end."

He rubbed his jaw, "Look, chief, I sure as hell don't wanna tell you how to do your job, but I'm 'on tell you what's a fact. My job's on the line here. You got to find this killer."

HB put his Stetson back on and cranked his truck.

"Mr. Dixon, I'm doing everything I can."

The foreman stood with both feet planted wide, gripping his elbows in his palms. As the truck pulled away, he nodded.

Was it as nod of assurance or did it say: Chief, you don't have a friggin' chance.

Later that night, as he climbed into bed, his mind was churning. Dixon claimed his foreman's job was on the line. But maybe the town council was coming after him, too. Lack of money, lack of forensic equipment, lack of personnel: none of that mattered. Small town folks can be loving and neighborly, but like a domesticated German shepard, they can turn savage. He had to spin gold out of straw, but this was no fairy tale.

* * * *

Rosie had on her best black pants suit and stiletto heels as she sipped an espresso at the counter, her nourishment for the day. Whenever a big event rolled around, she fasted, and today was high tea at the president's mansion, a slide show on Hildegard in honor of a visiting medievalist from Cambridge UK. Cucumber sandwiches and the university's 1855 silverware. Pinkies lifted, plaster of Paris smiles and an air of irony about all things grave.

Pretending to read the paper, HB observed as she recited sotto voce, patted her foot in rhythm and sipped. He didn't want to distract her; but he knew she'd want to know. And just as she was primed to knock 'em off their feet at the president's mansion. The dapper, old world President had a little crush on her; she knew it, HB knew it, everybody at the college knew it. And with just cause. Rosie was his show-off professor for prestigious academic visitors. And every now and then, a presentation at the president's led to grants and endowments.

"Fracas at the plant last night," he said, turning the page.

"Fracas?" she said and set her cup down. The foot tapping stopped.

"Two men fighting about Big Rig."

She wrinkled her nose. "Why?"

"One's a cousin, one of five working at the plant. The other was needling him about Big Rig and drugs."

She sat down opposite him.

"The foreman's worried," he said.

She leaned forward and took his hands.

Amazing, how her attention could shift in a nano second from an eleventh century German abbess to him, and she was right there with him, feeling, seeing what he saw.

"If I don't find the killer soon," he said, "all hell will break loose at the plant. The foreman's scared he'll lose his job. Plus . . . "

"Plus . . . what?"

"I think I might lose mine."

"The town council?"

He nodded.

Like hundreds of small birds settling into a tree, all the ideas and worries and fears of the recent months came to a head. He didn't just have a job. Their small town was home, where he was born, where he spoke to every person because he knew their PTSD father or helped rescue their mother's cat from a pine tree or from time to time sat beside their grandmother's bed because the family couldn't afford a nursing home. He was at the center of the tender tissue of trust that bound the town. Firing would rock him to the core.

* * * *

The checkout line at The Good'n Green was longer than usual, so he tramped back to the coffee section and picked up a second bag. Now that Mico drank it, the family went through a pound fast. When he returned, he was standing behind a towering Georgia Power linesman, white helmet, tools dangling off his belt.

Ahead of him, two women chatted.

"I'm puttin' in an ADT," the first said, leaning over on her basket and slipping her shoe on and off. "We got three kids under seven. No telling what kind of pervert is out there waitin' to kill us in our sleep."

"Frank sleeps with his pistol by the bed," the second said, as she mindlessly picked up a can of peas from her basket and read the label. "He says the chief ain't gon' find him. Says it's every man for himself."

"You think it'll come to that?"

"Frank says it always does. Got to protect your own when the law is as sorry as HB Alpata."

He shrank behind the lineman and hid. How many times in life are you permitted to hear judgment pronounced on you and your work by the people you're tasked to protect? As their conversation flowed, he wondered how long until the whole town, including the town council, turned on him.

* * * *

During pre-sermon refreshment hour Rosie whispered: "I wonder if you should say anything about the murder—from the pulpit, I mean?"

He dipped his marzipan into his coffee and bit. Wearing his navy blue blazer, brass buttons and a scotch plaid tie.

She wiped a fallen crumb from his lapel.

Before he could answer, Mico passed with a paper plate teeter- tottering with marzipan. He glanced sheepishly at his parents.

"I'm really hungry."

"When are you not hungry?" she asked.

"Once two years ago, just after English."

"You had a panic attack," HB said, grinning.

"I did. I broke out in a sweat and started to question my existence."

"Ha, ha," Rosie popped him on the arm. "You've been hanging around Nate too much. Don't make a mess."

Aubrey made a grand entrance through the front door, the court painter, long white beard, head high, glancing around, to insure that all eyes were directed at him.

Rosie nudged HB.

He wore a velvet purple blazer, a vermilion paisley ascot, light blue skintight leather pants, and boots with high heels. A ring on every finger, eight, faux gold to faux pearl. And a gold tipped cane.

He approached the Alpata's and held up his hands.

"Trophies from my last junket to my New Mexican artist colony. Rings make me feel present, you know, in the moment. More and more I need to feel in the moment. Tap into the cosmic energy that's waiting there. In our bourgeois throw away culture it's so easy to feel you don't exist."

"I like the pearl," Rosie said, and leaned down to examine it.

"Duke, I stopped in at Lizard's to stock up on his exquisite hickory smoked jerky and some corpulent dryad who claimed to be his cousin, said he was in the hospital."

"Lizard cut his leg with a box cutter, half-severed an artery. Nearly bled to death. I walked in just after it happened and got him to the hospital."

The dandy's face twisted under his long white beard. "Hmm. Well, I do hope you have a cutting communique from Mt. Sinai today. Something useful like how to get a paint stain out of my smock."

"Depends on the color," HB said.

"Red."

"The color of blood."

"Actually, blood is not red," Aubrey said.

"You're right," HB said, "the level or amount of oxygen in the blood determines the hue of red. It changes color depending on where it is in its cycle. William Harvey discovered the cycle 1628, Exercitatio Anatomica de Motu Cordis et Sanguinis in Animalibus. Before Harvey it was assumed blood was static in the body, but no one knew why its color fluctuated."

Aubrey smiled coldly. "How boring." He extended his cane and made his ostentatious entrance into the sanctuary.

"Why does he even come?" Rosie asked.

"His soul is empty. I think he knows it and it terrifies him."

They followed the painter in.

She sat in the pews; he mounted the dais and sat behind the lectern.

On his knee, he placed his fuzzy, beat-up RSV. As was his custom on the Sundays he preached, he prayed for the congregation, the five single moms, none with fewer than two kids, two working three jobs, husbands dead, disappeared or indifferent. He prayed against depression in the community, always stalking a kaolin town where the jobs depended on the kaolin market. Many of his people lived from paycheck to paycheck. Or those battling cancer, scared to go to the doctor, or those who won Round One, but weren't at all convinced they could hold out through Round Two. The adulterers, the envious, the addicts.

He prayed for Aubrey and Weeping Woman and Lizard Little and yes, even though he rebelled against it, for Happy Damon, Iraneus Loadholt, that a miracle would crack through the self-made masks the man felt compelled to wear, for Nancy Klein, that her adulterous heart would be transformed, for the old black gentleman at the 7/11, and for Dixon, Poteet and Scruggs at the plant.

His topic was hate, how our Lord tells us if we harbor hate in the heart we are murderers. The words and ideas flowed freely because he was on speaking terms with this particular demon. It destroys the hater, he told them. It robs your life of joy. And how well they understood. Their eyes showed it. The quick smiles when they recognized themselves or someone close. Besides, Christmas was approaching. They should be preparing their hearts for the Savior.

But when his eyes came to blond Roxanne, he was startled. Seated in the back, arms crossed, dressed in see-through material, she glared at him, through him, reading his soul. He recovered, continued and was reluctant to cast his eyes her way again, but finally, he couldn't resist and was met with the same fierce glare. He recalled her trashy mouth at the cemetery. That embarrassing moment stirred uncomfortable waves in his own household for days.

Roxanne had no family in town. She never talked about husbands or boyfriends, came to Georgia from Miami. Occasionally, she mentioned her hippy days and living in an Ashram in India for three years. The only Roxanne event that stood out was her annual exercise in public self-abasement when she got drunk and climbed the water tower. Dec. 25th, every year. It had become a town joke, part of an Ocopeeco Christmas like Santa Claus. Even Roxanne kidded about it at the bar and claimed it was her way of letting off steam. She said she had to let it all hang out once a year. What man or woman owns a bar and puts up with drunks week in and week out and doesn't need to let it all hang out at least once a year?

She always demanded HB climb the tower to bring her down. And today was Dec. 22.

* * * *

The knock on the back door came about 2 AM. After his usual night-mares of sand-swept IED explosions, he actually had a decent dream. He and Mico were throwing the paper route together. They rowed a swift, icy mountain stream in North Georgia, the water flowing under their canoe like the breath of heaven. The houses were situated so the owner could step out the front door, take the paper from Mico's hands and pay him on the spot. And the customers smiled and had exact change. The sun was bright in a cloudless sky, a trout leapt into the light like a sacred unveiling. He'd never seen his son so happy. Afterwards, Mico gave him a hug and said: "Dad, I wish you and I could do that every time." As the words tore at him, guilt and shame shook their unforgiving heads.

At the door was Davy, Mico's wide receiver buddy. "My dad says to tell you it's time for you to play Santa Claus again. He said you'd know what he means."

He sighed. He'd hoped she'd forgotten. Usually, she went up around 1 AM, which allowed him time to get some decent sleep. But the Christmas was mild and the night clear, perfect weather for a tower climb.

He slipped on his gym clothes, laced up his sneakers, and sniffed the coffee Rosie was already making. She handed him a thermos as he headed out the door.

Slogging through the dew-soaked grass. Clouds tattered, occasionally lacing their way like an old timey lantern show in front of a luminous moon. A head high blanket of fog passed into his eyes.

His gut was sour from Rosie's baking. The woman attempted to recre-ate a Christmas Rhineland bake market: cakes, cookies, candies, Weihnacht on the Ocopeeco. Once, he asked for a moratorium—for the sake of his blood sugar; her explanation told him how important this was for her. She struggled to adapt to a culture where university scholars weren't honored, but mocked and labeled snowflakes, where guns were not just a weekend recreation for a few, and every little town had a half dozen churches, but no opera house, as they did in the Rhineland.

A group of men stood under the tower smoking, drinking long necks: a few kaolin truckers who lived on the hill, where Mico threw his papers, Aubrey, Jim Jeffords.

A bottle shattered on the concrete.

He looked up and she waved, one hundred sixty-five feet straight up, high enough to provide the necessary water pressure. Each foot of height provided 0.43 PSI, pounds per square inch.

He waved back.

"Merry Christmas, Ocopeeco," she shouted, "you goddamned Sodom and Gomorrah rat hole of human misery!"

Aubrey puffed from his long stem pipe. He wore a beret and a Navy P coat. "Ever notice how booze brings out the eloquence in that woman?"

"Hadn't noticed," HB said. "Too busy figuring out how to keep her from breaking her neck. If her bar closed, we'll have wide-spread panic, a rise in suicides and divorces."

Jim Jeffords thumbed his overalls. "And you might have to do some real police work."

"Exactly," HB said, as he checked the bottom of his sneakers for mud and rocks. "With Roxanne out, my sinecure would be blown to hell."

"Chief," she shouted down, "You got a hot-blooded woman up here!"

He unscrewed his thermos, poured a hot cup full, and sipped.

"What's she so worked up about?" he asked. "She usually sings a few Neil Diamond songs and that's it."

The metal circular platform she stood on started to vibrate.

They looked up.

She was jogging around the tower, stumbling, grabbing the rail, struggling up to jog again.

The group moved around to follow her

"Chief," Jim Jeffords said, "You better get on up there. That rail was put up in nineteen sixty-three."

Before HB got a foot on the first rung, she threw up. Gobbets of pizza and hydrochloric acidized aerosol rained on them.

"Cut it out, Roxanne!" Aubrey shouted, as he picked pizza bits off his Navy blue pea jacket.

"Pepperoni?" HB asked, grinning.

In the past the steel rungs were so cold that gripping them and hauling his two hundred twenty pounds straight up was tough. Tonight, with the sweet scent coming off the river, the moon, the mild temp, his body seemed to rise up the side of the tower like a lighter version of himself.

The men below grew smaller and smaller.

He thought about the evil eye she gave him in church. It made no sense; he and Roxanne had no history. Occasionally, he stopped in at the bar, more to pick up gossip than to drink. Usually, the crowd clammed up when he walked in, but every now and then, a regular would let his guard down and reveal what was really going on at the kaolin plant or who was cooking meth and where. Apart from that embarrassing scene at the funeral and "Howdy, Chief" when he came in the bar door, she rarely interacted with him. And he always played along with the tower stunt. It was life in a small town. Somebody does something weird but harmless.

When he stepped up onto the platform, she was smoking and leaning back, elbows against the rail.

"That metal pipe you're putting all your weight on was made in 1963," he said.

She scowled and moved away from it.

"Old and shabby, like everything else in this piss hole burg."

"Coffee?" He offered her the thermos.

From the hip pocket of her jump suit, she pulled a nearly empty bottle of Old Grandad. The red cotton cloth form fit her still attractive figure. And whatever she did, shoving drunks, hauling beer boxes, blasting through town in her yellow Corvette, her blond hair never seemed mussed.

"Yeah, coffee. I'm sick of this booze, anyway." She flung the bottle over the rail. "Hot, strong and black."

"Now you're talking."

After he poured her a styrofoam cup full, she took it, and they sat down on the wooden bench that encircled the tower. In the past, the city allowed young couples to climb up and do what young couples do.

Lawyers put a stop to that.

She drank one cup and asked for another.

"Feeling better?"

"M-m-m-m."

Usually, he needed five or six before she came around, but tonight, two did the trick. But he had to be sure she was sober enough to navigate the climb straight down, one hundred sixty-five feet. It was a daunting climb, even for a healthy youngster. He could see the media coverage if she fell.

He made her walk around the track, once, twice.

She returned, sweaty, but clear-eyed.

Sober, she became the no non-sense bartender, who kept a Louisville Slugger behind the bar. If the bat didn't work, she had a Glock in a drawer under the register. He'd seen her swing the bat, two truckers at pool, rolling over and over on the mud-caked concrete floor. After she cracked their ribs, they struggled up, cussing her, bent over, staggering toward the door, which she slammed behind them with: "Nasty drunks!"

"My life is so screwed up," she said.

"How so?"

"I had an abortion years ago. Thought it would be a mild surgical procedure. The procedure was. It was what came later."

"Guilt?"

"Like hyenas cackling. And I ain't a Catholic goody two shoes. My confirmation vows crumbled the first time a boy touched my boobs."

"Sounds like you have a conscience."

"Ah-h-h-h. I don't use priest words like that."

"It's not a priest word, Roxanne. You heart's telling you something's wrong. God whispers to us in our pleasures; but he shouts at us in our pain."

She paced, gnawing her fingers. "Always preaching. I mean the things I hear folks say about you, praying for the drunks and reading the Bible to bums doing drugs. How'd a man like you, a special ops. stud, how'd you get all tied up in the church and the Bible?"

He hadn't intended to turn this into a counselling session, and he suspected she was just stalling. That was the problem with her. She didn't know what she wanted. She fumbled along until an idea popped up that looked good, and she snatched at it.

He stood up, stretched and screwed the cap back on the thermos.

When she saw he was about to leave, she reached for him.

"Roxanne!"

"You and me, HB. You and me."

He backed away as she squeezed her breasts and puckered her lips.

His heart pounded.

"You think I been bringing you up here all these years for nothing. It's time, Chief. It's high time."

Her dark eyes riveted on him, she pushed his body against the rail, tried to unzip him.

"No!" he shouted and shoved her backwards onto the bench.

She pouted, petulant.

"Chie-ie-f-f . . . "

His heart slowed down as clear thoughts returned and reclaimed their rightful place.

"Get up!"

"But chief . . . "

"Get up, I said! We're going down, now!"

* * * *

A week after Roxanne made her tower climb, Pain took to his bed.

He told himself his time had come. For weeks, a dog botha (evil spirit) had lurked around his cabin, ribs showing, mangy, snarled at him whenever he came home and unlocked the front door. He was bold, this botha. Put his front paws up on the porch bench and stared in the window into the living room, lips curled back, nose like a fox. Why a dog botha? Didn't he merit something more noble, an owl or an eagle? Not some scraggy mutt. But bothas had only one task and this one was performing it masterfully: destroy his spirit, his will to live. His inner thoughts circled more and more around his failure that day at the Shack, how he caused someone to suffer, probably to die. For that there was no forgiveness, no healing. His faith was not like HB's where forgiveness and reconciliation were always there for the asking. To Pain that was too easy. HB claimed no sin was too great for God to forgive. How could anybody believe in a god like that? No god worth his salt forgives.

He drank only poplar leaf tea and bone broth he made himself. The loss of weight gave him a clarity he had never known before, a confirmation he was doing the right thing.

One night, lying in bed he looked out his window across his grassy field to the edge of the pine woods. From out of the trees a figure came walking, regal, tall. Even from that distance, he knew a great man had come to visit. His long face was almost feminine, full lips, a rich red cloth binding his black hair and a large eagle feather dangling. He was dressed in royal robes, silver and red and a leather belt hung from one shoulder and crossed his body.

When he reached Pain's window, he smiled and removed his head.

Osceola!

The great Seminole chief whose head was severed at Fort Moultrie so the learned white scientists could study it.

The chief passed through the cabin walls.

"Asi-Yaholo," Pain said. He wasn't afraid. He sat up in bed. "Greetings, great warrior."

The chief spoke so softly, Pain could hardly hear.

But as the visitor whispered, he underwent a transformation. His regal attire turned to tatters. His magnificent headdress was torn. A wind blew his beautiful black hair until it hung down over his eyes and his lips cracked like watching an quake open the earth and blood oozed from his naked arms, glistening open wounds.

"O great warrior!" Pain cried out, "What have they done to you?"

The apparition gave no answer. Slowly, his image faded until there was nothing.

* * * *

Rosie stopped by daily, after she got home from school. Usually, she brought a magazine or a newspaper—her father-in-law didn't subscribe to any-thing—or she brought German pastry. Usually, he climbed out of bed to sit with her in the living room and eat and drink coffee.

One afternoon he told her about the red sticks and the white sticks.

"There were two brothers, strong, intelligent, many gifts, but the one brother was aggressive, loved to forge ahead and get things done, rather than pause and consider the consequences. The other brother was contemplative. He loved plants and herbs and talked to them and knew there were many mysteries no one understood. But they loved one another dearly. One evening they were summoned by Ibofanga to the vision quest. They rose into the clouds into an unknown land of fog. They separated and promised to return and meet at that spot. The aggressive brother joined a community and became a great leader among them. They wanted to prepare for war, so he showed them all the strategies and built all the weapons they needed. He taught them how to fight. The other brother also found a community, but he taught them not to fight, but how to read plants and listen to them for healing and nourishment. When the brothers were reunited, they rejoiced and shared everything. They were so happy to be together, but they realized they had both changed. One, the aggressive one, was the red stick; the other, the white stick."

"Go on." Rosie said.

"I'm a white stick. HB is a red stick. I abhor violence. Alice and I opposed the war in Iraq and Afghanistan, even though HB served three tours. When he started school, he stood out as an athlete. He was big and strong. He excelled at football, baseball and basketball—and he could fight. Boy, was he a fighter."

"My husband?"

"You haven't seen that side of him much. Here in Ocopeeco not much happens. I think that's why he stays here. Alice and I were called to the school so many times because some kid made an 'Injun' slur and your husband put his lights out."

"But you still love one another."

"We do. But there are times when that divide seems so wide," Pain said.

* * * *

In nineteen forty-four twenty- one Trappist monks left Gethsemane Abby in rural, mostly Christian Kentucky to establish the Monastery of the Holy Ghost in rural, mostly Christian Conyers, Georgia. Now, as Father Ignatius (Iggy) explained to HB, the monks were surrounded by Atlanta's urban, mostly secular sprawl.

They drank coffee in a screen porch that bordered the bonsai green house. Iggy poked the flame in the hearth, sleeves pulled up revealing the powerful, muscle-laced forearm of a one time All-American wide receiver for Alabama. He and HB played against one another for four years, The Georgia Bulldogs vs. Alabama's Crimson Tide. After their senior game (and a brutal Tide victory), they met in an Athens bar, drank the house closed and became close friends. In recent years Iggy had become HB's father confessor.

"The whole town's about to explode over this murder. I may get fired over it. Then what happens to my family? And then there's my congregation. So many living from hand to mouth."

"And it's all on your shoulders."

HB eyed him. "What?"

Iggy grinned. "You're not letting the Lord do any of the lifting here." He squatted on his haunches, still limber after twenty years away from the gridiron.

HB sighed, leaned over till their faces were six inches apart.

"I had a flashback," he whispered, "a bad one. I was in the woods outside town chasing this sociopath jacked up on PCP going at me with a flame thrower when it happened. Right there I was back in the sand with that demon Taliban on top of me so close I could smell his cigarettes and coffee."

"What'd you do?"

"I rode it out, leaning against a pine, shaking, crying. Hell, that flame-throwing nut could have grilled me."

Iggy popped up, twisting back and forth, and stretching to the floor.

"The worst thing though is what's happening to dad. He didn't embark on this Pain the Healer mission until after mother died. I thought: that's natural. Your spouse dies, you gotta keep busy, find an avocation. But the more I thought about it, I wondered: is he doing this to get back at me because I turned my back on his Creek world?"

"You two ever talk about this?"

"We skirt around it. But dad doesn't show his feelings much."

"Does he understand what you went through over there?"

"I've never told him about my breakdown and the year in the hospital, nibbling at nothingness. He just thinks I served my country, came home healthy and wiser, my brain kicked on, I found God and here I am."

"B., you need to tell him how you changed."

"I do."

"I hate to think of all the hurt you ran into over there. But look at what came out of it. You hit rock bottom which is where the Lord had been waiting for you all these years. Remember before your first tour, when I was considering the monastery and you looked at me like I had three heads."

HB nodded with a hint of a smile.

Iggy assumed a boxer's stance. "Almost came to blows one night in Manuel's in Atlanta. Remember? Just after I parted company with the Bucs. You insulted everybody from Thomas Merton to Mother Theresa, called them all a bunch of second rate losers, not an ounce of courage in the lot of them."

HB was chuckling now and shaking his head as he also assumed the boxing stance, and they stalked around each other.

Iggy went on: "I stood toe to toe with you, and said: 'B, shut your mouth, or I'm gonna crack every tooth in your head.'"

"Yeah," HB said, "and that little UGA freshman yelled out to me: 'Hey, mister, are you nuts? That's Carleton Cash, with the Tampa Bay Bucs.'"

The dropped their arms and looked into each other's eyes.

Iggy threw his arms around his friend. "I got your back, buddy. Always. You know that, right?"

"I do."

"I'm on' give you a tape book on Mother Theresa. It's meant the world to me. I want you to listen to it while you're driving back. And remember, we aren't called to understand folks, just love 'em."

He raised his hand over HB. "Lord, my buddy Big B here is hurtin' real bad. He's got a case of the 'I'm indispensables.' I know you run up against that little demon regularly, so I also know you can take him out with one good helmet in the gut. Lord, put on your pads for my buddy. Show him how light your load is, so he can lighten his. Amen and Amen."

* * * *

The old gravel road out of the monastery ran through soybean fields. HB stopped to admire the perfect rows and lowered his window to let in the January chill. He was driving Rosie's Toyota to save gas.

The peace of the well-tilled field and the cool air lulled him into a reverie he was awakened from when an engine roared up behind him. He turned around: a black army-issue Humvee, tinted glass so he couldn't see the driver. The big machine nudged at the Toyota bumper. He was about to get out, but his car started moving. He jammed his foot on the brake, but the Toyota was no match. The Humvee shoved him along the deserted road like a toy. He opened his window, leaned out and showed his badge and gun, but the driver refused to slow down.

He took aim at the Humvee's mirror and blasted it off. Still the thing kept coming.

He was bouncing up and down, his head hitting the ceiling.

Ahead lay a creek and a bridge. There were still no cars on the road as the Humvee pushed his Toyota away from the bridge to the edge of the creek and stopped. Below, the water ran swift and murky, the drop some one hundred feet.

He jumped out, rolled, took a knee, and fired. The Humvee driver in a ski mask leapt on top of the vehicle and returned fire on the Toyota with a M4.

The big gun ripped his car to shreds.

While HB sprinted for the nearest large pine tree, the ski mask got back in, revved his motor until the roar was deafening, barreled into the Toyota, and sent it flying into the creek. The mask leapt out, fired a long, arching flame and within seconds Rosie's car was a ball of fire.

After the Humvee wheeled around and disappeared down the gravel road, HB walked to the creek's edge. His .30.06 was inside, his cell, a notebook with info on Big Rig's case.

Then, he felt the cold on his head.

He reached up.

His Stetson!

Cursing, he kicked a log, and the pain threw him to the ground.

After massaging his ankle, he walked back to the monastery.

Had to be Damon.

He remembered what Sheriff Brown had told him. In the sheriff's younger days, a killer became obsessed with him. Stalked him, tried to ambush him, even went after his wife.

The monastery's waiting room was decorated in early twentieth century Funeral Home: austere, thick gray carpet, a giant oil portrait of Bishop Fulton J. Sheen, somber, black drapes.

He explained his situation to a Brother Chrysostom, a nervous novice, freshly shaved, nearly bald, a goofy, gawking grin and a midwestern accent. Seated at the glass-topped greeter's table, the youngster looked up and listened as HB unrolled his story.

"So, Mr. Alpata, you need to notify your wife that her car has been blown apart and burned and this was done by a known criminal in a ski mask who drove an Army-issued Humvee, a man you're currently investigating for murder. And his name or a least the name he goes by is Happy Damon with an Umlaut and he performs cover shows under the name of some obscure rock and roller called Jerry Lee Lewis."

"You never heard of Jerry Lee Lewis?"

"No."

"Where are you from?"

"Oshkosh."

HB took a seat on the sofa below the portrait of Bishop Fulton J. Sheen. He'd bet a year's salary the bishop had heard of Jerry Lee.

Wound up and tick tight, he breathed deep, using the technique Rosie taught him

"I'm not sure if I should allow you to use the monastery's landline, Chief Alpata," the young novice said. "Father Prior has strict rules about these things."

"Son," HB said, standing, "do you understand what I'm saying to you! My car was destroyed. Destroyed! I'm not asking you to call mommy to pick me up from band rehearsal!"

"We ..uh . . . we don't have a monastery band, Chief. Why would you say that?"

HB's heart pounded and he clenched his fists.

The novice realized he was in over his head. Leaning forward, he punched the intercom.

A elder's voice came on. "Brother Chrysostom?"

"Father, we have a situation here. I think you'd better send for Brother Ignatius and Brother Thomas."

"The big guys?"

"Yes, Father Prior, the big guys."

HB threw back his head and hollered. "The big guys! Praise God, son! Calvary's cavalry's coming!"

* * * *

"Their spot" was a deep black water lagoon where white sand jutted out into the Ocopeeco and made a perfect picnic swim site. A warm Saturday, low clouds meandering above them and the wind over them, they lay in their suits on the beach blanket, a bottle of Liebfraumilch and Rosie's tuna sandwiches for a morning out of time.

She rose and walked to the water's edge, turned, winked at him, and slipped off her suit. Forty years had unveiled such a flowering of her beauty, not the eye candy that captures a youngster, but the deeper life-molded loveliness of a brilliant woman.

He recalled their first meeting on the college library steps. Al and his wife and Rosie were coming out the glass doors and he was going in, book bag over his shoulder. Introductions, fumbling, Al cracking jokes, a magnet drawing the two of them, locking their eyes. As he walked away, turning, looking, stumbling, she giggled. Later, as a PTSD survivor, he worked hard to enter her good graces, and she made it so easy. She listened to his story and allowed him to escape his self-imposed jail of fear and shame and hate.

He joined her, au naturel. The black water covered over their shoulders as they embraced.

Afterwards, they lay on their stomachs on blankets.

"This man is obsessed with you," she said, as she rubbed oil on his back.

"Bad guys sometimes do that."

"You think the man is gay?"

"No. He just hates me. He has a need to confront and destroy me,"

* * * *

He pulled his truck into Roxanne's dusty parking lot.

A big sign hung on the door into the bar and said in Sharpie: "Aubrey Sold a Painting!"

"A Whiter Shade of Pale" was playing on the juke box, and the dusty parking lot was packed with kaolin-covered trucks and cars, except for one silver BMW and a black Benz, both from Dekalb County. The painter had landed a buyer on the board of the High Museum in Atlanta. Aubrey's work was going to hang in the museum's permanent collection!

HB thought about the arrogant, little bearded man, a leprechaun pounding sides of beef with a baseball bat in the woods, claiming that was how he became inspired. Most artists were phonies, but he acknowledged there were certain men and women, gifted, hardworking, who were struck by divine lightning and hurled into the great tradition. Was Aubrey really one of those?

He let his engine run in the cold and watched the smoke from his exhaust gather round.

It couldn't happen to a more obnoxious guy.

Just that morning at breakfast over brötchen and marmalade Rosie whistled and held up an article in the Atlanta Journal and Constitution. It showed a photo of the white-bearded Aubrey and a tall, blond twenty-five year old buyer, Boisfeullet d'Argent. The delicately handsome trust fund baby smirked at the camera, towered over Aubrey, and laid his hand on the easel where the painting was mounted. Rosie read aloud: "*The Orange Head Devouring his Children*. The painting is a virtuoso rendering of Goya, who depicted the frenzied Saturn, unable to control his lust for filiacide. The god is rough and naked, but in Aubrey's glorious transformation the disheveled hair is orange and combed in that obscene wrap-around style we cannot help but associate with a certain politician. The Orange Head also has an erect phallus, rendering his figure even more of an affront."

Inside Roxanne's, a thick cloud of overhanging cigarette smoke.

HB approached the painting where it sat on an easel in the middle of the crowded room.

Aubrey slipped up behind him and whispered; "Fooled ya, didn't I?"

HB shook his head. "Where's the hanging beef?"

"I told you, pounding the beef is only to kick start the imagination. It sends me to the place where the unconscious rules, where I set my sights on the real subject, the father and the son as they battle to the death. The father fears the sons. One of them will destroy him. The crass political angle came to me in a dream. But before all that, before anything happens on the canvas, I have to pound that beef."

HB removed his Stetson: "Aubrey, I actually understood some of that."

The elfish white-bearded artist threw back his head: "Hell, yeah, chief!"

"Does every one of your paintings demand a battle?"

"Only the good ones. Art is war. I know, that sounds like Nazi aesthetics. But as a child, I was short and mocked, ridiculed, so my muse is stingy, she hoards her gifts. I have to assault her head on and snatch her gifts from her naked arms. For the Orange Head we scaled her ramparts, breached her inner sanctum where King Priam was held up, terrified with all his wives and children, and we slit his throat. Then we watched him bleed out and we came away with $250,000."

Someone tried to thrust an open PBR in HB's hand.

"Nope," he said, "on duty."

"C'mon chief. Lock up the preacher and let the big dog run."

"I'd say the big dogs are running just fine without my help."

Aubrey relit his long-stem leprechaun pipe. Smoke billowed up, he waved the match and cocked his head up at HB. His eyes twinkled.

"Still think I gutted that child abuser?"

"Aubrey, you have enough pent up rage in you to single handed take out the Taliban."

The painter frowned, waved HB away and sauntered off.

Of all people, Weeping Woman nursed a beer at the bar, smoking. Her brown hair long in a smooth sweep down like Veronica Lake. The pose she assumed struck him as contrived, as if she was trying it on to see if anyone disapproved.

He eased onto the stool beside her as she gazed out at the dancers and the thick smoke. The cigarette was only for show. She hadn't taken a single drag.

He removed his hat. "Good to see you, Lurleen."

"You mean good to see me out of the bottle and the river?"

Clunk! He felt stupid. Rosie was so much better at chit chat.

"Can you believe that?" she said, nodding towards Aubrey passing through the crowd, shaking hands, basking in his conquest.

"He's really struck it rich," he said.

"Some Atlanta trust fund baby making a name for himself among the glitterati. And that painting!"

"It's not Rembrandt."

"No, it's Goya. That's what the little snot does. He picks a classic work and modifies it to bring out a political angle he knows will set the buyer class to drooling. He's like a showman who knows his audience."

"Didn't know you followed art."

She pounded her cigarette in the ashtray and smirked. "You mean how could a woman married to a misogynist child abuser with the politics of Attila the Hun have any idea what art is?"

He sighed.

"I apologize," she said and put her hand on his. "Before I had a family, I read a book. I've even been to a museum."

His eyes found the buyer, a real golden boy, tan, blond hair in glorious curls. Held his cigarette between his thumb and index finger. When he took a drag, he let the smoke dribble out and trickle up his face.

But after an hour of the twang and sugar-coated slide of country music, the yelps and the whoops and back slaps, the trust fund baby was in pain. His smirk sagged, and his eyes had rolled so many times they were sore. Aubrey had obviously twisted his arm to visit Ocopeeco and get a look at the squalid backwoods setting necessary for great art to emerge. Out of suffering and deprivation comes great beauty, and all that. HB suspected the kid would drive home to Buckhead, strip off all his clothes and have them burned.

Aubrey stood in a chair and banged a knife against his draft glass.

"Hear ye, hear ye, good citizens of Ocopeeco, my boon companions. I have lived among you now for five glorious years. Your hospitality, and generosity to me, an interloper, has touched my heart. You have not stinted with your care.

"But I have a complaint. No, a charge. It has touched my sensitive artist soul, among all the good fruit and good fortune my stay here has yielded, this one thing has tainted the water."

He pointed at HB.

"Our honorable chief, HB Alpata, you all know him, a man who combines the piety of Job with the shooting eye of Billy the Kid, has accused me of killing Big Rig Scruggs."

The crowd grew silent. Everyone turned to HB.

"Before God and you good people of Ocopeeco," Aubrey declared, "I swear I did not commit that heinous deed. What do you say Chief? Will you verify to the good folks here assembled that I am innocent?"

Weeping Woman whispered "That son of a bitch!"

Out of the corner of his eye, HB caught Roxanne standing by the cash register where she kept her Glock concealed in a drawer.

She blew him a kiss.

Someone pulled the music plug, and the silence seemed doubly quiet.

HB slipped off the high bar stool and put his hat back on. A trucker handed him a cold PBR, which he placed on the bar beside Lurleen.

"Why don't you drag him outside and pistol whip him?" she whispered.

He smiled at her, then turned back to the crowd.

"Aubrey, I want you to know how pleased I am at your success. I know how hard you work. I've seen the toll that lonely labor can take on a man, mind and body. And I congratulate Mr. D'Argent here, for his good taste. There are fine painters in Georgia, even in the smallest corners, polished and talented, and the powers that be need to give them the credit they deserve—and I don't mean the Howard Finster's. I know this painting will be a jewel in the museum's crown. And now—you folks do pay me to keep order, so I'll be off to do just that."

"Wait!" Aubrey shouted. "My good name! My character!"

"Oh, I suspect everybody here already has a good idea about your name and character. Night all."

He hurried across the dusty lot to his Ford, bright red under a street-light. Just as he slipped his key into the door lock, Roxanne slipped out of the shadows.

She wore a low cut, tight, gold glittering top, cinched snug at the waist with a wide leather belt, skintight leopard patterned tights, and heels, her lips flush and moist.

Her nails tip toed across his chest as she eased him back against his truck. Tenderly, her fingers clasped his, lifted them gently onto her breast.

He pushed her away. "No!"

"HB, drop the Mr. Clean act. I know you want me. It's in your eyes. They're a dead giveaway."

He shook his head. "Roxanne, you need to find somebody who'll love you, and not just ogle and drool after you."

He pointed at the bar. "Get out of that place for a start. You come in here every night tarted up like a cheap prostitute and taunt the husbands and the truckers and get off on their undressing you with their eyes until you've confused fantasy for fact."

She clobbered him and his knees sagged. He shook his head, dazed. What a punch!

"You son of a bitch!" she yelled, pointing at him as she backed away.

As she slipped back into the shadows, he dragged himself up off the truck, wiped his lip with his pocket handkerchief. In a minute, a car cranked and peeled out of her lot, her flashy yellow Corvette, spewing dirt and rocks until the wheels gripped the asphalt, the car fish-tailed and righted itself.

That night he emailed Iggy what happened, and the Benedictine monk sent back a string of sappy, teary-eyed emoticons.

Chapter Six

The door was locked, so HB slipped his key in and eased it open. "Dad?"

The cabin was dark and quiet, unusual. Candles and smoking herbs always gave his father's home a smoky outdoor feeling he loved. But today the air was clear, and silence reigned. Only the old grandfather clock in the corner ticking, all the way from Ocmulgee Oklahoma where Pain rescued it from the demolished home of his mother.

He tip toed to the bedroom door. It was cracked so he could see his dad lying on his bed, stone still, the bright red dye around his left eye like a target waiting for an arrow from Death's quiver. Asleep, hands folded on his chest. Denim work shirt, long sleeves, frayed jeans, and moccasins.

HB looked down at the shiny black package he'd brought: his dad's favorite coffee. Impossible to get except online and his dad didn't do online. He turned to slip out and let the sleeping body do its mysterious healing work.

"Son?"

He sighed. Mr. One Eyed Sleeper, prided himself on never falling too deeply into the dangerous, yet holy dream.

"Brought you some Tulsa Dark."

He set the coffee on the night table.

Pain's dry lips formed a smile. He touched his son's arm.

"It's so good to see you," he whispered.

After HB pulled up the old straw bottom rocker, he reached over and ran his hand over the thread bare red and yellow zig zag blanket made by his Mom.

"Pass me the water," Pain whispered.

HB handed him the glass. His dad took it with both hands, sipped and set it back on the night table.

His father gave him his full attention. "And what is the occasion for the High Chief of Ocopeeco to take time out of his busy day to pay a call on a feeble old injun?"

"Dad . . ."

Pain grinned, reached his grizzled hand out and HB took it.

"Remember all those times," HB said, "when you took me with you to the Bear Caves and I watched you do the rites. Any time somebody in the community or a kid at school was sick."

"And afterwards," Pain said, "we always stopped at the Dairy Queen that used to be up on the highway."

"Chocolate malts!" HB said.

Pain chuckled. "And that swamp woman at the counter, Miss B!"

"Miss B! I had forgotten about her. Lived way down in the swamp with her horse, FDR. Had him trained to paw the ground. Rode him to work every day."

"Called me Geronimo," Pain said.

"But you didn't take offense. You knew she had no education."

Pain's eyes glittered.

"I want to do the rites," HB said. "Relieve you of this guilt you carry about the Shack."

Pain raised up and frowned. "Guilt! That's some psychobabble word. It's not guilt. I offended Ibofanga! It's not some feeling you take a pill for."

"Easy, Dad . . ."

Pain's eyes closed, he sighed, and eased back down.

HB wondered if this was the right thing to do. He'd wrestled with it for days, prayed. Even e mailed Iggy, who said "Go for it!"

Softly, eyes still closed, Pain said: "I just want to know what happened. Did someone die because of me? I just want to know."

HB sat back and watched. The deep wrinkles around his dad's mouth quivered and his lips rose and receded.

Finally, Pain raised up again on his elbows, the dry dark skin of his neck stretched pale. His eyes locked onto HB's.

"You serious?"

"Yes. Look, I have powerful memories of those times. I'm a grown man now with a different faith, but maybe Ibofanga will honor that fourteen year old's belief."

His dad closed his eyes again, but not to sleep.

HB waited, crossed his legs. The bedroom seemed poised for an answer. Yes," his dad whispered. "Your heart was the heart of a boy. It was pure."

HB brought a spiral back notebook so Pain could list everything needed. They sketched an outline of the ceremony. At one point Pain stopped
and looked at him: "You remember all this?"

"Dad, when you're fourteen and you perform a thousand year old rite
in an ancient language, it makes an impression."

When they were finished, Pain lay on the bed, smiling at him.

HB stood, slipped the notebook into the book bag he'd brought the
coffee in. "There's one more thing."

"What?"

"I want to perform the rite on the Funeral Mound."

It took Pain a second to realize what his son was asking. Yes. It had
to be the ancestral mound by the Ocmulgee where the memorious spirits
lingered still from a time when the worship of Ibofanga was commonplace.

"I'll call Jim Rivers," Pain said, "He's retired, but he still carries weight."

* * * *

As he entered the Ocmulgee Indian Mounds, built around 1000 AD, the
gaudy commercial sheen of the highway gave way to a green world with no
human signs, no lights, nothing but trees and bush around and stars above.
He parked in the lot in front of the Bauhaus-style Museum the WPA built
back in the thirties, loaded everything onto his aluminum pull cart and
started down the long path toward the creek, then up and past the council mound. The grass was freshly cut and lay in long swaths, glistening in
the moonlit dew. He glanced a second across the trees to see Ft. Hawkins,
where the white settlers originally lived. Three more football fields until he
reached the funeral mound.

The bats and bugs seemed intent on preventing his reaching the top as
he pulled the cart backwards up the stairs. He had brought everything his
dad listed. Fortunately, the wood steps were built to support hundreds of
tourists daily. Behind him, the brown Ocmulgee was visible, easing through
the leafless winter poplars, sweet gums, and elm. And even though the twilight January air was chill, by the time he reached the top, he was soaked, his
back and shoulders aching.

He recalled his phone call with Iggy.

"Am I violating my ordination?"

"How so?" Iggy asked.

"I'm going to summon a pagan spirit, one that I once believed in. Like
Faust."

"The Lord's using the Devil," Iggy said, "to get what He wants."

"To heal dad."

"To heal your dad."

On top of the burial mound, the ground was hard. Pebbles and twigs, acorn shells, withered leaves. He swept a space clean. At the top he placed the cow's skull. Two black stones on the right below the skull and two red stones on the left. Two long sticks in parallel lines on both sides. At the end, opposite the skull, two more sticks in a V shaped connection. When he stepped back, he saw it: in Creek, a Honvnwv, a man.

He stuffed tobacco into his dad's snake head pipe, carved from cypress. Sitting near the skull, he smoked one bowl, then scattered honey suckle and jasmine over the red and black stones and placed his dad's squirrel skin medicine bundle where the man's heart would be.

He made the fire. When the blaze rose high enough, he tied on his dad's turtle shell rattles, two on each calf. He began the dance, slow at first, allowing his mind and limbs to call up the old memories of his boyhood years. As the rhythm settled into his legs, he arched his body, chanted and let his head bob and move to the beat. Those mournful, alien tones took him back to his confusion when he was torn between catechism and the animistic world of the Creek where little spirits were everywhere, and every tree and rock alive. It was painful, but he kept singing because he believed now more than ever this might be the paradoxical way, as Iggy said, that God would save his dad from suicide by starvation. Those words stabbed his heart. Not one, but two parents afflicted by the same disease. You could say, through the tears, that both your parents had died from cancer, but who could say both parents had starved themselves to death?

His reverie was shattered by a shriek.

From the other side of the mound a screaming flame barreled toward him. A man dressed as a Creek warrior with a burning pine knot plowed through him and cracked his skull with a blackjack.

When he woke up, his head throbbed a deep dull pain from his spine to his animal brain. It came in waves, throbbing his gums. He was tied spread-eagle to four metal stobs, Happy Damon grinning over him, naked, his body slathered in stinking Ocmulgee river mud.

"Wasn't that a brilliant entrance?" he said.

HB's tongue struggled.

"Yeah," Damon said, shaking his head and feigning empathy. "the old sapper does a number on your brain. Like my river mud?"

He twirled around like a hyperactive runway model.

"You're o' your 'eds again," HB said. His tongue was numb, no feeling.

"Ah, screw those meds!" Damon said, for a moment morose, his whole face transformed into the tragic mask. Then to the flip side and the comic mask was back. Pranced and lifted his head like a triumphant dancer. "I'm always on a natural high."

"Handy's 'aying you some 'erious overtime."

"That Jabba the Hutt jigaboo! No, Mr. Preacher Man. You are my own per-so-nal project."

He squatted beside HB's head, popping his blackjack in his hand. He leaned in to within inches of HB's ears and whispered:

"You see, Chief, I despise preachers. Self-righteous hypocrites. Like my daddy. Oh, yeah, my daddy was righteous 'fore God, righteous 'fore God. But when he got home . . . presto! The great man locked himself up with his Playboys and Hustlers. Come out, beat mama, poor terrified mama. Burned her with his cigarettes. Caught me with one of his play-mates one night. What? My son? Bone of my bone? Defilin' himself? Tied me up and flung me in the bull pen. Yeah, Mr. Preacher raised fightin' pit bulls. Great big curled up dog teeth, scars thick as your fingers. Threw me in with 'em and I had to scratch and claw and become a four-footed fighter to stay alive. Stayed in that pen two years. Till I was fourteen.

"No, you my own project, preacher. You and Ro-o-o-sie." He growled the syllables, gnashing his cigarette-stained teeth.

HB jerked at the ropes. His heart pounded.

"Ro-o-o-osie. Short for Roswitha. Me and Rosie won't be discussing medieval art when I give her a long, stone dose of Mr. Happy."

He strapped aluminum greaves over his legs and dragged a big wire cage out of the darkness.

"Like to get my victim's heart rate up before the curtain rises on the main act."

Using a long, curled snake rod, he drew out a half-dozen ten pound eastern diamond back rattlers, which he laid on HB's stomach. Tongues darting out, testing, they crawled in and over one another, like a mind amok, confused, but sure to kill.

HB breathed, counting to ten, holding his breath at the top, then expir-ing evenly and releasing his breath until he had emptied his lungs. He told himself they strike when they're threatened, only when they're threatened, or for food. Was he food?

He moved his left boot and felt a blow like a slap. Two punctures ap-peared near the ball of his booted foot.

"Ho, Ho!" Happy said. "A little love tap. My babies like you."

Happy took several camera shots. "Too dark, but no matter, got a buddy who's a genius with digital."

Then he was gone.

HB jerked his head around. Disappeared like a sprite.

A snake approached his head. He froze, the tongue moving in and out as if an engine guided its quick flickering. It came so close to his ear he felt the air move, but the snake showed no interest. Like a robot it pulled away, keeping its head fixed straight ahead.

After ten minutes they dissipated, seeking refuge down the burial mound and the green of the bush and trees.

The next morning the ranger appeared about eight, rushed to him, apologizing, and slicing the ropes with his Swiss army knife.

* * * *

Rosie massaged his back with her special oil, lavender and ginseng, lemon, and thyme. He lay on the bed; she sat beside him, leaned over stretching her long arms out, up and back, up and back.

He close his eyes, tried to release the stress.

"Your muscles are locked," she whispered. "Try to relax."

The warm oil soothed and his mind slowed down, and his body began to relax.

She hummed an old German Volkslied.

Her voice seemed a brother to the oils, his heart regained its easy rhythm.

"It's as if Big Rig's murder released something terrible in town," he said.

"Try not to think about it now," she said. "Just calm down and relax."

He wanted to take her advice, lie there, will himself into peace of mind, but he knew he couldn't.

He rolled over and took her hands in his. She smiled. He sat up and put his arms around her.

"This is what I need," he whispered in her ear.

He felt like a woman, needing to be held. But his trauma in Afghanistan had taught him it was okay to feel that way. And his dad said the same: "Never be ashamed of needing to be held and loved, son. Alice's arms brought me through many a night when the kids at school had wound me up like a top."

After a few minutes rocking, he said: "Had my first rattle snake bite."

"But you said they didn't hurt you."

"Not me. My boot." He reached down for it. The two holes near his arch had turned blue black against the red brown leather.

"And he was covered in river mud?" she asked.

"Green-gray. Slimy and stinky."

"Sounds like something a bad boy teen would do."

"A bad boy teen who's obsessed with this chief," he said.

"You think his story about the dogs and him being put in the cage with them is true?"

"Who knows?" he said.

She ran her hands through his hair until waves of peace broke down from his head and neck. He leaned back into her lap. He was so blessed, the suffering that lay beyond their four walls was beyond, apart. He was safe in his refuge.

"His story has the smell of truth," she said. "First, it's too bizarre to be fiction. Second, he's like the wild boy of Avignon. Uncivilized. Only in his case, because of the abuse by his father, he became hostile and aggressive."

"Are you defending him?"

"No, I'm explaining who he is."

"Should I be thinking of him that way, after he did what he did to me?"

"You're the preacher."

* * * *

That night he woke up around 2 AM. Rosie slept soundly. He slipped on his clothes, grabbed his Bible and set off down the dirt path from their front porch. The church back door still had the cut-glass doorknobs from nineteen twenty-one when the building went up. In that same year three black men were lynched not two miles away. He shone his flashlight through the kitchen and on into the sanctuary where enough light entered through the stained glass windows to adumbrate the cedar pews. He breathed in that scent he loved so, the old wood, the fuzzy-eared hymnals.

He knelt before the Cross. It was empty, befitting a reformed folk who preferred their savior risen, and not still tormented on the tree. But there were times he wished the broken and twisted body were there, visible, to remind them of his suffering.

He opened to Jeremiah and spoke: "Lord, you are in the midst of us and we are called by your name. Do not forsake us, O Lord, our God."

Had anyone asked him what about his job caused him the most stress, he would have answered: seeing beyond the law and surely, he had to do that now. So, he asked for mercy for a man so tormented he had lost the light of reason. On his knees and in his dirty jeans he prayed for the soul of Irenaeus Loadholt.

* * * *

That day at work, he began calling all the motels within a fifty mile radius of Ocopeeco, looking for a white Cadillac with a Jerry Lee Lewis logo on the side. By noon he was down to twenty.

He found him in a Motel 6 outside Dublin.

At four in the afternoon, after an hour drive, he pulled into the parking lot, a hundred fifty units, four stories, gravel lot. Nothing else around except for a Waffle House. The sky was clear blue, the air chilly. A row of leafless poplars behind the motel.

He pulled his truck off under a clump of winter dry mimosas and waited and watched room 12.

Around six, a bone skinny prostitute came out, smoking, staggering, pulling her clothes on and giggling.

A few minutes later, Damon emerged, a cigarette dangling from his lips, dressed in string-tied, blue jogging pants and a T shirt. He got in his Cadillac and headed toward the Waffle House.

HB followed, pulled in at the Waffle House lot and waited until the suspect sat down in a booth before he got out of his truck and went in. There were a half dozen customers. The hash slingers were all local teenagers with weaves and do rags and orange West Laurens High T shirts. A gray haired man, the boss, behind the counter eyed the big badge on HB's belt and threw him a perfunctory smile.

Observing Jerry Lee from the rear, HB noted the man gripped his fork in his fist like a bushman who's never eaten a civilized meal. Smoking while he ate, he had just stuffed his mouth with scrambled eggs when the chief slid into the booth, pulled his pistol under the table.

"What the . . . !"

HB learned across the able and whispered: "Ever notice nobody gets waffles at the Waffle House?"

Damon tried to leave, but HB tapped his knee hard with his pistol.

"Don't let me rush you, Mr. Pickwick. Stay and finish your eggs."

The face HB regarded was unshaven, eyes dark and cavernous, his teeth brown from his tobacco habit. He laid his long arms on the table.

"Think you some kinda Nietzschean superman, don't you?" he spit the words out in a malevolent whisper.

"That's me," HB said, grinning, "up in the sky. A Zarathustra bird!"

Damon gritted his teeth and his lips curled back. "Gr-gr-gr.."

"That's good," HB said, pointing to the man's teeth. "The pit bulls teach you that or was that tale just another fantasy like Jerry Lee Lewis? My guess is you actually went to prep school, then Yale and dropped out because you were convinced the world of stage and screen had need of your talent."

Damon put down his fork, lit a Gauloises, took a deep drag.

"You know the French don't make those anymore," HB said.

"I care."

A waitress twitched her nose, punched a co-worker and pointed to Damon and his cigarette.

Damon smiled. It wasn't friendly gesture, more of a threat. An idea was dawning. He was one of those men you can observe as a notion begins to form and eventually rises to expression.

He leaned forward. "You ever consider a leap of faith?" His eyes were steady now on HB. He wasn't joking. "I can't beat you, I know that now. But I can do something to rise above you, something you can't touch."

HB held his gaze. Did this fool understand the meaning of a 'leap of faith.' No, but his demented mind gleaned some dangerous energy from the sound of the words.

"Never understood that phrase, myself," HB said.

"You do something so complete there's no going back. Give yourself one hundred per cent. There's a purity about that." His voice grew soft.

"I'm gonna have me some of their pure orange juice." HB said and motioned for a waitress.

Damon stared at him, studying him, antsy, legs shaking.

The waitress came over, took out her pencil and pad and jotted down HB's order, wrinkling her nose as she left.

"Everything is so tainted, so lacking innocence," Damon said.

He wasn't speaking to HB now, but to someone else or just speaking off into the universe, his eyes electric.

"Those eggs are getting cold," HB said, nodding toward Damon's plate.

The man stamped out his cigarette in the metal ashtray, squashing it violently until the tobacco split through the paper and he popped the butt in his mouth and downed it with coffee. "You know what I mean, don't you?" Damon said. "I see it in your eyes. You know the bright abyss."

HB shook his head.

Damon nodded, over and over, as if he finally understood something. "Yes, yes, and yes."

He bolted.

HB raised his Beretta, but an older, gray haired couple walked in, and Damon plowed over them. HB slipped his weapon inside his jacket to conceal it, made for the door, but getting by the elderly pair proved tricky. The woman slid to her knees and sprawled across the entrance way. She reached up, grabbed HB as he tried to slip by.

"Ma'am, I'll get one of the kids here to help."

He called one of the employees, then pursued Damon who didn't get in his car but fled on foot across the parking lot.

"Stop or I'll shoot!"

Damon never looked back.

HB knelt, fired, and clipped him in the right shoulder.

Damon staggered, but got back up. He dashed up the metal motel step. The shot filled him with energy.

Before HB could get to the steps, he heard customers coming out of the restaurant shouting. He turned back to see them pointing to the roof.

"Don't do it, mister!"

"Please, mister, God loves you!"

"Life's always worth living!"

When he looked up, directly overhead, Damon teetered on the edge of the fourth story, arms out, grinning down at what, by now, was a crowd.

"See if you're good enough to wing me on the way down, Chief! I'll bet Rosie could do it!"

With that, smiling, Jerry Lee Lewis launched a great ball of fire in a swan dive, arms spread wide, a red splotch on his shoulder from HB's bullet, headfirst into the concrete.

The crowd screamed, hands over their faces, at the sickening crunch.

Nausea swept over HB and he nearly lost his balance. An iron weight crushed him. He could not move forward toward the body.

Damon landed so his right arm was twisted under him, his face splayed on its side in a pool of blood streaming out under gnarled lips.

A small elderly group from the motel appeared, curious, but frightened. In the dressing gowns and night coats, they approached the body like well-behaved children, whispering and trembling.

After the oohing and ahing, "Look at that!" someone said. "It's a river of blood."

A tiny man in a walker leaned over, squinted. He pointed with shaking hand to the body while he reported to the rest, "I seen a wreck on I 16 like that. Two little teenagers racin'. I come up on one left a red Mississippi all up and down that highway."

HB hustled to his truck, opened the glove compartment, and fetched his prayer book.

He passed through the crowd, who gave him an up and down look, as if to say, who are you.

He knelt beside the body, felt the pulse.

None.

As he said last rites for the dead man, a woman in a red corduroy bath robe and flip flops whispered: "Must be a Roman Catholic." She uttered the first syllable of Catholic as if it were a dread disease. She whispered to a neighbor from the back of her hand: "They claim suicides is going to H-e double hockey sticks."

Kneeling on the concrete, HB prayed: "Merciful Father who creates in love, we entrust to your merciful hands this man who has taken his own life." He continued silently and as he invoked the saints as he recalled his own stay after Afghanistan in Atlanta's Crawford Long Hospital, a time when, like Happy Damon, he could have turned to the darkness.

"'At's just awful, Chief," another woman said, as he looked up from his kneeling. "Did you know the young man?"

"We had met before."

"Was he always troubled?"

"Yes ma'am, I didn't know him well, but I believe he was."

He invoked the archangel Michael to protect Damon's soul from judgement and begged for mercy for the poor man.

He lost track of the time.

When he looked up, the others had left, and he was alone in the parking lot with the corpse.

He contacted the Laurens County Chief's office. When he asked if they wanted him to contact the coroner, the deputy on the line said: "Are you the chief over in Ocopeeco?"

"I am."

"The preacher/chief.?"

"I suppose so."

"You really pray for your crooks and druggies? I heard you get down on your knees with meth heads right there in the cell and pray with 'em."

"I have been known to do that. You have a problem with that?"

"I just don't see why you'd go out and arrest somebody, rough 'em up, even shoot at 'em and turn around and pray for 'em. Don't make no sense."

"Deputy?"

"Sir?"

"Do you really believe that, that what I do doesn't make any sense?"

"Yessir, I do."

"In that case I'll be praying for you, too."

* * * *

The atmosphere in the monastery cell assigned to Father Ignatius of the Heart of Mary was electric. HB and Iggy sat on the edge of a cot munching Frito's and drinking bottled water as the Falcons broke into Tampa Bay's red zone for the first time that afternoon. Score: Bucs 7, Falcons 3. 1 min. left in the fourth quarter.

The tiny TV required them to sit twelve inches away, sound low.

"B, I can feel it. Ryan's due."

He removed his cowl, his just shaved bald head glistened, his always five o'clock shadowed face rippled with worry, his big prognathic jaw thrust out.

HB grinned and rubbed his friend's scalp. "O, magic cue ball, put your fumble fingers mojo on Matt Ryan."

Iggy knocked his hand off.

"Hey, don't mess with the nether deities. Look at who coach has put in at corner back. I can't believe it."

"Back Peddle Peters!"

"Back Peddle can't defend Julio Jones. Julio' ll head fake, spin and bingo, Mattie Ice will nail him on the numbers and voila, first and goal"

The ball was snapped. Jones head faked, spun, and Ryan hit him on the numbers. Back Peddle missed the tackle and Jones strolled into the end zone, bowing extravagantly left and right.

Iggy snapped the TV off.

Standing, hands on his hips, he breathed in and out deeply, facing HB. A stressed out Jolly Green Giant.

"Am I addicted to football?"

"You do get excited," HB said, looking up. "Remember that Saints-Panthers brawl when Cam Newton plowed over three tacklers to win the game and you smashed your hand against the wall?"

Iggy held his right hand in his left. "Still smarts in cold weather."

A white envelope slipped under the door.

Iggy grinned. He reached down and opened it. "Father Prior. He always gives me the Tampa Bay score."

The note read: Falcons 10, Bucs 7. Julio Jones catch on the ten yard line.

"He know you have the TV?"

"He pretends he doesn't."

Iggy lay down on his cot while HB pulled up the rocking chair.

"So," HB said. "I'm not a bit closer to finding Big Rig's killer."

"You were sidetracked."

"I can still feel the goose bumps when he jumped."

"Worse than Afghanistan?"

"Different. This time was seeing the last act in a long series of bad choices, cruel parents, crime, despair. All ending in a swan dive into concrete."

HB rocked; Iggy lay looking up at the ceiling. Outside his door some-one passed, his sandals flip-flopping.

"So, if I lock Lizard up—which I should have done a longtime ago—I'll never find out where he's stashed his cash."

"How much?"

"Maybe a half a million.."

Iggy rolled over. "So, lost lucre. What's the big deal?"

"The big deal is Handy."

"The drug king pin in Atlanta."

"He's already sent one psycho down. But another Handyman will show up on our doorsteps, soon, prowling for the cash."

"Or a half dozen handy men."

"Don't say that!"

"Doesn't Lizard believe in banks?"

"Lizard Little is a grandchild of the great depression. His parents died in a car crash and he was raised on a houseboat by his granddaddy, old one eyed Zeke Little, who ran the only bait and tackle shop on the river for forty years. Mr. Zeke stashed his cash in a tackle box till the day he died. Lizard got a right smart inheritance from the old man, but he was also bequeathed that same tackle box mentality. He's got a nook or hideout somewhere he's squirreled all his illegal cash away."

Iggy pursed his lips. "Crazy. He a ladies man?"

HB rolled his eyes. "He scotch tapes his glasses, sweats in the winter, smokes two packs a day, and he lives in a double wide."

Iggy made a funny face. "He tryin' to run 'em off?"

HB stopped rocking.

"What's the matter?" Iggy said, sitting up.

"A ladies man . . . yeah . . . that's it, Ig. That's it!"

Chapter Seven

In the Ocopeeco High library AV room, stuffy and cramped, packed with Pac Man era computers and videos of such avant garde classics as *Song of the South* and *Goodbye Mr. Chips*, he unearthed a nineteen-eighty annual, Lizard's junior year, blue cover, darker Blue Jacket logo. He thumbed through the pages. Nothing. He tried '77, '78, and '79. Each time he wound up with little more than a pitiful photo of a small, pinched face boy glaring out at the camera, a look between rage and loneliness.

His own senior year, during study hall, he enticed a cheerleader into that same room, Rhoda Willis, of the constant chewing gum and long ponytail. Without much prompting she dipped her head down and around, faster and faster, until that ponytail spun like something at the fair. Then they made out. Who came up with that phrase? They made out. He's the make out king. Where'd you make out, front or back seat? If you said back, it was serious.

The clamorous class bell startled him out of his reverie. He gathered the annuals for reshelving; but nineteen - eighty flipped open to an ad at the back. Black and white, it depicted the three officers of The Key Club, a short, chubby, black boy with braces and bow tie, the effervescent Grace Daniels, tennis champion and honor student, her tanned, healthy smile stealing the scene. Last, transfixed by the school goddess, his skinny limbs leaning towards her, his pimply, pinched face yearning and his mind awash in teen fantasies, Lizard the-would-be-lover Little.

* * * *

The six tennis courts at Ocopeeco High were surrounded by towering pines that shed cones on them. Coach Daniels had the girls walk back up to the PE office, bring down the brooms and sweep. Then the cones were gathered and returned to the cone room, where they were saved for Christmas, and all other holidays. The coach did not believe in waste.

HB reminded himself of that as he observed practice from his truck. Coach Grace Daniels was a beauty, but she stood more in the lineage of Joan of Arc than say, Lady Godiva. A faithful Catholic, she grew her own food, raised chickens, and kept a spice garden the locals loved—for a fee. On weekends her tennis girls earned brownie points by working the spice garden cash register. Customers drove up to the curb, paid and picked out a sack of anise or ginseng, or thyme.

He puffed on Simeon, his seventh smoke for the day and considered how Simeon became Simon who in turn became the rock upon which the Lord built his church. Number seven always gave him a magisterial feel, rock solid foundations. Good to close the day with. Then he remembered Grace's clean living gospel and stubbed the cigarette out, fumbled in his glove compartment for mouth spray and decided to conduct the interview outside his truck.

His wheels were stuck in the mud. He wasn't one inch closer to getting Big Rig's killer, but this business with Lizard involved the whole town's safety. He had to do something and Grace Daniels, he hoped, held the solution.

One of the girls had trouble with her serve. Grace brought over a basket of balls, waved at HB and he waved back to insure her he was in no rush.

Grace tossed the ball high and powered through to meet it precisely at its zenith. The blazing serve dropped in. She handed the racket to the student and observed as she attempted the same. After a few tries her serves began to fall in.

In a few minutes Grace joined him.

"I got your text and I thought, Grace, you forgot to pay a parking ticket and now the high chief is on your trail."

They hugged, politely.

"I can't remember the last time I issued a parking citation. Heck, we only have forty-five parking meters."

"I heard what happened to that poor Jerry Lee Lewis guy. Was it drugs?"

"Partly."

She leaned back against his truck, took the rubber bands out of her air and it fell gloriously around her tanned and freckled shoulders.

"Do you remember Lizard Little?" he asked.

She tilted her head, quizzical.

"Ronald Little. I hated that nickname. I see him, occasionally, up at the store on the highway."

He explained everything, how Lizard and Big Rig got into the pain killer business, how they made the kaolin-fentanyl exchange, then, how Big Rig ripped off Mr. Handy and Mr. Handy sent Damon to Ocopeeco to get his money back; but Damon became obsessed with him, HB, and wound up jumping off the motel. At first, he suspected Lizard killed Big Rig. He did have motive: get at Big Rig's cash he made selling fentanyl himself on his Savannah runs. And he was sure Lizard had all the money. But he doubted Lizard did the killing. Plus, he was sure Handy would not give up. Soon, another of his thugs would show up.

"So how do I fit in?" Grace asked.

"I need you to help me find that money and get it to Handy."

"How?"

"Use your feminine wiles."

She made a face. "What? You want me to seduce Ronald Little?"

"Well, seduce is a strong word. What about persuade?"

She giggled. "Wow, HB, I've had guys ask me to do some weird things. But this . . . "

She toweled off and pulled out her lipstick and applied it. "Sorry," she said, "I've got to be somewhere in about thirty minutes, and I won't have time to get home."

"So?"

"You know, I once had a guy ask me to sit still for a half hour while he recorded my breathing. No words. Just silence. He said he would take the tape home and play it back and in that way we could become soul mates."

"What'd you do?"

"That was our first and last date."

HB took off his Stetson and wiped the sweat from his head band. This was a mistake. Grace was too straight laced, too much in control of her life to risk something this weird.

As she continued to apply rouge and comb her hair, he recalled how Rosie did the same, the same arms and hands moving in a tried and true pattern. And like Rosie this woman didn't need anything.

"You're asking me to play a role, be an actress for a time. You're playing on my vanity and his vulnerability to get what you want."

"Yep."

"Has it occurred to you how cruel this will be to Ronald? He did have a bad crush on me."

"Grace, I'm trying to save his life."

She looked directly at him. That thought sank in. "You know, I haven't done anything crazy for years. And you think this will save his life. But . . . "

"But what?"

"I'm dating a guy, a football coach at Georgia Tech. Long distant love."

"Great."

"Yes, but he must never find out about this. HB, I really like this man, plus, he's, well . . . "

"Jealous?"

"No, he just believes mature adults should observe boundaries."

"Are you worried about not observing boundaries with Lizard?"

She laughed. "No, of course not. But you understand, don't you?"

She wanted to help but she also wanted some assurance.

"Look" he said, "I'm trying to keep Lizard out of bad trouble, deadly trouble. I can't tell you for certain how this will play out. I just know we've got to get that money back or our town will suffer, especially Ronald Little."

"That's not reassuring."

"Trying to be honest."

"Ronald Little," she said in a reminiscent tone. "You know I had to tie his shoes for him. He got so nervous around me, one time a shoe came untied, he tried to lace it up and couldn't. Finally, I reached down and did it for him."

"Can we say you will wrap him around your little finger?"

* * * *

Grace stooped to run her hand over the frost on the metal steps of Lizard's trailer. The February morning air was freezing. She wore a brown leather jacket, a paisley scarf with her hair done in a long pig tail. Her high heeled boots were the problem. Carefully, she stepped up, balancing the heavy platter, and spotted Lizard through a large window watching the View. She knocked.

The squeak of a Barcalounger coming down was followed by footsteps approaching. The door opened to a suave, barefoot Lizard, his droopy moustache, his undershirt hanging below is knees, his baggy pants. She thought: put a pirate's hat on him and he's Yosemite Sam

He blinked, removed his scotch-taped glasses, wiped them on his undershirt and put them back on..

"Grace?"

"Good morning, Ronald. I heard about your run-in with that awful Jerry Lee Lewis person, so I brought you something."

Wrapped in Saran, a chocolate cake. He took it, unsteady.

"Here," she said," let me set it somewhere. Where's your kitchen?"

He made a whimper. "Well . . . sort of . . . sort of everywhere."

She spotted an empty place on a counter. Stepping over a stack of empty pizza boxes, twisting between a turned over chair and a discarded TV, she made her way to it and put the platter down.

He pointed to the old TV. "Got a new giant sized screen last week at Walmart. Like it?"

"It's a fine looking set."

"You . . . you wanna sit a spell," he said.

"Ronald, I would love to sit a spell. We have a lot of catching up to do."

Leaving his trailer that morning, she was certain her life span had been cut short five years by the cigarette smoke she inhaled, so she made sure their next meeting would be at her place, a one story open air, half house, half farm, that sat sprawled on the side of the last hill that Mico had to climb for his paper route.

In Lizard's mind these visits unfolded like a lost world recovered. As for Grace, she was walking a tightrope. On one hand, she was courteous, hospitable, but distant; on the other, she offered Lizard hints that more than her favorite vegan doughnuts (sugared Kleenex) would soon be forthcoming. On Saturdays they rode bikes. On Sundays she took him with her to St Joseph's in Macon. In the evenings they drank wine.

Grace texted HB regularly. His return texts always ended: "Find out where his money's hidden."

After two months of courtship, with Spring bursting out in Ocopeeco, wildflowers and golden rod and wisteria, they sat one night on her patio, sipping Merlot, listening to Oscar Peterson. Grace wore a sunny green dress, her hair golden in the fading sun. As always, she sat, back straight, one arm over the old fashioned outdoor glider, one leg stretched across it.

Lizard slumped in a comfy chair, dressed in new hush puppies, white socks, tan pants, an old, frayed belt with holes that looked gouged out with a butcher knife and a once blue polo shirt that revealed his bone skinny arms. Beside him an ashtray she provided. Her rule: only three cigarettes per night. At first, he objected, but she tightened the reins, threatened and scolded, until he agreed.

Whenever she turned her back to pour or clean the table, he stared at her with the same moon-struck face from high school, only now his big moustache drooped over his mouth. From time to time he removed his Scotch-taped glasses to wipe them clean on his shirt and revealed deep, gray shadows beneath his eyes. It was as if a sightless sea creature had come up from the deep into the light. He blinked, put the glasses back on his face, and the creature returned to the darkened depths.

She poured the wine freely. And poured again.

He worked up the courage to move onto the sofa beside her. She smiled and nodded and made a place for him. He sat and leaned over.

"Wanna know a secret?"

"Hm-m-m-m-m. Yes, I would," she said. "Secrets turn me on."

He raised up, blinking. "Really? Get ready to be turned on like a house a-fire."

His glasses slipped to the tip of his nose where sweat gathered and dropped off.

Waving his finger back and forth, he whispered: "I'm a rich man, Grace."

She took his hand. "You are. You're rich in friends, you live in a precious small community where you know everyone and . . . "

"Wait!" He thrust his index finger up. "I don't mean that kind of rich. I mean cash rich! Cash, Grace! Moola, dough, the green kind that buys pretty things like cars and boats and houses."

She stood. "Well, I think we've had about enough to drink tonight. What say we head to the car and you let me take you home?"

He leapt up, unsteady. "What! You think I'm not tellin' the truth! You think it's the wine talkin' and not me!"

"I didn't say that."

"But that's what you thought, ain't it, ain't it?"

He stormed around the patio, harrumphing and teetering.

When she grabbed him to steady him, he drew her close, reeking of wine and smoke. "I'm gonna show you something will blow your mind!"

Miffed, she straightened her mussed hair. "Now I have told you several times about that, Ronald."

He backed off, hands raised. "Okay, Okay, I'm sorry, I'm sorry. But let's take a ride to the river so I can show you something."

"Show me what?"

"Grace, please!" he shouted.

Two hands firmly on the wheel, she steered her yellow Cooper down the steep hill through Ocopeeco, turned onto River St. and followed it to the old river road, a two lane, rut-filled challenge for her tiny car. Lizard, his face and lips like a slug, slimed the window. Through thick fog they turned down a dirt road to the river and a water-logged shell of the houseboat he grew up on.

She helped him through the dewy weeds and golden rod to pine planks stretching from the bank to the boat. The fog covered everything so she jumped when a whip-o-will sounded off behind them.

The upper portion of the houseboat looked flimsy, plywood and rusted corrugated aluminum; but the lower half appeared solid, asbestos-covered square logs.

`She paused at the water's edge. The planks to the boat were fresh, but still, she hesitated.

The snooze sobered him up. From behind, he whispered in her ear.

"What's a matter, girlie, chicken . . . "

"No, just careful."

She made her way across the planks and stepped down into the boat. Lizard descended into a room below that was dry, the floor covered with new indoor outdoor carpet. Someone had done work here—recently.

Glossy photos from magazines covered the walls, young women displaying the way God made them.

"Do you spend a lot of time out here?" she asked, averting her eyes from the images.

He leered at her. "Unh-huh." .

"Fishing?"

"Naw. Makes you stink."

He slouched in an old fashioned lawn chair, canvas and wood; she remained standing, examining old photo of his parents and pictures of school.

"Oh, I remember this one!" she said, picking the frame up. It depicted a group of teens, standing grim and stiff in front of a red brick building. "That was our class picture. So, you come down here and reminisce?"

"Nope. I talk to my babies."

"You've got pets?"

"I'll show 'em to you, if you'll be real nice."

She bristled. "Ronald!"

He slipped out of the chair onto the carpet and found an up-turned corner. He pulled it back, revealing a brass handle.

"What's that?"

He looked up at her, grinning and sweating, his glasses fogged. "Most every day I come down here and we have us a good old chat. Just me and my babies."

"Ronald, you're scaring me. I think I'd like to go."

He pulled the top of the hold and hauled out three large tackle boxes, brand new, with their shelves and cubicles stripped away.

"All my babies," he whispered, "safe and sound. . ." He opened the boxes and there they were: a half million dollars in hundred dollar bills.

* * * *

HB passed mansion after mansion as he eased his Ford down West Paces Ferry in Atlanta. The houses all sat high and faraway from the road at the end of immaculate lawns dotted with Renaissance statuary of gods and goddesses. At a miniature mill and a water wheel, he pulled his truck into the Handy driveway. It wound around gazebo's and ponds with swans and willow trees until it opened onto a rising terraced lawn, green and freshly cut in redolent swaths of grass, and dotted with Lady Banks roses. At the top of the hill, a three storied Gothic mansion seemed to have sprung out of the Atlanta granite. Gargoyles and gryphons perched atop parapets glowered down at all who dared trespass on their grounds.

The palazzo was built in the thirties by a bootlegger named Frog Feinberg. The Frog was so fascinated by a certain castle from The Black Forest, he brought it over the Atlantic, stone by stone, and reconstructed it in Tara land, in a time when pedestrians still walked around downtown Atlanta shoeless. His childhood dream in Newark had been a swimming pool filled with hooch. He got his wish. On his thirty-fifth birthday, he and his fourth wife were found floating full of holes on large yellow rubber duckies in a pool filled with Vodka

HB wore a blue blazer, a light blue Oxford button down, starched, a tie and a red striped handkerchief tucked in his blazer pocket. He even polished his boots. It wasn't every day a lawman returned a half million to a drug lord.

He was breaking the law, that much he knew, but he had to take the risk. If he turned the money in to the GBI, Handy would come after him and Lizard. This was the only way to make the man happy and keep him and his thugs out of Ocopeeco, but he felt sure this violation of protocol would come back to bite him.

The entrance way into the Handy Mansion soared three stories and was wide enough for the Atlanta Falcons to march through, arm in arm. HB rang a button that looked like a mermaid. A J Arthur Rank gong sounded inside and a small door within the larger door opened. A bald, dour-looking white butler with a monocle stepped out.

"Ye-e-e-e-s?"

"Chief Alpata to see Mr. Handy. He's expecting me."

The butler searched him up and down, then gave the red Ford a long look. His nose twitched.

HB stepped over, reached in the truck bed and hoisted out a large leather satchel.

When he turned back to address the butler, the man had already disappeared inside. He hurried through the door into a dark, tall ceilinged room with swords, lances, mace, cross bows, long bows hanging on the walls. Occasional light beams slippered down the darkness, dancing in golden nuggets of dust. After passing through several rooms where the furniture was covered, they entered a more modern carpeted chamber. A dozen men sat or stood around the walls, mostly lost in their phones, dressed in black. Shoulder holsters and AR-15's, each weapon embossed with DuBose Handy.

The butler clapped his hands and the doors opened letting in a cool scent of lavender and weed. They stepped inside.

Leaning close, the butler, smelling of citrus and oak moss, whispered: "It would be wise if you refrain from mentioning the unfortunate Mr. Damon."

HB whispered "Of course," and pretended to zip up his lips.

Sneering, the butler spun around in a precise military move and marched out, leaving HB facing the great man himself who was being served by a half dozen women of various races. One Nordic lass stood by his side, feeding him grapes.

"Greetings and salutations, Chief," Handy said, smiling.

The man's voice took HB by surprise. It was a dead ringer for James Earl Jones, whose DVD of *Othello* Rosie had played until she had to order a new one.

"I see you come bearing gifts," he said, nodding to the satchel.

"Indeed," HB said. He had the urge to bow.

The man before him was a mixture of races and types. Eyes slightly oriental, hair curly and glistening with oil, his face was massive, his skin flawless. His nostrils expanded with each breath. Large hands glittered with rings and a gold chain bearing a sundial hung around his neck. Trickles of perspiration through an archipelago of skin tags could not be air- conditioned away.

"Timeo Danaos et dona ferentes." Handy said, rolling off the "r" of ferentes.

"I fear the Greeks, even when they come bearing gifts." HB translated. "Mr. Handy, there's not a Greek bone in my body."

"Yes, but I understand there are plenty of Creek bones."

"Now, there, you've got me. I'm half Creek Indian."

"Carlotta," Handy said to a tall, languid brunette girl who lounged at his feet, "Fetch our half-Creek chief here a PBR. Tall and cold, right, chief?"

"You've done your homework."

"I have. The chief of Ocopeeco is a populist."

The girl slipped away, sneaking a shy glance at HB.

"We have a lot in common, you and I."

"How so?"

"I studied classics at Harvard."

"Impressive."

They stared at one another, silent, Handy strenuously grinning, spitting grape seeds into a silver cup, HB arms crossed in front, military fashion, Stetson in his hand.

He thought: this guy has ordered murders, and who knows what else, yet enjoys the *Odyssey*? What's done in one cerebral room is concealed from the room next door.

Carlotta handed him the beer. He took a sip. The cold tingly liquid awakened his senses.

"Good?" Handy asked, eyebrows raised as he nodded. The man genuinely wanted his guest to feel comfortable.

HB nodded. "Delicious."

"I'd like to show you something. Sarah, be a love and fetch the two books on my desk in the study."

HB watched as another girl ascended an old-fashioned spiral iron well of stairs and disappeared into a room. She returned with two books and handed them to her boss.

"Come closer," Handy said.

HB approached. Handy offered him the volumes. *The Iliad* and *Odyssey* in Greek.

HB opened, thumbed through, and closed the book.

"Sing, goddess," Handy said, "of the wrath of Achilles, son of Peleus."

By heart HB recited the next fifty lines—in Greek.

He sang the dactylic hexameter, although he had no lyre to accompany him. The orotund euphony, the compilation of five, six vowels, pay-lay ee ah-day-oh, rolled out, building momentum, higher and higher like a thundering ocean wave that seized control of the room.

Handy's eyes opened wide.

Even the girls around him perked up and blinked. Here was something they had not heard on Snap Chat or Instagram.

"Wow!" Handy said, when HB was finished "So it IS true."

"What?"

"You're a Greek prodigy."

"Started as a sixth grader. Had an old LP, played it till it became too scratchy. Summers digging ditches in high school I recited Homer and Apollonius in meter to keep time with the shovel. My memory skills didn't really kick in till I joined the army and wound up with lots of down time. Recited and memorized to keep myself from being bored."

"What do you think of the binding? Two octavo volumes bound in 19th c. blue calf, gilt. With the Aldine anchor and dolphin device on the title page and the verso of the final leaf in each volume. Fine copies"

"Set you back a penny?"

"Two hundred K."

HB whistled. "My old Homer's falling apart. Got it in a used bookstore in Istanbul."

Handy's eye lids sagged. He sighed and stared away into the emptiness of the large wood-lined room.

At first HB thought he was about to faint. But he wasn't, he was . . . bored?

After wiping his lips with a lavender napkin, the massive man slouched back in his chair.

"Ugh! Here we are enjoying the fruits of the highest culture. You a many-sided man whose appearance—a character out Cormac McCarthy—belies an extraordinary knowledge of classical Greek, and I, one of the few connoisseurs on this pitiful planet who appreciates such refined accomplishments, outside some ivy-clotted bastion of woke fragility, and what are we compelled to do? We have to talk business."

He pushed a button and two of guards in the other room entered. They stood at parade rest with their AR-15's.

"Chief, Lizard Little stole my money. If my half million is not in that satchel, you and your little village of Ocopeeco, along with all its potato-fed peasants, are in for a world of hurt."

HB grinned. He opened the satchel, stood back and took a long cold slug of his PBR.

One of the male guards brought the money to Handy, who reached inside and plucked out a packet of hundred-dollar bills.

"The retired chief of Bibb County," HB said, "Bang-Em-Up Brown has a list of those serial numbers. He knows I'm here. In fact, he's listening in right now."

HB held up his phone and a gravelly voice said: "Howdy, DuBose, remember me? I'm the one chased your sorry-ass out of Macon years ago, back when you were just getting your feet wet."

Handy rolled his eyes. "Oh, my God, Chief. I'm surprised that a man of your accomplishments would have anything to do with such riff raff."

HB put his phone away. "Mr. Handy, I'm asking you to keep out of Ocopeeco, permanently. No more Happy Damon's. No more anybody. Forget this kaolin-fentanyl scam and we have a deal."

"Chief, you will lose your job."

"Maybe, but I won't lose my town. Do we have a deal or don't we?"

"So, you're going to let me have my money and in return I will pursue my enterprises elsewhere, just not in Ocopeeco."

"That's the idea."

"Carlotta, more grapes, sweetheart, my palate is so dry."

The girl plucked a bunch of red grapes which she brought on a silver platter. He tilted his head back as Carlotta inserted a grape into his open mouth.

"M-m-m-m!"

He chewed, slowly, eyeing HB.

He could have me shot right here, HB thought. But Sheriff Brown would be a witness. He turned back around toward the guard standing by the door. A tall, shaved-head African, the light from the windows above turning his scalp into a surface so smooth it didn't look human.

"Now," Handy said, "Do we seal this deal by cross my heart and hope to die, or maybe swear on a Bible?" After he daubed his lips with a napkin, his large mouth eased open into a serpentine smile.

* * * *

Iggy grunted as he heaved the two hundred fifty pound bar over his head until his arms were fully extended. He trembled and sweat dripped off his nose.

"Now," HB said, standing behind him, both arms half-raised. "E-e-easy down. Easy does it . . . "

The monk let the weight down until it reached his chest where he released it and it thundered, bouncing off the cork and pine foundation Father Prior had allowed him to build in an unused barn.

Iggy rotated his shoulder.

"Good?" HB asked.

"It's holding."

After HB handed him an ice pack, which he taped to his shoulder, Iggy opened a Styrofoam cooler and pulled out two orange Gatorade's and they flopped down on a ratty sofa with stuffing emerging like fuzzy intestines.

"What did Handy say when you handed him the money?"

"He laughed and said he had never known a cop to break the law so a dumb ass redneck could keep on drawin' breath."

"That a quote?"

"It is. I memorized it because it's so pithy in a ghetto sort of way."

"Well, Handy knows you should have turned the money in. You worried, I mean about the feds finding out what you did?"

"Of course, I'm worried. Handy may have somebody on the inside. I just have to live with that. But if I had turned the money in, all kinds of bad would break out in little Ocopeeco. Handy would get his pound of flesh and on top of that, the GBI would show up with their own brand of well-meaning chaos. This way Handy's happy, Lizard's alive, a little heart-broken and there'll be no more Happy Damon's coming to call."

"You trust this guy?"

"Not at all. But he's a businessman. He doesn't want to deal with all this hassle."

Iggy did twenty side straddle hops and sat down, panting. He guzzled Gatorade. "And you're positive Damon didn't kill Big Rig?"

"Positive, too messy. And too intimate. Damon was a projectile man. Long shot to the head. No, Big Rig was killed up close by somebody who knew him well, somebody he was on good terms with."

Iggy stood, grinning. He nodded down at the bar. "Wanna have a go?"

"Don't think so."

"What? HB Alpata, Mr. Forearm in your Face?"

"All right, now . . . '

"I'll take fifty off."

HB sighed, gnawed his lip. He looked up at his friend. "Why?"

"Well, you haven't been lifting in a while. Don't wanna hurt you."

"So—you think the reason I don't want to lift is 'cause I CAN'T lift it?" Iggy blinked. "What?"

HB removed his Stetson, took a swig of Gatorade and stepped up to the platform.

Moving up to spot him, Iggy chuckled.

HB popped his knuckles, stretched. Ten sissy squats. Ten side straddle hops.

Then, he gripped the bar on the floor. Red faced, he brought it up to his chest.

"That's what I'm talkin' about!" Iggy said, his eyes lit up like a kid's. "Look out, Tide, the big Dog is back!"

A smile crept across HB's face. His heart was pumping and his muscles humming. Oh, it felt go-o-o-o-d! That energy he had forgotten was back. What was the Simon and Garfunkel "Hello, darkness, my old friend . . . " Hello, hamstrings, my old friends! Hot throbbing, his thighs and his back, his groin and his gut—they all joined in. Now, sucking in breath, he heaved up, two hundred fifty pounds of dusty black iron, higher and higher until his arms quivered and Iggy shouted.

"You got it, buddy! You got it!"

He did, he had it! His entire body trembled. From his head down to his toes, he had it, he had it.

* * * *

The odor of the Ben Gay Rosie rubbed on his back reminded him of the Georgia Tech game, his senior year, when he gave it everything and then some. They won, but at a cost, his back. Then, Old Chloroform Wiggins, the Dogs' trainer, slathered him up with Ben Gay and lectured him on the proper way to tackle.

Rosie commanded the language better than old Chloroform and her hands weren't covered with callouses. On the other hand, his wife was so mad at him he yearned for those steel brush hands, instead of the hands of a woman who knew her man had done something worthy of a pubescent teen who'd stolen his daddy's car and wrecked it.

She'd rubbed for a half hour. Not one word.

"That feels good," he said, just to break the ice.

She opened oil of wintergreen, poured, and up and down his spine she pounded with her fists.

"Easy, sweetheart . . . "

She pounded harder.

"Rosie!" he said, raising part way up.

"You are such an idiot!" she hissed through her teeth.

He deserved it. A real beating. When would he grow out of the sixteen year old who needed to win at all costs? Time had caught his body. It wouldn't let him go off chasing this challenge or that gauntlet. He hadn't lifted a weight in what . . . three years. He was a racehorse with a bad leg. Fired up, horsey juices flowing, ready to rip out of the gate. But when the bell sounded, and he tore out, he fell straight into the dirt. Over and over. Same gate. Same bad leg. Same dirt.

"It was Iggy's fault", he said, grinning back.

"It was not Iggy's fault," she said, "but he's your enabler. I may have to call Father Prior and inform him his favorite former NFL linebacker is a danger to my NFL wannabee husband."

"Father Prior lets him keep a tiny TV in his room."

She shook her head.

"In Germany, the Benedictines still self-flagellate."

"They whip themselves?"

"To feel the sufferings of Jesus. And Iggy is glued to the TV watching grown men dress up and prance around knocking each other over for millions of dollars."

"Guess we're not as tough as you Germans."

"You're not."

She brought out the dreaded yellow and black plastic roller stick, leaned into it with all her weight, up and back. A small steam roller crushing every muscle.

"Ow-w-w-w-w. Rosie, please-e-e-ese . . . "

* * * *

Two months later HB tapped on Lizard's door. Summer was slowing life in Ocopeeco down to a crawl. Kids were out of school and the town was fishing or relaxing on porches serenaded by the cicadas. He was hoping Lizard had mellowed.

Rosie said it was one of his major character flaws that made her love him so much: a chief who couldn't stand to make an enemy or lose a friend,

"Who is it?" Lizard said.

"It's HB."

Barcalounger squeaking, muttering.

"I ain't got nothing to say to you, Judas Eye-scare-ree-yot!"

"C'mon, Lizard. I saved your life. You know I did."

Grumbling, beer can pop top, remote clicking on. Through the glass window he watched Whoopy Goldberg appear with long worm dreadlocks and her Ben Franklin glasses.

"And you can tell that two timin' Jezebel, Grace Daniels, I ain't never speakin' to her again!"

He knocked again, twice, but it was futile, so he stepped down and headed back to his truck. With time he might come around. Then again, he might not. Folks in Ocopeeco held long grudges. Old Mr. Titus Little, Lizard's grandad at the candy store houseboat, was one of the worst. He used a big hunter's sling shot to chase off the bad kids who ripped off his candy, and even after they were dragged back by their parents to pay and apologize, he still brought out the sling shot the next time they came to buy.

He was fumbling with his truck keys when the trailer door ripped open.

"That was my ticket to the good life!" Lizard shouted with a half sob, as the door banged against the trailer. Standing in his underwear, sleep deprived, clutching a tall Millers at 9AM, he hurled an accusatory hand between whose index and middle fingers a long-ashed cigarette burned.

"I didn't get to go to no fancy college, just barely got outta high school. Work my fingers to the bone hawkin' jerky and swabbing john's and here comes a cool half million just drops in my lap, once in a lifetime, like God is finally havin' mercy on me, but no-o-o-o. Mr. unconstitutional Preacher-Chief has got to stick his self-righteous nose into my bidness. You're a thief, HB Alpata! A two timin', two-faced, half-injun thief!"

HB cranked up, wheeled away.

No kindness goes unpunished.

Out on I 16 the traffic into Macon was light. The raised highway passed over small houses where folks raised chickens, grew tomatoes and beans, but also worked in town. Kudzu creeping over sheds and garages, one or two trucks in most driveways. He passed a rare sight: a chicken truck. A rattle-trap hauling about a dozen cages: wood frames and chicken wire. Three hens to a cage. The driver had looped ropes around the whole thing to secure his cargo; even so, the whole contraption looked like a rolling house of cards. He pulled up beside the driver and waved. The grinning man returned his greeting, young, red beard, Duck Head overalls.

The old Georgia. Most folks waved as a sign of . . . what? A common set of values? A common Protestant faith? A common speech and accent? Easy to wax nostalgic, but he knew better. He'd grown up half-Creek. He knew what happened in those days to people who looked different. His daily school run-ins included charming phrases like the one Lizard just used, "injun," or "half breed," or "redskin," slurs heard in movies or on TV. Many days he came home bloodied, shirt ripped, knees ripped in his jeans. But as he grew in high school, lifted weights, and became a football star, the bullies backed off.

At the college he pulled his truck into the faculty parking lot—Volvo's, BMW's, an ancient Benz or two—and hung up the parking pass Al scored for him on his mirror. The new redbrick gym was massive, signaling how well the school was doing. He grabbed his gym bag as several coeds passed him, eyeing his cowboy hat and his Sam Brown, giving him the come hither once over.

Al Praetorius was already in the locker room next to the racquetball courts. They dressed and then warmed-up on the court.

Al's first serve blazed low and deep into the corner, almost impossible to return, but HB's long arms gave him a piece of the ball which he lifted high onto the front wall. Al backed up and caught it as it came down and fired it inches off the front, normally a kill shot; but HB anticipated and was there when it struck. He tapped it lightly and Al was too far to the rear to get to the front wall and make the return.

They played three hard games.

Afterwards, they showered.

"That back sprain's still slowing you down," Al said, opening his locker and slipping on his watch.

"A little. You just played well, today."

With a towel wrapped around him, HB stood in front of the long mirror. There were no other faculty members present. He examined his beard and face.

"Man, my hellacious week has etched a whole new crop of wrinkles."

"You sound like an ad for L'Oréal, but yeah, I did hear about some of it from Rosie in the faculty lounge."

"A guy pours rattlesnakes all over you, then dives headfirst into the concrete—you rethink some things."

Al eyed him, quizzically. "Such as?"

HB stepped into his jeans and snapped them up.

"I was ten," HB said, "Mom was accused of adultery. I'd made a lot of friends, so I was ashamed of my own mom. Heck, I didn't know what an adulteress was. I didn't even know what sex was. I just knew people were saying my mom's name and that adulteress word in the same breath and then they'd stare at me like I was the scum of the earth."

"So you blamed her."

"Of course. Fast forward fifteen years. You and I take that New Testament class with Dr. Colwell on the Gospel of John and the man was working on the woman taken in adultery. I was ripe fruit."

"And he plucked you."

"Gave me books, I got into it, wrote a great paper. But I was still confused. The woman in the pericope was accused of adultery, but I was confusing her with Alice Alpata. That ten year old was twenty-five but still trying to forgive his mom."

"So, have you?"

HB sighed. His mouth and face relaxed as he stared up.

"Hard to say. How do we ever know? Better dreams? Better sleep? A sense of peace? Am I gushing?"

"Like a fire hose. Put Oprah on the back burner and let's go get a PBR."

Chapter Eight

It was a perfect Sunday afternoon for the Alpata clan to destroy stuff. A breeze blew up from the river and clouds muted the sun just enough for them to bear the Georgia heat. They were sitting in fold up chairs around the old bootleggers' trash pile where Rosie had just related how, in a meditation class at the college, she learned to concentrate better and shoot straighter; but when she told the instructor why she was there—to improve her aim—the woman denounced her as a fascist war monger and booted her out.

HB chuckled. "Bet you've never, ever been kicked outta school."

"Wrong!" she pointed at him, "I took a field trip to Aachen once and some crazy kids and I wrote 'Charlemagne was a male chauvinist pig.' on his statue. Three days suspension. We were bad ass radical feminists."

"Mom!"

She pointed at her son. "But here's the part you're going to love. The sisters informed my straight back father and he summoned Mr. Justice."

"Who's Mr. Justice?"

"A two handed oak paddle he used on me and my six siblings. No time outs. No standing in the corner. And no therapist to deal with my unresolved issues. Just a session with Mr. Justice and a raw butt."

"O-w-w-w!" Mico reached for his behind.

"Spare the rod, prepare the delinquent," Nate said.

"Now," Rosie said, "I need to shoot!"

She placed ten long necks on the ground side by side as the males—Mico, HB and Nate—observed.

With HB clocking, she moved laterally, squatting, the pistol held out in front with two hands. Ten bottles in twelve seconds.

"I think the class helped," he said, handing her a Gatorade.

She sat down beside him, took a long swallow and wiped her mouth with the back of her hand.

"Bet they didn't teach you to guzzle with gusto at Our Lady of the Most Sacred Heart Convent School."

She pointed her finger at him. "No, you taught me that, you big American brute," she reached over and kissed him.

"Mo-o-o-o-om," Mico said, wincing.

"Yeah," Nate chimed in, "do you know how traumatic it is for the boy to witness his parents reenact the first coupling archetype?"

"Oh, no!" Rosie said, feigning shock, "First Freud and now Jung."

"Hey," Nate said, "know thy opponent. First rule for an apologist."

"So, it's down to Weeping Woman and Aubrey?" Rosie said to her husband.

"Yep," HB said, wiping the sweat from her brow with a napkin. "Slim pickings."

Mico raised up from texting, his thumbs twitching like a dead frog whose legs still have life. "But Dad, you said Weeping Woman wasn't strong enough."

"I did," HB said, raising his index finger. "But suppose she hired someone."

"A hired killer?" Rosie asked. "Right here in River City?"

"Why not?" her husband said. He lit up a cigarette, leaned back and enjoyed his first long puff.

"Which tribe is that?" Rosie asked.

"Poor, unloved Gad, son of Jacob and Zilpah, Leah's maid servant."

"Unloved because he was the son of a maidservant?"

"Exactly, those ancient Hebrew siblings were mean little guys. Probably played keep away with his yarmulke or pin the tail on Gad."

Mico's thumbs were back flying on his phone.

"What's so urgent?" Rosie asked him.

"I'm texting Davy the news. A real hit job here in Ocopeeco."

"Spud," HB said, shaking his head. "I'm just speculating. Davy doesn't need to know that."

"Aw-w-w-w, I never get to share all the cool stuff you do."

"It's for your own good," Rosie said. "In a small town news like that could get back to the Weeping Woman and if it turns out to be true, then she'll know Dad suspects her. No telling what she might do."

"She might creep over in the middle of the night," HB said, reaching over and squeezing Mico's knee, "and cut your throat."

"Ha, ha."

"Plus, last year just before Thanksgiving Big Rig sold his worm farm for a million and a half."

"For worms?" Mico said.

"Takes years to build up rich worm beds."

Mico stopped texting and was lost in thought.

"What?" HB said.

"So . . . Big Rig was . . . rich?"

"Think so," HB said, puffing. "He wa-a-s rich. And now Weeping Woman inherits all that."

Rosie gathered more bottles and handed them to HB. "So why," she said, "keep singing in the river? Why doesn't she leave with the boys and buy her a fancy place in Atlanta?"

"Beats me," HB said. He stood and threw the bottles high for Rosie to shoot. Three bottles, three hits.

Sitting, leaned against the truck with Nate on his shoulder, Mico asked: "Mom, I know about great grand dad the German sniper and all that, but really, why you are such a good shot?"

"Yeah," HB said, as he sat back down, "It's embarrassing. Here I am, the high chief, feared by a few, admired by a few, yet the whole town knows my wife's a better shot."

Rosie grinned. "You really want to know?"

"Yes," they said in unison.

"Curiosity killed the cat, the coon and the cow," Nate said.

"Don't listen to him," HB said.

"It's partly genes," Rosie said. "Partly love. I love to shoot. But lately, I've been particularly motivated to improve. Tack up one of those human targets." She nodded to Mico.

He bounded to the truck, pulled out the box of targets, fetched a hammer and nails and nailed a paper target in the shape of a woman in a large pine trunk.

Rosie loaded her Glock.

"I imagine I'm aiming at a certain, shall we say, persona non grata."

"I warned you," Nate said.

"Okay," HB said. "Who are you gunning down in cold-blooded murder?"

Rosie took aim. "Roxanne Sapp!" she said, then emptied the Glock into the defenseless figure's heart.

* * * *

"Tell me again what happened when you saw Big Rig abusing his boy."

Aubrey shrugged, wiped his hands on a paint-spotted cloth. After packing his long stem pipe, he flopped down on a decrepit porch glider, rusty, in his paint-flecked flannel shirt, open, showing his pale sunken chest.

His wild grey hair bound in a ponytail. Next to his easel: a table with half-drunk glasses of red wine.

He looked up at HB, still standing, and poured isopropyl alcohol over his bare feet and massaged his toes.

"Bugs and rocks and chiggers! Ugh! And I have to paint barefoot.Get in touch with Gaia's cthonic energy."

He went on and on about mother earth and how the true artist "sells his soul" to her. Knowing she was always there, feeding him, encouraging him—that was so vital to his success. So he needed to have his bare feet touch her, talk to her, love her.

HB listened, bored, wondering if this was some spiel he'd picked up the way one picks up a cold, unconscious, just reciting the standard artist's talking points, or was it an honest philosophy of life he'd developed by trial and error over the years. If the latter, he felt sorry for the poor guy.

The sun-baked clearing was Aubrey's latest en plein air painting spot, surrounded by loblolly pines. Near his easel a make shift metal rack, the side of cow hanging like a just-hanged prisoner, swarming with flies, pale maggots, and who knew what else crawling over it. Aubrey claimed the more disgusting the meat, the better he painted.

"Duke," the painter said, drying his feet with a towel, "don't you do tape recorders or even take notes? How many times do I have to go over this sordid little tale?"

"I have my methods," HB said. He sat down in the glider and it groaned. His polished brown leather boots shone in the sun.

"As I said before, there I was, cheerfully ensconced in my new spot, perfect light, perfect shade. Then I hear whimpering. At first I think it's an animal. Then I realize it's a child. So, I crouch, detective style, and head down through the trees."

"Still barefooted?"

"Of course."

"And there they were. Big Rig twisting the boy's arm, the child whining, on his knees, begging his daddy to stop, but he wouldn't stop. He kept saying: 'You got to learn, boy, You got to learn.' Chief, I saw a man decapitated in Syria, been in two earthquakes, a typhoon and a tsunami in the Philippines, but nothing got to me like seeing Big Rig torture his own boy. Man, I'm an old peacenik, but it sent me into a rage. I charged him with the limb. He turned just as I swung, and it cracked him right across the face. Felt go-o-o-od. I really whopped him. Didn't faze the brute. Sneered at me, blood streaming from his eye."

"Let's go see."

"What, now?" He pointed to his easel. "I'm on a schedule. This is a commission."

"I'm on a schedule, too. This is a murder."

In HB's truck they drove down the river road, crossed the old Hitchiti bridge and turned up toward the caves. Black bears had returned to middle Georgia. Each December a group was allowed to hunt them.

The caves sat high above the town, visible if the two men looked up through the oaks.

Aubrey found his former painting spot.

The ground was covered with clover from a break in the oaks that allowed sunlight in. HB could see why the painter was drawn to the spot: It had an Arcadian feel, soft celestial light pouring through the trees, a group of oaks in a circle.

From there, they descended to flat, treeless ground dotted with weed, vines and pebbles. Hard, barren clay. It was July, so any tire tracks were long gone from November the previous year when Aubrey came up on the boy and Big Rig.

"His truck was parked here," Aubrey said.

HB scoured the soil, squatting, picking up bits of paper. He plucked up a used condom.

"Kids park here," he said, squatting, his biceps straining through his red-checkered, long sleeve shirt.

"You came up on them," he went on, looking up at the painter, "and attacked with the pine limb. But look around: there aren't any trees here."

Aubrey's face seemed to shrink. "I brought one with me, a limb, from up there. I figured I might need some protection."

"A weapon."

"Right. I don't carry a gun."

HB stood and dusted off his jeans and removed his hat. He wiped sweat off his neck with his red bandanna. "Did the boy try to run when you hit his dad?"

"I don't remember," Aubrey said. He raised his hands like drawn pistols. "No, wait, he did. He ran, but he slipped down, and Big Rig grabbed his leg and dragged him back, screaming."

"The boy was screaming," HB said.

"Hell yes!"

"So, he throws the boy into the truck. Did he fight back?"

"Like a wildcat," Aubrey said.

"He's lanky, strong." HB said.

"He is."

Crouching, HB semi re-enacted the scene. "Now Big Rig tries to lock the cab door to keep him from escaping. Must have been hard, the boy screaming and fighting."

"I can't remember. I was scared out of my mind. All I could think of was: did he have a gun."

"Why didn't you run?"

The shocking reasonableness of the question stymied the painter. His face grew small. He shook his head and tried to smile.

"I was frozen, I guess. Like an animal caught in the headlights?"

"So, let me get this straight. After you pounded Big Rig and saw it didn't faze him, you stood there while he struggled to stuff his ten year old boy, fighting like a wildcat, into the cab, him fumbling to get out his keys, to lock the door and you, knowing a three-hundred pound weightlifter's about to break your neck—you just politely stood there like a schoolboy, waiting?"

Aubrey shook his head. "Why. . .why are you doing this?"

HB folded his arms as he glared into the painter's eyes. "Cause you're lying, Aubrey."

The painter seemed to recede, his face grew smaller.

"What?"

"I talked with the boy last week, Darrel. He was never here, and this never happened. His dad abused him, all right, but it happened inside the cab up near the kaolin plant after school."

Aubrey bolted up the hill, but HB tackled him hard, his big body crushing the small painter.

Aubrey crumpled and wept.

"I didn't want people to know. I'm not mean. Please, Big Rig had a family."

"What are you saying?"

"He and I met once a week. He . . . he . . . "

"For sex?" HB asked.

"Yes! Goddammit! Are you stupid?"

HB squatted. He lowered his voice. "Look, I'm not judging you."

"Of course, you are. Just like everybody else in this rat hole town."

"You met once a week. What happened?"

"Love happened," Aubrey said. "He was really a sweet man, down beneath all the macho armor. I loved him." He whimpered softly.

The lunch whistle from the kaolin plant sounded.

Aubrey put his hand on HB's arm. "I did, I really did love him."

After he dropped the painter back at his easel, he drove to the chapel, parked in back and came in through the rear entrance. The sanctuary was empty, cool and dark, the smell of flowers hanging in the air.

He found his pew, sat and scribbled notes about what he had learned, what he didn't know, what was missing and who he needed to talk to.

Silence arrived slowly. It was like a shy little animal, frightened and timid, hanging back to see if it was safe to emerge. When it did arrive, he began to see clearly. Aubrey was telling the truth. He knew because of the way that truth had come to light: with pain. The painter fought hard to keep it at bay, but the truth demanded the light of day. The painter was ashamed of who he was. Odd, since he was an artist, and they're supposed to be non-conformists, flaunting society and it's middle class values. And middle class values themselves were changing. Yet, Aubrey remained ashamed, however much he strutted around town like Little Lord Fauntleroy.

He knelt on the kneeler and asked forgiveness for his own sin and asked mercy and peace for Aubrey. The painter was tormented in ways that he, HB, would never comprehend. But he understood enough to know a fellow sojourner, one who suffered as he tried to hide who he was and stood in need of prayer.

* * * *

Pain awoke to the sound of a drum beating a slow, steady, rhythm outside his open window. Wood smoke drifted in, as well. He sat up, his long gray hair wild and unruly. In the near dawn light, the red dyed circle around his eye glowed. He padded barefoot over his pine wood floor to see outside his window a row of archaic Creek elders standing on his lawn. In the front: Osceola, dressed in a gold, long-sleeved tunic, cut off at his waist. His black hair was bound with a red bandanna and a rich black and white feather protruded from it. In his left hand he held a musket. His moccasins were dyed vibrant orange and his calves tightly bound in black leather and buttoned to his knees.

He peered into Pain's heart. Pain had long expected a reckoning, but in his paltry imagination, he had conceived of nothing so formal, so unsettling.

He stepped through the wall onto dewy grass, its cool droplets between his toes. A layer of smoke hung above them, a tutelary spirit that kept the great morning sun at bay as the Seminole led them over a hard-packed, clay path centuries of runners had pounded into near concrete. Into the impenetrable woods they embarked, single file, silent, resolved. Pain wanted to talk to someone. How would they punish him? Would they use one of the ancient ways, cutting off his nose or a hand? Or, the worst, would they cast his soul into the darkness for the bothas (evil spirits) to torment, never again to know the anogetchka, the deep love he shared with Ibofanga. He was tempted to turn around and ask the elder behind him, but he knew that would be blasphemous. A mission to meet the sacred entailed total silence.

The sun rose, the sun set. They followed a rocky creek for days, hopping from dry rock to dry rock, careful to avoid the slippery stones worn deadly smooth by millennia of rushing water. They came upon three buzzards feeding on cow carrion. One of the chiefs stepped forward, shielding himself from the stench with a blanket over his head. He asked their permission to take the skull.

"Why only the skull?" a buzzard asked. "Why not some meat?" A long, glistening thread of entrails dangled from his beak. "Brother cow was fat, and his flesh is delicious."

"The skull summons the spirits," the chief said, "It will tell us the future."

The three buzzards cackled, holding their sides. "Fool! There is no future."

At these awful words, darkness descended. Clouds swirled in kaleidoscopic fury, and the pines writhed in agony, screeching.

Pain covered his ears at the terrible noise.

Osceola shot three quick arrows into the blasphemers.

Their feathers turned into three long snakes, bothas all, gold and black. They slithered off into the trees.

The great chief glared at Pain. "This is what you have done. Now the bothas pursue us to the great round house."

Pain wanted to defend himself, but he knew it was futile, even dangerous.

After a week's walking, they arrived at the Boiling Waters. They descended a steep bank, vines and weeds ripping at their legs and pebbles flying loose until they stepped into the shallows. They turned north, against the current staying to the shore, keeping an eye out for alligators. Soon, a hungry granddaddy trailed behind them.

Osceola turned and bowed: "Greetings Brother. I hate to disappoint you, but we are too tough and stringy to make you a decent meal."

A deep, gravelly voice spoke: "On the contrary, Brother Two Legs, I see fatty thighs and a bulbous butt on more than one of your clan." He chuckled. "Beware of the slippery rocks. They are well placed just below the surface."

Osceola leaned down to Pain and whispered. "Our long tooth brother is waiting, Pain. Take care, lest you fall and fill his belly."

Pain winced as he glanced back at the two bulbous eyes trawling behind them.

They climbed the muddy bank straight up until they came to a green, then far away, the smoke of the village. They crossed the open field, enjoying the breeze and seeing the smoke already pouring out of the top of the council house. It faced east toward the rising sun which brought knowledge, knowledge of what man needs to do. The male fire of the sun entered the womb of Mother Earth and there the community could discuss and out of those debates the truth would emerge

At the entrance, Osceola stooped, and the others followed. The passageway led deep within the mound, cool, smelling of clay and wood smoke.

Pain's heart pounded! How many times had he dreamed of coming here, but not to be shamed and humiliated. He'd dreamed of a triumph, of praise for a great deed performed for Hesegadamasse.

They arrived in the council room. A hardened clay fire pit fortified the Creek connection to the earth, 'down' being one of their seven sacred directions. A central opening in the ceiling allowed the smoke to rise, another holy way. Maintained all year long, the fire itself was kindled with four logs arranged in a cross, each log serving as another sacerdotal marker.

Osceola positioned himself at the head, facing the sun.

The elders moved counterclockwise, each sitting in one of the seats patterned around the fire in a circle.

Behind them, a boy entered carrying a large clay pot of asi. As he came forward reverently, eyes cast down, a deep masculine hum arose. The elders held a clay cup up while the poured the black drink. After they drank, the older men's faces stiffened and their necks tightened. Some of the younger men immediately vomited.

The drink came to Pain. He quaffed it, and his throat was seized by the bitter yaupon taste. Once inside his stomach, the thick liquid boiled and rumbled. Then the thirty six cups of caffeine ripped his insides and out of his mouth poured a greenish waterfall. He rocked, groaning, head throbbing. He saw tiny golden spots and his heart slammed against his ribs like a wildcat clawing out.

Time sauntered away.

Mumbling and chanting, the men filled the room with tobacco smoke. When the pipe came to him, he couldn't puff. His chin and mouth trembled so his mouth could not even grasp the pipe.

They sang, deep basses, archaic diddies, children's songs, high shrieks like women screaming in child birth.

The asi came around again. The elders' faces ran rivulets of sweat and their eyes fluttered, while their heads, out of control, bobbed around and around.

Half-reclining, trying to breathe, Pain trembled and twitched, his stomach muscles jerking like a snake after his head's been severed.

Finally, Osceola stood.

He removed his colorful garments until he was naked. After he raised his sweaty, bronze arms, wings and feathers emerged from them; a beak grew from his nose and even more feathers covered his face. Last, his powerful naked legs shrank into the scaly, yellow flesh of the eagle.

He motioned for Pain to mount his back. Together, they rose through the opening above and soared over the village into the clear blue sky.

They were met by a bank of wind-boiled clouds and as the eagle twisted and dodged, sped up, slowed, Pain grabbed a knot of feathers like a horse's mane. The wind grew freezing cold. Pain buried his face in the feathers that still smelled of tobacco smoke. The massive wings clicked and groaned like the mast and rigging on a sailing ship. Eventually, they set down on the side of a mountain.

Pain slipped off the bird's back. The eagle's fierce eyes glared at a vine-entrammeled cave opening whose cool, musty air Pain could already feel. Still a little shaky from his wild ride and the black drink, he entered. The way forward was hard-packed and free of rocks, as he moved ahead, wondering. His granny back in Ocmulgee OK told him how the clan cut off her father's fingers each time he broke the sacred law, the Mahaga-ajagidos. When the young man wound up with only the thumb and index fingers of both hands, he finally learned to obey. As a second grader, Pain wrote and ate with only his thumb and index finger to see what it was like because he knew he would break the laws. Granny said their bear clan was forgiving. In other clans the first item under the knife was your manhood. After that, few would dare disobey.

But had he disobeyed? When Hesegadamasse summoned him to the shack, he went. And when he found nothing, no one, no signs of a struggle or a crisis, no heart attack or a murder, he kept searching. But he knew: That was not enough. For Hesegadamasse, failure was not an option. The Creek was not like the soft-belly white with his forgiving God and his knee-crawling Son. To the Creek, wrong was wrong and it had to be punished—which is why he felt much more at home in the eye-for-an-eye Old Testament than in the New where God gave his only-begotten-Son.

They came to a well-lit room and a granite throne occupied by an Owala (a prophet and emissary of Ibofanga). The throne was ornamented with eagle feathers and pelts, fox, wolf, bear.

The Owala had the head of a donkey, only his two eyes were not aligned. Long, floppy ears and twin horns curling out from under them like a small ram. A single curved horn grew from the top of its head. Human hands, donkey feet, two legs.

"Give me your finger," the Owala said. His voice was deep and gruff.

Looking around, no one there, Pain panicked. He was going to lose a finger. Not much. Maybe he could do without one finger. But not his index. That was for pointing. You point all the time. Everybody does. How much is that book? You point. Don't touch my food! You point. He couldn't imagine not pointing.

He thrust out his pinkie.

The creature reached and gripped the digit and pulled it away as if it were made of wet Kleenex. Pain felt nothing. There was no loss of blood.

The Owala pulled off all ten fingers.

Dazed, but not hurting, Pain looked at the stumps. Why had he felt nothing? He could feel the cold hard clay on the soles of his feet. He could smell wood smoke and burning yaupon leaves.

The prophet reached out again and pulled Pain's left arm off. It, too, gave way easily, like wet paper.

Then, the right arm.

Pain backed away, shaking his head . . . .

"No . . . no more . . . This is too much. The punishment doesn't fit the crime!"

The creature laughed, a sound like a big-toothed saw tearing into wood. Blood dripped from its long teeth.

"There is no punishment," it shouted, "no punishment that corresponds to your depravity!"

Pain screamed, but he couldn't move. The prophet had already taken his legs.

* * * *

Mico shouted as he pounded his granddad's chest.

"Grandad! Wake up! Mom! Dad!"

On the porch carefully hauling in a pot of chicken soup Rosie and HB put the food down and dashed inside.

Mico was sitting on Pain's chest, pounding, and screaming. The old Creek lay still as a stone, his eyes closed, his colorless lips compressed.

When Rosie brought out the smelling salts she had started carrying on their visits, the old man swung his fists, eyes still shut, and teeth gritted.

"The punishment doesn't fit the crime!" he shouted.

HB stood, gnawing his lower lip, hands on his hips. "He's still there, wherever there is. Spud, get a CD, Count Basie. Put in on. It's one of his favorites." Mico rifled through the collection and soon the room was filled with the sound of Basie and his band "Stomping at the Savoy."

Eyes fluttering, Pain rejoined them, spittle dried in the corners of his mouth.

He kissed Mico's hand, crying.

Rosie and HB slipped to the other side so all three of them could put their hands on him.

He shook his head back and forth. "I'm so sorry. I've frightened you all yet again."

Mico laid his head on his grandfather's chest and fought back tears. Rosie joined her hand with her husband's.

Memories poured into HB's heart. This was how his mother died. Intense dreams, family gathered around pleading with her to eat, loving her but hating the fast, telling her it was all right that she couldn't forgive the woman who accused her. Humans are made that way. But his Mom was convinced that just as the Lord told his disciples "This kind only comes out with prayer and fasting," her spirit of unforgiveness would come out with the same remedy.

Rosie brought a cup of soup. Pain took a few sips, then pushed the rest away with "Makes me nauseous." Rosie didn't even protest. She had tried so many times to get her father-in-law to eat.

HB wore a giant yellow cardboard star that read "I'm Marshall o' this here town!" Grace Daniel had called in her IOU and cast him as the Marshall in the high school's production she herself had written closely based on *Oklahoma*.

Pain raised up. He blinked as he took in the star.

"I'll bet you one of Miss B's chocolate malts you won't preach in that outfit."

They all chuckled.

Mico turned to his Dad, then his grandad. "Whatever happened to Miss B?"

Pain and HB exchanged looks. "You tell him, son." Pain said. "You were fourteen. Your memory's better."

HB took in a deep breath, he was finally relaxing. He grinned.

"One Saturday we were playing a pickup baseball game on the grassy field back of the church. I was at the plate when I looked up and there was FDR. Still had his saddle on. He nudged me, backed away and pawed the ground. The whole team stopped and gathered around him. Then he turned and started walking back the way he'd come. We followed, a dozen boys. Now, some of the boys had heard scary stories about Miss B and FDR, living in the swamp with alligators and witches and such, but I felt comfortable, so I kept up the pace and about a half dozen dropped out. The horse found a dry hard path that cut right through the swamp: cypress and lily pads and some deep water on both sides, but we were dry and fine. We spotted her cabin. A corrugated tin and plywood shack, not too poorly put together. Coon skins and rabbit hide everywhere. Chickens in a pen. One black, speckled rooster started to crow soon as we showed up. There was a bad stink.

"FDR stopped outside the entrance. When we went in, she was lying on her bed. She raised on her elbows. 'Holy Boy!' she said, 'I knew old FDR could find you.'

"We rigged an Indian style carry-up and FDR dragged her back to town and a waiting ambulance. She died of liver cancer a few months later, but before that, she sent us all a thank you card. FDR passed on in about a year. I can still taste her chocolate malts."

Pain nodded. "I asked her once what her special ingredients were. She winked and said. "If I told you, Geronimo, you'd up and start your own shop."

Chapter Nine

Rosie sat at her freshly waxed desk in the big lecture room, sipping her morning coffee, perspiring from her early morning workout and sizing up her new semester's crop of students as they hemmed and hawed down the tiered steps to find a seat. Immediately, they pulled out their phones. Didn't speak. No "Hey, how ya' doin'?" or even a nod at the person beside them. Well, that was part of her job, wasn't it? Get them out of their narcissistic digital universe to peek into the real world as it was nine hundred years ago. Most pulled out a laptop for notes, but a few had pen and paper still.

In the top back sat an older woman, wearing a starched blouse and black skirt.

Wait! It was Lurleen Scruggs, Big Rig's wife. In her medieval art class!

Worlds in collision! Ocopeeco didn't fit at the university, at least not in Rosie's mind: she had to adjust her sights. Lurleen noticed her staring and waved, so Rosie waved back. This was going to be interesting. About fifty kids—and Weeping Woman, who sang in her straw bottom chair in the river at night.

As part of her presentation the first day she always asked the college players to put on a medieval mystery play to give the class an emotional door to step through. This time they outdid themselves with a rendition of the harrowing of Hell. A group of bedraggled souls wandered onto the stage, a loud rock guitar playing cacophonous heavy metal, some crawling, all groaning in misery, bruised, cut, half naked. They were herded by a trio of devils: odd horns from the side of their heads, wart-studded noses and long tridents with which they prodded the unhappy souls. Gradually, the devils covered the lost souls with a red rubbery plastic substance until the audience could only see the hands and heads of the dead as they pressed into the malleable imprints of their bodies. Then came Christ in white with blinding glow and the dulcet sound of a lute and angels singing.

Even though some of her students were still trapped in the hell of their phones, Lurleen was transfixed. Her eyes bright, she sat on the edge of her seat, gripping the seat back with white knuckles, that neatly-coiffed Veronica Lake look so out of place with the shaggy youth around her.

But even as she looked forward to having an adult in class who was paying attention, she could not forget that this woman may have had her own husband murdered.

At last night's supper of Kohlrouladen (stuffed cabbage rolls), sauerkraut, and Liebfraumilch, HB explained Lurleen's bank records showed no large withdrawals, which would be indicated if she hired someone to commit murder. Likewise, her phone records showed nothing unusual, either. No calls outside Ocopeeco. He'd also checked the mileage on the family Toyota. It was consistent with travel out and about Ocopeeco for a year. There was one grocery store in Macon she visited once a week to buy T bone steak Big Rig liked. HB telephoned the butcher who confirmed Lurleen appeared like clockwork on Thursday every week for five T bones.

Rosie stood and began her class by reading excerpts from Hildegard's writings.

"She writes: 'Not in stubbornness, but in humility, I refused to write for so long that I felt pressed down under the whip of God into a bed of sickness.'"

Rosie commented: "She had experienced wonderful visions from God, but her male advisors cautioned her against writing such things down. She repressed them and it made her sick."

She showed a slide of one of the visions. It depicts a woman seated with a writing tablet on her lap. Overhead are five bizarre tongues descending.

"This portrays her awakening, like the awakening of the disciples at Pentecost when tongues of fire cast out their doubt and uncertainty. Hildegard cast off her illness and began to write down what God had shown her. Subsequently, she tells us what a deep and profound exposition of books came upon her, a program that took up the next ten years of her life."

When the lecture was over, as the students filed out, Lurleen remained.

Rosie climbed up to the top row seats and sat down. "I'm so delighted to see you! Are you enrolled as an auditor?"

"No, as a student." Lurleen closed her laptop and turned to look at Rosie. Her face glowed.

"Well," Rosie said, "What did you think?"

After a long sigh, the woman took Rosie's hands: "You're a brilliant teacher!"

The force of her words moved Rosie. She felt tears well up but fought them back. Like many teachers she lived with a nagging sense she taught into a void.

Lurleen squeezed her hands. "And I already love Hildegard. I know what she felt. I always have felt squelched and beaten down, too. I hope someday to have my Pentecost moment."

Chatting, they left the art building and found their way to a massive magnolia where they sat and sipped coffee and ate power bars.

"I majored in Art History at Emory," Lurleen said, her pinkie catching a crumb at the corner of her mouth.

Rosie noted how delicately she bit into her power bar. Was this really Big Rig Scruggs' wife?

"Art history and drawing. I was the best copier in the department."

"Well, it is a skill."

"I did a Durer, one of the rabbits, pen and ink. As a joke, we slipped it into a department wide Durer lecture—evening "do", tuxes, posh buffet. The three profs on the panel gushed on and on about the detail, the light and shade. In the middle, one of my buds, a TA, slips in and whispers to one of the lecturers that there was a screw up and one of my copies got mixed in with the real etching. Caused a mini scandal."

Rosie paused, trying to think of a way to ask the question, politely.

Lurleen grinned and asked it first. "So, how did I get mixed up with Big Rig Scruggs?"

"Yes!"

Lurleen giggled. "Sex."

Rosie laughed as she grabbed Lurleen's arm. "You know, I did a guest lecture at the high school back in the spring and I saw a photo of him back in the day. He was a stud."

Lurleen rolled her eyes. "M-m-m-m, you got that right. He owned a gym in Little Five Points. Grungy little hole in the wall, but he loved that old place. I had an apartment on North Highlands. I would visit him at night after his weightlifting class. We got married and I got pregnant. He didn't want to raise his child in the big city with all the crime and drugs, so we moved back to his hometown. I had no idea what he would turn into."

Rosie squeezed her new friend's arm. "Oh, sweetheart, I'm so sorry.

The sympathy brought tears to Lurleen's big, brown eyes. She reached into her purse for Kleenex.

While she wiped her eyes, Rosie noted how her new friend stood out because of the way she dressed: a trim, black skirt, a starched cotton blouse, her Veronica Lake hair-do perfectly coiffed, hanging on one side and iconic red lipstick. A film noir moll, only one who drew as well as Durer.

Students passed them by and threw furtive glances their way. Eventually, a tall, shaggy-haired black boy approached. He wore a T shirt showing an upraised fist in front of a backdrop that said: BLM! Leather wrist cuffs, chains, the odor of weed.

Rosie bristled. She bit into her power bar and glanced at Lurleen who seemed calm.

Arms folded, the boy stared at Lurleen. He nodded to some inner rhythm.

Before Rosie could intervene, Lurleen spoke up: "Excuse me, do I know you?"

Chuckling, he stroked his beard, a young man trying to look old.

"Yeah," he said, "You do. In another life. You and your husband ran a plantation. Had me whipped, clapped in irons. Your husband raped my wife. When I tried to escape, you sent dogs after me, tore off my arm."

Calmly, Lurleen sat down her coffee. She lit a cigarette and blew a long stream of smoke. But she said nothing.

"You hear what I said?" the boy yelled.

Again, no answer.

The silent treatment infuriated him. He muttered something, head shaking.

Rosie reached for her friend's hand.

Now the boy raised his head. His eyes glowed and he breathed hard. His nostrils flared.

"You think you're better than me, so you won't talk to me. Just like the damned folks that enslaved my people."

By now a crowd of students had gathered. Rosie could tell they were mostly under class men and women. Lately, this kind of brutal confrontation had become too commonplace. Someone passed out yellow leaflets about a protest and a march.

"Answer him, bitch!" somebody yelled from the crowd.

"Yeah," another shouted. "Your silence means he's right. Your people enslaved his people. Treated them like dogs."

Now students were running from across campus toward the gathering. Like piranhas, Rosie thought.

"Do you know who I am?" she said to the ringleader.

"Yeah, you teach some privileged for whites only art class about dead old white nuns."

Lurleen stamped out her cigarette. She looked him directly in the eye.

"A year ago, my husband was brutally murdered, but not before he abused my three small boys for years and warped them for life. But I have refused to become bitter and hateful. The words I heard from you were spoken by a sad boy who's also been deeply hurt. But he's allowed that pain to make him bitter and take control of his heart and soul. Bitterness will destroy you. It will turn you into a monster who can only hate and hate some more. Only love will give you peace, the peace that passes understanding. And that is what I wish for you today, my friend. Right here in this grove of academia, in front of all your friends, I wish the peace that passes understanding come into your heart. God bless you and everyone who loves you."

* * * *

Rosie chopped onions, wiping the tears from her eyes with her elbow, but giggling. "You should have seen that crowd," she said. "Total silence. The ringleader skulked away as if he'd been scolded by the Pope and the crowd dispersed. I wish I'd had a camera."

"And this was Weeping Woman?" HB said. "The same person who sings in her straw bottom chair in the river?" Munching onions, he had his boots on the table. Against his usual, spiffy-at-all times protocol, he had rolled his sleeves up, revealing his big, hairy forearms. "So, what do you think?"

She stopped chopping, scraped the onions into the chicken salad bowl, stirred briskly with the wooden spoon and handed him a spoonful.

He nibbled and smacked his lips. "M-m-m-m, a tad more mayo."

After she reached into the fridge for the mayo and stirred in a spoon-ful, she said: "I think Lurleen Scruggs is an enigma wrapped in a riddle whose solution will lead us to a mystery."

He rolled his eyes. "Ro-o-osie . . . "

She pinched his cheek. "We do not know this woman. She's articu-late, smart, cultured. Not twenty-four hours after that confrontation on the quad, she dropped a set of pen and ink drawings in my faculty mailbox done from Hildegard's *Scvias*. They're incredible."

"So, she can draw," he said, "But did she figure out a way to have her husband murdered without withdrawing money from her bank account, without using her credit card, even without telephoning anyone outside her normal circle of acquaintances?"

Rosie beat her salad faster. "I don't kno-o-ow . . . "

"Plus," he continued, "Come November, it'll be one year since Big Rig was murdered. I was in the post office yesterday. Guess who I was trapped in line with for half an hour, and who gave me the third degree about why I was taking so long to find the killer?"

"Gussy B!"

"Judge Gustavus Breckenridge, he of the tart tongue and the speedy gavel. The city council session is coming up in a week. He wants to know what I can report."

"You've eliminated two suspects and, well, you're looking closely at a third."

"That's what I said. He wasn't impressed."

She covered the salad in saran wrap and slipped the bowl into the fridge. "I'll ask Lurleen for supper Friday night. Maybe, you can come to some closure on her, as a suspect"

"Baby" he said, raising his voice, "I don't need closure. I need to find the killer!"

Saturday morning following the Friday night supper with Lurleen Scruggs, HB sat down at his desk and made a journal entry:

Last night I had the opportunity to eat crow. I usually eat a lot on this job, but last night was particularly galling. Lurleen Scruggs explained to Rosie and Mico and me what she planned to do with the money Big Rig left. She's donating a million dollars to Rosie's university for a medieval art center with Hildegard of Bingen as the main subject. We had to pick Rosie up off the floor. The two women bawled and hugged, Kleenex and more Kleenex, then they bawled and hugged some more. Other money goes to the high school to establish an art department and new tennis courts for Grace Daniels. Still other money to a Center for Abused Children in Macon. The rest she set aside for the boys' education. Oh, and lest I forget, she did splurge on herself. She had her old mailbox replaced.

There went my last suspect. A wife who hires a killer to do her husband in does not turn around and donate the money for a medieval art center, and tennis courts and a center for abused children. Lurleen Scruggs, I am both happy and sad to say, is not our killer.

* * * *

The high school principal's office offered the city council the most elegant meeting space.

Behind the desk, the chair was occupied by Judge Gustavus Breckenridge, Chief of the Superior Court of Twiggs County, known at Roxanne's as "Gussy B.", a short, rotund man, a full head of hair, a three piece charcoal gray suit. His walrus moustache and dimpled smile belied an acute, if archaic, prosecutorial mind.

The judge pounded his gavel.

"Don't you ruin my desk with that thing!" Ann Glynn said.

Unaccustomed to any challenge, the judge seemed to shrink. He tugged his tie and started again.

"Now y'all know I'm an elected official, so I don't have any business being here, but Ann and Grace asked me to sit in in an ex officio capacity just to help out, you know."

Seated to the judge's left, a perky black girl, tiny glasses on the tip of her nose, pecked at a laptop. She grinned and waved to the council.

Beside the judge, in the witness stand, sat HB, hat in lap, looking out at the council seated in a semi-circle. Fifteen minutes before, in the parking lot, the conversation was cheerful and normal; but now, nobody would look at him. Grace kept her eyes lowered and Jim Jeffords stared straight ahead, even though HB had tried several time to make eye contact. And Mrs. Beasley, always eager to see him, would not meet his gaze. Even Ann Glynn, a long-time friend, seemed cool.

Gus Breckenridge leaned back, squeaking. "HB, I don't want you to get the wrong idea here. We called this meeting out of concern for you."

The council nodded.

"You see," the judge continued, "here we have a case of unquestionable malum in se—I'm referring of course to Big Rig's murder. Now it's become an insidious presence, a corrosive eating away at those invisible but vital bonds of friendship, loyalty and fidelity that are the very nexus of any healthy community. It's been over a year now."

The judge stroked down on his moustache with his right index finger, his face hypertensive pink.

"I've eliminated three suspects," HB said. He looked at Breckenridge, then out at the council. His stomach was churning.

He explained why Aubrey, Lurleen and Lizard Little could not be the killer.

"And you're certain about this?"

"Pretty certain."

Ann Glynn shook her head. "HB, I can't help but think you're too close to this case. Heck, you know e-v-er-y-body. You grew up with Big Rig. Can you be objective?"

They all stared at her.

"What?" She glared back at them as she held out her arms. "I'm only saying what we've all been thinking."

HB fiddled with his hat. He felt naked without it, but the judge had made him take it off.

"Ann, I've followed standard protocol. But hey, my resources are limited. I pay for my own weapon, my own bullet proof vest, I slap a chief's insignia on my own bought and paid for Ford truck. That's thirty thousand dollars I save the council. If I want high tech equipment I have to go to Macon which I do three times a week. I even use my own laptop."

The judge thumbed through his notes. "And in Macon you sometimes seek the counsel of former chief, Bobby Gene Brown, otherwise known as 'Bang- 'Em Up Brown.'"

"Correct."

"And he has served as a kind of mentor to you?"

"He has. Chief Brown is still beloved because everyone remembers how he walked the trailer parks, and ghettos, white, black, Latino, armed with only a big smile and an uncanny ability to remember names."

Ann Glynn shook her head. "Yeah and he walked the courthouse with a Louisville slugger in his hand. And he wouldn't know Microsoft Word from a mad dog turd."

"Ms. Glynn!" the judge said, pounding his gavel.

The principal folded her arms and turned her head to the side, revealing her freshly shaved, glistening scalp.

The outburst caused Mrs. Beasley to blink, rapidly.

The judge opened his briefcase, pulled out a dozen letters written on a yellow legal pad in sprawling pencil."

"And now Lizard Little writes me once or twice a week. He's got himself a 'so-called' lawyer and plans to sue the town for his money. Chief, I've got a full docket. I serve three counties. I don't have time for this."

A mumbling and muttering ensued: "Such a disappointment!" "He's become a menace." "Used to be a nice boy."

"HB, your solution to getting rid of the money was risky," the judge said, "but you did save the town a peck of trouble, but here we may have a lawsuit on our hands."

HB shook his head. "I know the lawyer. And I hate to criticize people, but the man struggles with alcohol and the truth."

"If it does come to trial, that'll cost money—even if the case gets thrown out the first day. Heck, it costs money just to have Callie Cousins here sit in and type the council's notes." The judge nodded to the reporter.

She made a pouty face, so he grinned and to console her, reached over to pat her knee.

"Judge," Ann Glynn said, "do you think fondling the court recorder in front of the town council is behavior befitting your office?"

The others giggled.

Caught in mid-pat, his short, stubby judicial fingers resting on Callie's knee, Gussy B's face twisted into an expression of guilt, anger and pleasure deferred.

Recovering quickly, he thumbed through his notes. "And that brings us to the GBI. Why haven't you asked for their help?"

The sweat trickled down HB's back and made his freshly starched shirt stick to the chair. He wrenched his body to unstick himself.

"You okay?" The judge asked.

"A little stiff. Look, judge, the GBI does a thorough job. They will turn over every rock, including some we don't want turned over."

"What's that supposed to mean?" Ann Glynn asked.

"Ann, they will investigate everybody, including the principal of Ocopeeco High, a hard working woman whose tough discipline and excellent record on academics—high test scores and such— should by every right outweigh the inevitable questions the GBI will raise about her non-conformist private life."

The judge raised his eyebrows.

"I'll sue their homophobic pants off!" Ann said.

"And you should. They have no business poking where they shouldn't. But they'll think your lifestyle's a weakness the criminal mind can exploit. Why bring that trouble into our town to begin with?"

The council murmured and the judge pursed his lips, as HB gave them his best non-committal smile.

Mrs. Beasley whispered to Jim Jeffords she failed to understand why anyone would investigate Ann Glynn's personal life, except to hint to the poor girl that most sensible men are not attracted to her awful, mannish haircut; but she was not aware that the GBI or any law enforcement agency considered it their responsibility to dictate hairstyles.

The council continue to consider the pro's and cons of calling in the GBI until Mrs. Beasley stood, shiny purse clutched close to her body. Mico's now retired second grade teacher wore a light green blouse with small, puffed sleeves and a full billowy dress. The thick moist folds of flesh on her face seemed about to slide off, along with several layers of face powder.

"HB, I have he-a-a-rd that you . . . I mean there are those who claim or, is it possible that . . . oh, my goodness! HB, do you pray for the crooks?"

For the first time, he was on home turf. "Mrs. B, when a crook gets caught, that's G-d's way of saying, 'this is your non plus ultra, the point beyond which you cannot go.' But the fact is, and G-d knows this, there is nothing, apart from that person's conscience, to prevent them from going farther. Most do. They go to jail, serve time, get out, do it all over again: car jack, sell drugs, rape, you name it. Only a heart transformation can bring that cycle to an end. So, yes, I definitely pray for the crooks because that is usually the only way they will change their life."

The judge winced and pursed his lips, and his face underwent a bizarre series of wrenching and stretching. He hated it when religion sneaked into his court.

"Seems to me, HB," Jim Jeffords said, "That ain't right." In his overalls, the owner of the general store spoke deliberately. His big bald head, and sagging jowls moved up and down in synch with his voice. "Chief's supposed to lock 'em up and that's all. A law-man ought not be dabblin' in religion. Leave religion in the church—where it belongs."

Mrs. Beasley nodded and looked around to all: "Why I would no more take my religion outside the church walls than I would smoke that awful marijuana."

Grace Daniel, the only Roman Catholic in Ocopeeco, stood and faced Mrs. Beasley and Jim Jeffords. The blond, attractive high school tennis coach had on her white tennis togs "I disagree. Our Lord made it clear in the Gospel of Matthew that we Christians are to go forth and make disciples of all nations. How can you do that if you keep religion inside the church. What HB does is right, and I support him."

The judge was sweating. He bobbed his head a round and twisted his gavel in his hand. The religion talk upset him so, he called for a lunch recess.

The council retired to the judge's house; HB stayed put and ate Rosie's tuna fish sandwich plus Kohlroulade.

When they returned, the judge got straight to the point.

"HB," he said, leaning forward with his elbows on the desk, "with the vigorous exception of Ms. Daniels, the council has decided to expand our horizons."

The tennis coach sat, pouting, arms folded.

"Mr. Blake, here," the judge continued, "He's the plant rep." A young man stood at the back of the room.

HB had noticed him and wondered why he was there and now he understood.

"His uncle, Mr. Dupree, as you know, is the plant owner. He will finance a new chief search. We've already picked three men after a considerable effort. Son, I hate to do this to you, but we've got to find this killer."

HB closed his eyes and breathed in deeply. He'd anticipated some complaints, a dressing down, but this? And did they think a real lawman would come to Ocopeeco? The pay alone would drive the good ones off.

"And" the judge went on, "Mr. Dupree has agreed to up the new chief's salary."

Grace Daniels stood: "That's not fair. It's an insult to HB!"

"Grace, I'm not crazy about it, myself, but Peyton Dupree pulls a lot of weight in these parts."

The door flew open and there stood Lizard Little, brandishing an antique double-barrel shotgun and swaying from the two six packs of beer coursing through his veins. His duct-taped glasses down at the tip of his nose, he swept the room with the shotgun and shouted:

"Woo-wee, got all the vermin in one corner, the money-thieving chief, his Jezebel side kick, the lesbo principal and the crooked judge. Lord, I must be livin' right."

"Put the gun down, Lizard," HB said.

"Oo-o-oh, look at Mr. Cool. Ain't gon' ruffle his feathers, no siree."

"Lizard Little," the judge said, "I'm warning you!"

"Now, judge, this man' ll steal all your money right out from under your nose and tell you you're his buddy in the same breath. He's a cool customer, folks."

"Lizard," HB said, "if you put the shotgun down, this won't turn out so bad for you. Do it now before you hurt somebody."

"Naw, I ain't puttin' my gun down. I wanna sit in on this meetin' of the rich and powerful and see how this here town operates."

With those words he stepped forward and tripped on a lip of the indoor outdoor carpet. He fell forward, the gun went off, and two shells ripped a five foot wide swath of the carpet to the wall.

Gussy B. landed on his back with his cute court recorder lying across his chest, squealing and kicking. Jim Jeffords lay face down on top of Grace Daniel's. Lizard lay sprawled in the floor, his hands covered his ears and his duct-taped glasses twisted on his face.

HB rushed to Mrs. Beasley. He lifted her up; her mouth opened and closed like a fish and her thick face powder was imprinted with the xxx pattern of the carpet.

Later he would ask himself why he thought he'd be able to determine anything about her defibrillator by sticking his hand inside her dress.

She jerked and her eyes opened.

"What are you doing? Get your paws away from there!"

Her lashes fluttered as she slapped at his big hairy hand

* * * *

In handcuffs, walking ahead of HB, Lizard trundled down the tile steps from the principal's third floor office as the council observed at the rail from a safe distance above.

"I ought to throw you in jail up in Jeffersonville!" the judge shouted down, "meet some tatted-up Tango and Cash boys, some of Captain Cody's men and the perks and dillie pushers. Teach you some manners!"

"You better be glad the chief's a preacher!" Ann Glynn shouted.

HB had talked them down. A stay in the big jail wasn't warranted, he maintained. A few nights in Ocopeeco's luxurious facilities, deprived of PBR's and smokes, would hopefully bring Lizard back to his senses. The condition for getting out would be to enroll in the kaolin plant's AA program. Lizard would hate it, but he would do it and it would give HB a way to monitor him.

He drove Lizard to the church on main street. They parked in front where HB jimmied the meter so he could stay beyond the city-prescribed limit. They passed through the dark, quiet sanctuary, exited the back door and walked the twenty yards through uncut sour grass to the jail, a concrete block building with one door, a cot, one barred window, a toilet and a sink.

Once settled on the cot, Lizard put his head in his hands.

HB sat beside him. He looked around at the tiny concrete block cell. Usually, Saturday nights were the only times he locked anybody up, a drunk from Roxanne's. Being here in the afternoon felt strange.

Then, it hit him: They had fired him!

He was out of a job! No way to support his family. Worse, he'd have to face the townsfolk every day as the failed lawman. Heck, he'd had Mrs. Beasley himself when she was a young teacher. Gus Breckenridge had represented his Dad back when Gus was a young lawyer. Jim Jeffords coached Mico's Little League team. The unsolved murder scared them, and he hadn't realized until that moment how much. To the town a murderer was loose in the community and the community was so small they had begun to wonder and look around and ask themselves who among their neighbors was it. Those bonds of friendship, fidelity and trust. And he had failed to pick up on all that. To him the case was a puzzle to be solved, but they were scared. Rosie had told him more than once: "The grocery clerk asked me again about the murder."

Lizard wiped his duct-taped glasses on his shirt. His eyes were dark and sleep deprived and accusatory.

"You done this!" he said, glaring at HB. "You the one made me go and get drunk and get out my granddaddy's old shotgun. It's all your fault."

HB took the cue. He rose to leave.

Lizard threw himself onto the cot, mumbling into the scratchy wool blanket.

"What?" HB asked, bending down to hear.

Lizard raised his head. His lips were pouting, the face of a child, lost, alone.

"Ain't nobody left!" he bawled. "Granddaddy, momma, daddy, sister—they all dead and gone. Got no friends. Ain't nobody! Nobody!"

HB slipped out into the sunlight and texted Rosie he would be a little late getting home. Then he walked down to Jim Jeffords store, bought sandwiches and hot coffee and returned. They sat down on the bed, ate the food and drank as Lizard talked about what it feels like to wake up one day when you're fifty years old and find yourself without friends, without family, without anyone to love.

Chapter Ten

He moved through the trailer park like a jungle cat, his knee-length buckskin boots with fringe crunching the gravel. Thick black hair and Native American features, high cheek bones, he wore a faded work shirt, first three buttons open so you saw the layers of his muscled abs. The shirt, too tight, showed off his bulging biceps and chest. Besides his holstered .45, he carried a machete with an ivory handle.

HB and the judge sat on a bench at the park entrance where, with binoculars, they observed him slipping from unit to unit, sniffing. Apparently, the man had an olfactory GPS.

Once a week, HB inspected the trailer parks. Today, he decided to let the new applicant for his job do it, get a feel for what he was about.

The judge focused the binoculars. "Feel like I'm watching an old black and white western," he said, "Randolph Scott, or Joel McCrae."

He tried crossing his stubby legs, grunting, but gave up and lit his pipe.

HB took the binoculars. Pedro Murietta claimed he didn't drink or smoke or do drugs. They dull your senses, and a lawman is like an animal: he needs his senses. HB had never thought that way, but there was obviously something to it. The man's perfect white teeth and buffed body showed he lived what he preached. And when he squinted at you with those dark eyes, he resembled an amused animal.

"The Tijuana deputy I talked with said he's the best tracker he's ever seen. But, he has some personal habits we might not approve of."

"Like scalping," the judge said.

"I told the deputy we weren't concerned with his personal habits, as long as he can live on chicken feed."

The judge patted him on the back. "Now, son."

"I'm trying." HB said, and handed back the binoculars.

"A fellow judge I talked to in his district says the man worked against the cartels. I'm thinking: the cartels? In Ocopeeco. You don't need a shotgun to kill a fly."

"That is one bad Harley he rode in on," HB said, "drove it all the way across country. Camped out and ate at farmer's markets."

"He'd make a lousy judge," the judge said. "I asked him about drugs in Tijuana. He said 'Users use, suppliers supply. You gotta get rid of one.' No Latin or sociology or long legal words. Just: 'You gotta get rid of one.'"

"Dad would love him. Concision, son, he used to tell me about writing."

"How's he doing?"

"Not so good. He mostly stays in bed. Watches Native American documentaries. Weak as a kitten."

"Like your mom."

"Exactly."

The judge looked at him, but he remained silent.

HB jerked up, focusing the binoculars. "I think he's got something."

They drove to where Murietta was crouched low beside a rusted out double wide, two new Ford 150 pickups out front, one black, one white. He pointed to the top of the trailer where a pipe emitted smoke, then to propane cylinders beside him.

He whispered: "Those cylinder valves are blue. That means anhydrous ammonia."

The ammonia odor was strong.

HB drew close. "This trailer hasn't been here more than a week. It wasn't here the last time I came through."

"Makes sense," Murietta said. "Not much trash yet. No guard dog or signs to keep out. They just got here."

The judge put his handkerchief over his mouth.

"You okay, judge?" Murietta said.

"Yeah."

"Then let's get to work!"

With that the man from Tijuana leapt onto the wooden steps to the front door, pulled his .45 and blew the lock off. The three trailer occupants screamed as they exited the other end.

HB tackled two, but the third got away.

Murietta sprinted to his Harley concealed behind plum bushes, sped across the park after him and within minutes he returned with the third man cuffed and riding behind him on his bike.

They chained the three to HB's truck and returned to the lab where the judge snapped pictures.

Standing with his arms crossed, Murietta waited until the judge was finished.

"Now if we had a forensics team . . . " the judge began, but before he could finish his sentence Murietta slashed into the beakers and jars and bottles with his machete. HB and Gus threw up their arms to keep the glass from their eyes. The man cursed and spat as he destroyed. "Spawns of Satan, go back to hell, where you came from," he shouted, as he shattered and leveled everything, including the chairs and a ratty red sofa in the corner.

When he was finished, he stepped outside, wiped his blade with a rag and stood with eyes closed, breathing deeply, and smiling, face to the sky.

The judge leaned in the doorway, not sure whether he should say anything.

Eventually, he relit his pipe.

"Son, maybe I'm overstepping my bounds here, but I'm assuming down Tijuana way, you boys don't much go in for warrants."

* * * *

Wet and icy November weather forced the Ocopeeco Panthers to practice in the gym. Wearing socks, but all their pads, the team ran plays on the basketball court, no hitting. In a golf cart the three hundred pound coach putt putted back and forth from offense to defense, calling out directions and comments with a bull horn. Beside him in the cart the team manager, a pony tailed senior girl with acne and thick glasses took notes on a laptop while another student filmed with a camera on the sidelines. The coach sipped from a giant-sized cherry slurpy in a Styrofoam cup. From time to time he handed his slushy to the ponytail who used the plastic straw to better distribute the ice.

Ann Glynn led the group, the judge, Jim Jeffords, HB and Pedro Murietta, into the gym. HB noted her butch cut made her naked scalp glisten more under the gym lights.

As usual, Murietta said nothing. He observed from under his crumbled straw hat, muscled forearms folded, pects and abs exposed. At least he had sheathed his machete.

HB recalled his own days at indoor practice, listening to the older boys explain to the underclassmen how to avoid the clap.

Ann led the group in front of the second and third stringers who sat on the bench along the side lines. Most smiled politely to the principal and her guests. Most recognized the judge and knew better than to wise crack when he was around. But one skinny blond, a third stringer, smirked as they passed. He addressed Murietta who was last in the group..

"Hey, Sittin' Bull, who you gon' scalp with that blade?"

The man from Tijuana stopped.

The other adults moved on.

Around the boy his teammates cringed, heads low.

Murietta walked back, leaned down into the boy's face, his high cheek bones, and wide Native American nose. "Excuse me, what'd you say?".

The boy did not back off. He gave off a cocky grin.

"I said, hey, Sittin' Bull, who you gon' scalp with that blade?"

The boy next to him popped him on the arm. "Knock it off!"

Up and down the line the boy's teammates took note of the stranger's muscled calves and cold stare.

Ann Glynn rushed past HB.

"What happened here?" she asked Murietta and the boy.

His teammate said: "It was nothing, Ms. Glynn. Just Weeks here mouthing off."

She folded her arms and glared down at the boy and the light of recognition dawned in her face. "Oh, ye-e-e-s. Mr. Winter Weeks." It was clear she knew the boy well. "Mr. Murietta, I do apologize. I'm sure you've had to deal with smart-aleck teens before."

Murietta would not look at her. Arms folded, he glared down at the boy. "Miss Glynn, you apologized, he didn't." He nodded at the boy.

"Mr. Weeks," the principal said. "Mr. Murietta is our guest. We Panthers do not insult our guests. Now, I don't know what you said, but tell the man you're sorry."

The boy's chin slipped down into his neck as he looked lazily up at the visitor. Then he turned his head to the side and mumbled into his shoulder pad.

"What did you say?" Ann Glynn said, bending. She glanced back at Murietta who stared holes through the boy.

"I'm sorry . . . " came out in a muffled, half-hearted effort.

Murietta shook his head. "Where I come from, that's not an apology. That's an insult."

By now the others looked on. HB noted that Ann Glynn kept up a tight, pained smile and blinked a lot as she looked back and forth from Murietta and the boy and HB and the judge. He felt sorry for her; trapped between a wise-cracking kid and a hard-nosed, play-for-keeps cop.

He pulled Murietta to the side. "You need to let this go. This boy's a notorious punk."

The man from Tijuana growled, sucked his clean, white teeth. "Let one get away, the next' ll do something worse."

After Ann Glynn suspended the boy for three days, the adults moved on to the lunchroom, but HB noticed, as they exited the gym, Murietta paused at the door to burn the boy's features into his memory.

At the end of three days, Mrs. Weeks telephoned Ann Glynn to inform her that Winter would not return to school for some time.

"Why not?" the principal asked. She noticed a tenseness in the woman's voice.

"He can't talk."

"Oh, oh. Too much smoking, Mrs. Weeks. I know he hangs with that bunch by the wall after school . . . "

"It's not his smoking, Miss Glynn!"

Ann realized something else was going on. She lowered her voice. "Mrs. Weeks, what happened?"

"He was walking to the spot behind our house where we burn trash. Somebody jumped him from behind and chopped him in the throat. A doctor in Macon says his vocal chords are damaged. He has to have surgery."

"So, he was assaulted? Any idea who?"

"The boy won't say a thing. He just lays there on his bed fiddling with his phone. My husband thinks one of his buddies got revenge because Winter stole his girlfriend. He says let 'em fight it out. It'll do 'em good."

After she hung up, Ann Glynn telephoned HB.

She explained what Mrs. Weeks told her.

"Do you think one of our high school students could deliver a chop to the throat like that? Enough to damage his vocal cords?"

"No way," HB said.

"Are you thinking what I'm thinking?" she said.

* * * *

Murietta invited the council to his place for some authentic Indian-Mexican food. Ann and HB decided they would not mention the Weeks business. They didn't have enough information and Winter Weeks may have gotten involved with some bad guys. Plus, it was clear to everyone that Pedro Murietta had the skills to track down Big Rig's killer.

They offered to put him up in a Motel Six, the only tourist accommodations in Ocopeeco. It was located near the plant for executives or engineers whenever they came for extended inspections or repairs; but the man from Tijuana, sitting like the Buddha on his Harley, took one look at its glowing neon 6 sign, and informed them he didn't like sleeping with people over and under him. He could hear what they said, smell what they cooked and hear them making love.

Thus, a chilly Friday night the council in four vehicles found itself on a rocky, dirt road near the swamp, surrounded by a cathedral of spidery leafless autumn kudzu and intermittent swamp water. Murietta had discovered a dilapidated shack, propped up the sagging ceiling with four by eights, recovered the roof with shingles and cleared the vine and bush-clotted yard with a bush hog Jim Jeffords loaned him.

The council had to negotiate a twin pine plank bridge over some muddy swamp water to reach the porch where the host stood beaming, arms crossed. He wore a gold buttoned red blazer over a blue polo shirt and a pair of stylish leather open-toed sandals. Tiny glittering jewels in both his ear lobes. A feather, black and white, hung from his hair and curled down over his shoulder.

"You should try some ear jewelry," Grace Daniel whispered to HB as they crossed the wooden planks. Give you that manly feminine touch."

"Jewelry? I don't have a job, remember?"

The host had to cross the planks and carry Arlette Beasley across on his back.

In the side yard, their tantalizing, well-roasted main course was turning on a motorized spit.

The chief-to-be served white wine in paper cups, followed by a fresh guacamole and tomato salad with crackers. He moved from person to person, grinning and congenial, serving onto paper plates on individual fold up tables. In the background, tender but passionate music.

"Who are we listening to?" Grace asked.

"Arigon Starr of the Kickapoo Creek," Murietta replied. "You like her?"

"It's . . . different." She took a bite of the guacamole salad. "M-m-m! This is delicious!"

Murietta was stooped over, spooning salad onto the judge's plate. He grinned over his shoulder to Grace. "I found an old Negro woman who grows avocados near the kaolin plant. She says the white clay gives them a special taste. I swapped her for some gemstones."

"Pedro, you are one resourceful guy," the judge said, as he beamed up at the man he would be working with. He spread salad on a cracker. "And you saved us a bunch of money by not using Motel 6."

Murietta became animated and friendly with food and drink. "Judge," he said, wiping the lime juice off with a towel, "I was brought up poor. Do you know, I was sixteen years old before I saw more than twenty people in a group. And that was all my family. We had iguanas for pets."

He brought more salad, which the council devoured, and he asked HB: "Chief. What led you to get a PhD in Greek and then become a chief?"

HB retold his story, but he noticed Ann Glynn was about to jump out of her seat. "Ann, it's Okay. Folks?"

"I get such cravings with food," she said, looking around, apologetic.

They all nodded.

"Go on, Ann," Jim Jeffords said. "I know the feeling."

She exited the cabin, fumbling for her vaping device and the planks clattered as she crossed the swamp water and soon large puffs of bluish smoke emerged from the open window of her little car.

Murietta stepped out to check the meat.

"I'm so glad I never started smoking," Grace said, delicately nipping a cracker.

"It affects people in different ways," the judge said. "Take HB there. He has smoked twelve cigarettes a day ever since I first met him. He names 'em after the twelve tribes of Israel"

"Wha-a-at?" Murietta said, entering with an enormous platter dripping with meat.

Jim Jeffords grinned. "The main course!"

Talk of the evils of smoking ceased as the group dove in.

"The lime and avocado whet your appetite," Murietta said, as he dished out a dripping chunk onto Arlette Beasley's plate. Her eyes grew large and she went to work and soon her mouth was stuffed. "M-m-m-m. This is so juicy!"

Now the host handed out cold PBR's.

Ann Glynn returned and joined the feasting.

"Wow!" she said. "Years ago, I had a Chateaubriand at the old Four Seasons. This is better!"

"Son," the judge said. "where did you learn to cook beef bar-b-que like this?" He removed his jacket and rolled up his sleeves. Even though it was chilly outside, he was sweating and grinning.

The host squatted in the center of the group, pleased at how much the council enjoyed their food. They were all eating heartily.

All except HB.

He poked at his meat, took note of the brown, thin gravy it was steeped in and recalled that in the hills and caves of Afghanistan, he often was forced to share the locals' food. While the town council was gobbling with the gusto of a college tailgate party, he drank his beer, smiled and attempted to be sociable.

* * * *

The council had to meet in the church sanctuary because Ann Glynn's office was being disinfected. No one mentioned why it had to be disinfected, but the council members thought they knew: Ann was vaping in her office—again.

At supper, the night before, Rosie vented her anger: "It's an insult!" she said. "They're firing you and yet they're invading your church to do their dirty work."

HB pushed his Kohlrouladen around on his plate.

"Oh, you got a call today on our land line," she said.

"Don't tell me it was a council member."

"Nope," she said. She sat with her elbows on the table, smiling grimly, which always made her dimples leap out. "Your tower climbing friend. Wanted to know when you'd be in. Said it was important."

He shook his head and dove into the food. "Roxanne. I wish I could help her. I really do. But I'm not trained to do what she needs."

Rosie chewed hard. "I don't think I want you to give her what she needs."

* * * *

Beside the first pew, HB stood with his hat in hand, as everyone filed in to sit and the judge mounted the dais and plopped down above him in the big oak chair where the preacher usually sat.

The judge rose and nodded to Callie Cousins, who typed beside him on a fold-out table. Christmas decorations were still up, so the judge was obliged to push aside The Three Wise Men on camel back. The camels' wheels squeaked as he eased them off to the side of the dais.

"Y'all" Ann Glynn said, "I'm sorry about my office. Some fool senior put dead fish in my air conditioner over the weekend, so we had to disinfect."

Since the podium was designed for HB, the much shorter judge was forced to sit atop Vol. I and II of Calvin's Institutes for his head to be visible from the pews.

"Judge," HB said, from the pew below, "you were predestined to sit on top of Calvin."

The judge gave off a feeble smile as he gripped the podium to keep his balance.

Arlette Beasley squeezed her black, shiny purse and her chin rose: "Hmph! I doubt even that curmudgeon Calvin condoned eating dog meat!"

Grace chimed in, "These were posted all over town for a week." She held up a cardboard poster:

Lost: Black and brown German shepherd. His name is Earnest.
Please return to Miss Samantha Smalls, Ocopeeco Middle School."

Ann Glynn shook her head. "The misogynist jerk. And he was so proud, said he fattened the poor creature up for a week! Said everybody did it where he came from!"

"What'd he feed him?" Jim Jeffords asked.

"Chicken," she said, staring blankly ahead.

"Finger lickin' good," Jim Jeffords quipped.

"Ha ha," Ann said.

"That explains those two calls I got last week from the plant," HB said. "Two guys claimed somebody was stealing their chickens."

"Son," the judge said, looking down over the podium at HB, his big eyebrows shaggy and mournful. "I guess you have thrown up your hands in despair over us. I'm so sorry it turned out this way."

"Better to find out now than later," HB said.

The others nodded, relieved that the man they were firing had such a big heart.

Grace reached over and gave him a pat on the knee.

He could see they were beginning to think they had made a mistake.

Rosie: "Of course, they see. They made a colossal mistake! But they don't have the decency to reinstate you!"

As usual, Rosie was right. They had no intention of reinstating him. How could they? The next applicant was scheduled to arrive from Dallas in a day.

* * * *

Buckminster "Bucky" Lamotte dressed like a white haired pro golfer: a navy blue polo, embossed with Augusta National, cream colored slacks, black and white saddle oxford golf shoes. Although the tire around his stomach clashed with the suave sportsman look, he overcame it with a constant toothsome grin and his Rolex Submariner.

The town council was watching his Power Point, aerial photos taken from his own plane, of every street, corner, alley and lane in Ocopeeco. He zeroed in on River Street, the main drag, with his laser pointer. Bucky wanted surveillance cameras everywhere.

"There's my store!" Jim Jeffords said and nudged Arlette Beasley next to him.

She threw him a scornful glance.

"Indeed," Bucky said, pointing with his finger at Jim. "Now, you 'll sleep soundly, knowing your store is protected."

"I did get robbed once," Jim said, proudly. "Back in '84. Fool broke in and stole a dozen chicken bitties."

"I think we're the only school in the state that doesn't have cameras," Arlette Beasley commented. She sat, holding her black shiny purse in front like a protective shield.

Jim Jeffords looked puzzled. "I always thought it was just those big city schools with all their bad kids needed cameras."

Mrs. Beasley rolled her eyes. "Do you think we have no bad kids here?" She blinked, squeezed her purse, and flashed him a fake smile as she recalled his son, a boy who cupped his hand in his armpit to fake a fart and on her blackboard scribbled *Mrs. Beastly.*

At the mention of school, Gus Breckenridge apologized for Ann Glynn, the principal, called away on a last minute emergency.

Bucky gave him his toothsome smile. "Well, I'm more than certain she'll be pleased as punch with cameras all over her school. When I worked security for AT & T, we installed units in over five thousand schools. Back then, that was forward thinking. Now it's standard."

"Except in Ocopeeco," Mrs. Beasley noted.

"You worked for AT&T?" Jim asked.

"Twenty years. Seattle, Boston and Chicago."

"I wish you'd show me how to pay my bills on my computer. My wife says she's tired of fooling with all that paperwork."

Bucky approached and laid his hand on Jim's shoulder. His Rolex glistened in the light of the Power Point as his voice grew soft and fatherly. "I'd be glad to help."

Jim nudged Mrs. Beasley. "Now we got us a real chief." He settled back, content.

Bucky walked back to his AV cart, switched off his machine and turned on the lights. He returned to the front and stood, arms crossed.

"Folks, I'm your complete package. Twenty years AT &T Security. Retired and independently wealthy. I won't need a salary."

Grace sat up. "You don't want a salary?" Her voice rose.

"I do not. Little lady, years ago, I was blessed to receive some wise investment tips. So, no, I don't need the money. After the judge and I talked, and he explained that you all were desperate to solve this crime, I said to myself: 'Bucky, you can help these folks.'"

"But what can you do that other candidates couldn't do? " Grace asked.

"I know folks. Especially forensics folks. There's a unit close to us right now, Flashback Data, out of St. Pete. A six man crew, two devices, working on a project for the town of Milledgeville over on Lake Sinclair. One phone call and we could have them over here in a few weeks and solve this murder mystery."

"How much do they charge?" Jim Jeffords asked.

"Depends. You want an expert witness to testify?"

"Absolutely," the judge said. "I mean, even if one of us understood the info, the law says you have to have an expert explain it, otherwise it's inadmissible. That's just what we need, right, HB?"

HB nodded. "That would be great."

"Who's side are you on?" Grace whispered.

"It's just the truth."

"Bucky," the judge said, like a father introducing his all American son, "that's an endorsement from a fine lawman. Meet HB Alpata, the man you're replacing."

HB stood and stepped forward to shake hands. Bucky stood a head shorter, but he wasn't intimidated.

"Boy, chief," he said, looking up, "I've got some big boots to fill."

"I think you'll do just fine."

The judge grinned and nodded at the other council members.

After the awkward moment passed, Bucky slipped onto the edge of the judge's desk. Knowing now which person in the room really knew what was going on and amused that the council had imposed on this obliging man to help them find his own replacement, he leaned over towards HB. "So how many sites will you need?"

"At least three, the river, the shack and Big Rig's house."

Bucky nodded. "Then I would guestimate between forty and fifty thousand for the whole project."

"Fifty thousand!" Gus said, throwing up his hands.

"You don't have to pay, Judge," Bucky said. "I will."

HB scrutinized the new applicant. What possible reason could this man have to be so free with his money? The rich are usually frugal, unless they're passionate about a cause. What was Bucky LaMotte's?

After the shock of the offer wore off, and the council realized that his refusal of a salary and his offer to pay for the forensics team meant their troubles were over, the council decided Bucky should get to work ASAP.

As they filed out, HB presented the judge with a box of dog meat.

"Rosie marinated it for a week to kill any vermin. We had some last night. Even Mico liked it."

The judge snatched the box, sneered, and waddled out.

* * * *

Bucky's brand new Black Mercedes SUV wheeled into the parking lot of the high school. En route the judge played with all the high tech gadgets while Bucky explained, employing an arsenal of technical terms. When the judge exited the vehicle, he held his head high, a man initiated into the lofty realms of techno speak.

The two obese men struggled up the three flights of outdoor steps to the principal's office where HB was reading St. Maximus the Confessor. Maximus had his hands chopped off in the 4th cent. for publishing sermons the emperor disliked. As a fellow persona non grata, HB identified with the church father. The council had refrained from chopping off any of his members, but their actions had achieved about the same effect on his mind and heart. Ocopeeco was his home. Now he walked the streets and the faces he met knew he was a failure, and they showed it. And the signs posted on telephone poles and buildings showed it, too: "Chief wanted: one that will actually do his job."

* * * *

So, all the speeders he issued tickets to, the town tough guys he'd confronted at Roxanne's, the perennial parking violators—they all found a voice now. Just that morning he had found his truck with white lettering on the door sign in paint: *HB, get out!*

As for the folks who stood up for him and gifted him and Rosie fried chicken and chocolate cakes—those folks hung back, as if he had suddenly acquired some highly contagious disease and talking with him meant catching it. For the first time as chief, he felt like an outsider in his home. A middle schooler, he had fought his way through those feelings, coming home once a week with bloodied knuckles and lumps on his head, but he always assumed those years were behind him.

He began spending too much time in his office on the computer. The demons from Afghanistan were stalking around him. He could smell their sulfur and knew the signs. Long walks in the woods didn't help either. He visited places he hadn't set foot in since he was a boy, trying to recapture his love for his home, but he was hurt and mad, and it made his body tight, his breathing short. At night he lay sleepless, so he took Ambien, which didn't help much.

Behind the office counter, Mrs. Coleman, the secretary, was typing. Her jowls jiggled, and the fat under her upper arms kept the same rhythm.

Flipping through their phones, three students waited to see the principal.

The secretary raised her eyes over her glasses. "No phones allowed in the office," she said.

The students rolled their eyes, but they obeyed and put their phones in their bags.

HB grinned. St. Maximus would be pleased. Obedience is basic. The old saint should know. He obeyed and it cost him his hands.

Lately, his dreams conveyed what his obedience would cost him. After that first day, when they fired him, he was visited again in his sleep by the crazed Taliban warrior, choking him in the sand, but that image morphed into a dozen Creek warriors who penned him down naked in the same sand for wolves to rip open and vultures to peck at. When he looked around him, the townspeople stood side by side, grinning and wagging their fingers. "We know who you really are, you half-breed failure."

HB rose, closed his book and greeted the judge and Bucky LaMotte.

"Millie," the judge said, "where's Ms. Glynn? She was supposed to meet us here."

Millie removed her glasses as she approached the counter. She wore a navy blue sweater over a white blouse, around her neck a set of pearls amid a scattering of flesh-colored skin tags. "There was a fight in the lunchroom. Ms. Glynn got spaghetti on her pants suit. She 'll be back in minute."

She gave the applicant the once over.

"Oh," the judge said, "Millie, this is Bucky LaMotte. He's interviewing for the chief's job. He wants to identify spots in the school where we should put surveillance cameras."

Millie glanced at HB who looked back, as if to say: 'Please don't announce my firing to the world.'

"Put your first camera in the girl's bathroom," she said. "The things I hear go on in there."

By now the three students were up and listening in.

On the counter Bucky appeared oblivious to HB's presence. He unfurled a schematic of the school. With his laser pointer he highlighted the spots where cameras would do some good. HB noted he was wearing another golf shirt today, this one white, embossed with a gold Pebble Beach.

Soon Bucky had the students and Millie involved in a discussion about where the real in-school mischief happened.

"And put two or three extra ones in the boys' bathroom and cover them with steel plates," Millie said.

The students giggled. "Millie, you believe too much of what you hear. Most of the time, kids are just trippin'"

Bucky turned to HB. "What say you, chief. The bathrooms?"

"Put 'em high," he said.

Millie nodded. "The little demons. They will dismantle 'em."

Bucky guffawed and slapped HB on the back. "The more things change, the more they stay the same!"

HB tried to smile.

The glass doors swung open and the principal blew in.

"No! The more they change, the better they get!" she said. "You must be Bucky LaMotte, the man who's going to save Ocopeeco! I'm Ann Glynn." She thrust out her hand. "I hope you haven't believed all the lies these two have told you."

Bucky's face dropped a second, but he recovered and shook her hand and gave her his best toothsome grin.

The group—Bucky, Ann, HB and the judge—headed out the main door toward the science wing, which Bucky had asked to see.

Ann had to answer her walkie-talkie, so she slipped away and leaned against a brick wall, trying to keep the conversation with her Assistant Principal private. It was obvious the lunchroom fight was not resolved. Parents were unhappy, and the AP was having trouble.

Meantime, Bucky huddled with HB and the judge. He handed out Tic Tacs. "Boys, this is a fine school. How long has Ms. Glynn been principal?"

"Five years," HB said. The breath freshener was mint and hot. He motioned with his thumb to Ann. "She has turned this school around. We had the lowest test scores for our size school in the state. Now we compete with the big boys in Gwinnett and Dekalb."

The judge sucked on his Tic Tac at the front of his lips, so he looked like a fish. He confirmed HB's high praise. "Ann is a fireball, Bucky. You'll love working with her. Now, she can be prickly, but that's because she cares for her kids. And don't ever play her in Pickleball, she's a beast."

HB grinned at Bucky. "Truth to tell, she and I don't always see eye to eye. "

"Yeah," the judge said, "Mr. Greek here tries to tell her how to structure her curriculum. And that was her dissertation topic! But, heck, last time I looked you two were still friends."

"Yeah, Bucky, she's all modern languages all the time. I've tried and tried to push for some Latin at least. But it's all Español, Francais and Deutsch."

The judge looked Bucky in the eye. "But you wanted to know how long Ann's been here. What's your question?"

The Texan removed his cap and wiped the sweat around the sweat band. "Oh, nothing."

HB noted his toothsome grin was slipping.

"Just like to know as much as I can about the folks I'm to be working with." Bucky said.

"When's that forensics team arriving?" the judge asked.

"Oh, uh, week after next. They're really busy."

Ann was called away again.

"Mr. Alpata remembers the way to biology, don't you chief?" she said, grinning.

He threw up his hands. "Ya' got me, guv. My worst subject. How could I forget?"

The advanced biology class consisted of twelve seniors. The walls of the well-lit room were covered with colorful charts of the human body, the Krebs Cycle, and the major contents of the cell. The three men slipped in quietly and sat down at an empty table.

The teacher came in from Macon three times a week just to teach this class. An endocrinologist, he drove an antique Volkswagen and was considered by his professional colleagues an eccentric rebel, but he was also a genius, who studied genetics for pleasure. HB whispered all this to Bucky as they watched the man writing furiously on a white board.

Paul Bunyan red beard and tattooed forearms, a faded Navy work shirt, an Atlanta Braves baseball cap worn backwards, cutoff jeans and open toed sandals—Dr. Bob Bellinger was unorthodox.

He stalked back and forth tossing a Sharpie.

"So, Mr. Evolution, C. Darwin, believed the cell was a blob of protoplasm! The man who first determined that the earth was several hundred million years old, who reordered our understanding of the animate world, the man who transformed all our major universities from faith based to science based within twenty years, that man thought the cell was a wad of spit! Is that funky! Or what? Mr. Charles D Double Dog Darwin! Boom shakalakalaka boom!"

The kids loved it. They typed furiously on their laptops so as not to miss a word.

Bucky pushed back his chair, stood and addressed the teacher in a loud voice. "So, you believe Darwin was right?"

The kids turned around.

The judge reached for Bucky's arm; Bucky snatched it away. His toothsome grin was gone.

"Excuse me?" Dr. Berringer said.

"The earth is six thousand years old."

The judge introduced Bucky, awkwardly.

"The earth is 4.543 billion years old," Berringer said. "The geology proves that." His voice was deep.

"No. The earth is six thousand years old and was created in six days. That's what the Bible says. What you're teaching these kids is a lie straight from the pit of hell."

Now HB understood Bucky's cause, why he was willing to pay for everything. He was a fundamentalist.

"Who do you think you are?" Berringer said. He stepped forward. "Judge, what's going on here?"

"Uh, Bucky," the judge said, "you're interrupting the man's class."

"Somebody needs to interrupt it," Bucky said. His jaw was fixed like a bulldog. "Really, judge, I'm surprised you allow this man to spread his atheistic lies to your children. This is what's wrong with our country."

HB grabbed the Texan's bicep. "You need to step away," he said, "This man has a PhD from Duke."

Bucky wasn't having it. He glared at the man. "Duke, Nuke or Fluke—I don't care. What he's teaching contradicts scripture. And you two sit here and condone this?"

"Bob, I apologize," HB stammered. "Bucky, I think we'd better leave and let the man get on with teaching."

"I will NOT leave. Somebody needs to defend the truth against this godless charlatan!"

Before anyone could stop him, he marched to the front of the room where he erased everything the teacher had written on his white board. Quickly, he sketched a genealogy of mankind, beginning with Adam and Eve down to Noah and the flood.

Everyone was too shocked to speak or act. Bucky was well into the post-Noachian period when Dr. Berringer slammed two desks out of the way as he rushed to within inches of Bucky's face. "Look, I don't know who you are or why you're in my class, but you had better not utter another word of that retro anti-science garbage in my room."

"I'm not afraid of you, you godless, hippie freak!"

The teacher ripped a right fist into Bucky's nose, sending him flying backward across a table and onto the floor. Blood covered his golf shirt.

"Good shot, Doc!" one of the male students yelled.

The students gathered around Dr. Berringer, complimenting his boxing skills while the judge and HB helped Bucky out the door to the nurse's office where they set him down on the side of a bed. Cotton staunched the blood flow, but it couldn't staunch the flow of abuse from his mouth. He talked half to himself, half to HB and the judge.

"I tell myself: here's a tiny burg, an itty bitty blip of a place. A place where all the perversions and godless ideas haven't taken root, where folks still honor Biblical values and good common sense, and what do I find? Not only is the high school run by a man-miming pervert, but some tattooed quack is indoctrinating tender, innocent minds into the godless doctrine of evolution! Do you people realize what you're doing here?"

HB stood in the doorway while the judge pulled up a chair. They exchanged glances.

"So, you're a young earth creationist?" HB asked. His arms were folded, revealing powerful biceps.

Bucky tilted his head back as he spoke. "I was a main contributor to the Arc Encounter."

"That's the replica of Noah's Arc in Kentucky?" the judge said. He stood and straightened his tie in the nurse's wall mirror, then groomed his Yosemite Sam moustache with a small metal comb.

"It's a roaring success," Bucky said, dabbing gauze against his nose. "People want the truth. There was a real Noah. There was a real Arc. There was a man who answered God's call and thereby saved the whole human race. People even come from other countries to learn the truth, and not the lies spun by the likes of that godless pseudo-intellectual in there."

HB unfolded his arms. He massaged his left shoulder, still sore from the weightlifting fiasco. "Bucky, looks like you'll survive the shot to your nose, so the judge and I will leave you to recover. Stick around if you want. The nurse here is one of the best."

Bucky nodded.

"Bucky," the judge said, "about that shot to your nose . . . "

"Oh, hell, I'm not vindictive. I know he was defending what he believes. I just hope you two understand. I can't work in a place like this with people like that. So, I withdraw my offer of the funds. Find somebody else to be your chief."

The two men found the bank of soda machines, a half dozen, offering every sugary drink made in the USA.

"Name your poison," the judge said, as he popped in coins for a Pepsi.

But HB had already pulled out a Dasani water.

"How do we frame this?" the judge said and took a swallow.

"Well, first, let's hope Bucky doesn't change his mind about pressing charges."

"But what about the other issue?"

"We don't mention it," HB said. He unscrewed the cap off his water and took a long swig. "Ann Glynn has fought discrimination all her life. I know, teachers are a liberal lot, but I also know old, entrenched values die hard. We keep quiet."

The judge belched. "You're right. Don't won't to lose Ann."

"No, we don't."

They finished their drinks.

The judge pulled out his phone. "Number three arrives day after to-morrow. This bird's bringing a horse named Zach."

HB shook with laughter.

Chapter Eleven

Chill Wilkerson's only visible drawback was his gimpy leg, but he man-handled it with such vigor and good cheer it became a plus. A string bean in old jeans, his face weather-beaten as hammer-pounded leather, a beat-up, dishwater-colored cowboy hat, the front cinched into a roll by a kite string so old it had worn a brown groove in the fabric, he was pure Texas, easy to talk to and easy to chuckle.

From inside his horse trailer, he chatted with the council while he held the leg of his palomino over his knee and gouged red clay in big chunks out of the shoes with a pocketknife. Straw covered the trailer floor; the walls were lined with old rodeo posters, bronc busters, hands waving, atop unbroken stallions.

"Yee, doggies," Chill said, "I never see'd such clay, like con-crete. Old Zach felt it, too. Me and him took us a little jaunt down through the plum bushes behind that Motel Six by the kaolin plan. No sooner had he set foot on this here Georgia ground, he looked back at me and said with those great big eyes of his: 'Chill, old pard, what in hell kinda mud is this I'm walkin' in?'"

But his complaint was laced with a twinkling eye and a grin. His long, stringy fingers and hands were brown and wrinkled and the veins on his forearms rode high like a yard full of mole tracks.

"Yessir, we eased on down to a sweet little creek, followed it a ways to a river. Zach gimme a nod and we eased in till it come up to my knees. I could see this weren't no kiddies wadin' creek, so we backed ourselves out, set on the bank, and watched an old bull frog glued to a limb over the water."

Zach stirred.

Chill spoke softly to ease the horse's worry, but the creature was upset about something.

HB stepped up into the trailer. He took the horse's leg from Chill.

145

"You step around and stroke his muzzle," HB said, "while I dig the mud out. I did this in Afghanistan for the local freedom fighters. Some rode horseback ,so I helped out with the care and feeding."

Soon, Zach stood calm and content as HB cut the mud out in big pieces.

After Chill was finished, Grace led the group on foot to the athletic fields where PE was in progress. Even though the hard ground was covered with pebbles and twigs, the country boys played touch football without shoes. The council stood on the chalk sideline while Grace explained to Chill and the others that three touch games were in progress at the same time so as many boys as possible could play.

A skinny, shirtless quarterback, long, tattooed arms, bad teeth, taunted a rusher, a heavy set boy who got just close enough to nearly touch the QB: but each time the older faster boy juked out of his grasp. Fists balled, red faced, the rusher returned to the line of scrimmage after every play, madder and madder.

"Keep it up, fats," the QB yelled from the offensive huddle. "You'll catch me—in the next century!"

The boys in the huddle laughed and pointed back at the fat tackle, who glared at them.

The center's snap sailed over the QB's head. The ball took wild whacky hops until the QB scooped it up. When he turned to sprint his way out of the tight spot, he was steam-rolled by a two hundred twenty pound flesh train, full speed. Legs and arms went sailing. The rusher threw in a forearm to the throat and sent the hotshot QB gagging and writhing around in the dirt in a fetal position.

Fats stood over him, laughing: "Boy, I nailed your sorry ass!"

The other players, panting and sweating, gathered around. The QB hailed from The Bottom, a swampy public housing where the poorest of Ocopeeco lived. In The Bottom every male carried a knife and the QB was no different. He got up to his knees and pulled out a military Schwartz Gambit, sharply curved to a flesh ripping pointed tip, the blade embossed with a spider web.

"What the hell!" Fats yelled, backing up, his sweaty, flabby navel jiggling as it stuck out under his T shirt.

They circled, crouching. The QB grinned, waved the knife. "I'm 'on gut your flabby ass."

"You crazy, boy!" the fat one said.

HB struggled to break through the crowd, but they had formed a wall. He picked one up, but another took his place. He was stymied. And he didn't want to be charged with assaulting a minor to save a minor's life.

But Chill eased around to the other side and penetrated the crowd. Then there were three: the QB, the fat boy and Chill, the stringy, weather beaten cowpoke.

"Gimme the knife, son," Chill said, holding out his hand.

"No way, old man. Get lost!"

The crowd shouted at him.

"Get on back on your horse, old man!"

"You're way outta your league, old timer!"

"You gonna get hurt, Pops!"

As the QB turned his attention to his supporters in the crowd, Chill cracked his forearm with his .45 and the knife fell to the ground. The Texan picked it up while the boy whined, holding his forearm.

"Son, this is Marine issue. How'd you come by it?"

"None of your bid-ness. Who are you?"

"Chill Wilkerson, son, Texas born, and Texas bred. Now turn around so I can cuff ya."

Dazed and still nursing his forearm, the boy winced as the helpless old timer produced a pair of rusty cuffs and with an effortless move snapped them on.

* * * *

Later, in Ann Glynn's office, the council served coffee and cookies and fruit. The judge, with Ann's permission, had even yielded his chair to the guest of honor. But no sooner had the Texan sat down than he leapt back up and informed the group: "Folks, it's nothing personal, but I'm a behind the scenes sorta feller. The limelight gives me the heebie-jeebies."

He found a wall to lean against where he drank his coffee and nibbled an Oreo.

"Chill, that was a mighty smooth intervention out on the PE field," the judge said. He was back in his seat and had pulled out a cigar; but Ann Glynn caught his eye and solemnly shook her head. He put the tobacco back in his jacket pocket.

"Kids just need a strong hand," Chill said, "gentle, but it's gotta have some bite."

HB sat on the edge of the big desk, sipping coffee. "How long have you had that headgear?"

Chill chuckled, removed his hat. The top of his head was bald and pale white.

"This here belonged to my Uncle Wadie Wilkerson, he was a lawman, too. Raised me after my mama and daddy was killed in a bad wreck outside Lubbock when I was three. Lawmen didn't make no money back then, so after he got off work, Uncle Wadie helped sneak wetbacks across the border for the cash. I know, it don't make much sense nowadays, but if you'd lived down on the borderlands back then, it would've."

HB noticed Ann picking lint off her black pants suit with more than her usual nervous energy.

She approached the Texan until they stood three feet apart.

The rest of the council sensed something was afoot. The judge leaned forward in his chair; Arlette Beasley picked up on the fresh electricity and blinked several times; Jim Jeffords folded his arms and observed.

"Chill," Ann said. She lifted her chin, so she seemed to look down at the Texan. "You do realize that I'm a Lesbian."

Behind his paper coffee cup, Chill's eyes glanced around the room at the others. Considering his response, he puckered his lips.

"Ann . . . " Grace whispered, as she put her hand on the principal's arm.

"Grace, please, let's allow Chill to speak."

The Texan slipped his hat back on. He gazed at the principal with eyes gentle and quiet, like his voice. Direct questions made him uncomfortable.

"Yes, ma'am, I do," he said, nodding. "But you know, the way I figure it, that ain't none of my bidness. I hear tell you're one hell of a fine principal and that's good enough for old Chill. And, I have to add, that's good enough for Zach, too!"

Ann threw back her head and howled. "And that's good enough for Zach!"

The two hugged and the council collectively breathed a sigh of relief.

When Ann pulled up a chair in front of the Texan and they began to chat, the others gathered around,

"I needed to ask you," she said to Chill, "because these two (she pointed to HB and the judge) tried to keep me from finding out that we just interviewed a homophobic candidate, and I didn't want that to happen again. Get all your cards on the table, I say."

"Busted," HB said, grinning over at the judge.

"Dadgummit, Ann. There's no way you could have found that out," the judge said, leaning forward in his chair and wrenching his face into confusion.

Everyone turned to Ann. She closed her eyes and rolled her head. "Judge, you know that huntin' dog you're always bragging about, how she can smell birds so far away?"

"Esther," the judge said.

"I can smell one, too, only it's not a covey of quail."

HB nodded and pointed at her. "That first day when you came into the office?"

"Exactly," she said. "It only lasted a nano second, the expression of shock on his face when he got his first good look. After that it was all smiles and sweet talk. But in that unguarded moment Bucky La Motte told me all I needed to know."

* * * *

HB and Chill eased down the kudzu slope to the river's edge where their horses took a drink.

"There's a sand bar here," HB said, pointing to the white just visible beneath the black river.

He clucked and popped the reins; the animal stepped into the water. Fast flowing current swirled around his legs until the horse found the sand.

On the other side, they dismounted. Chill slipped a feed bag onto Zach's muzzle while HB unrolled a green tarp over the kudzu. They lay down on their sides, HB nursing a cold PBR from the saddle bag and Chill cross legged, tobacco string in mouth, rolling a smoke.

"The king of snakes!" HB said, pointing to the river.

Chill peered out a second, then realized HB was fibbing.

"You hear that tale where you're from?" HB asked, grinning.

"Oh, yeah," the Texan nodded. "My Uncle had a cousin, poor woman, lived in a trailer all alone. Drew circles and squares and triangles in a yellow pad all day long. Had stacks of them things. Got so bad Uncle Wadie and his other cousins had to go and clean the place out. He claimed she saw the King of Snakes one night and the critter took the woman's wits. I believed that story till I was about twelve when I was at the doctor one day and the nurse told me my daddy's cousin had taken some bad drugs in college. It did something to her mind. No King of Snakes."

Chill was easy to talk to. HB told him about his Dad and the Shack and how Pain was slowly starving himself because he believed he caused someone to die. Then he explained the Scruggs' case in detail. Chill listened, nodded and offered insightful questions and comments. HB realized that this man was sharp. His lackadaisical manner put some people off, but it was an effective strategy for a lawman.

Picking tobacco off his lower lip, the Texan sat up in a yoga-like pose, his long, skinny torso, shriveled tan hands on knees.

"So," HB said, "think you can solve it?"

"Can't say for sure. Way I work is this: I lay back, listen a lot in the background, meetings, stores, post office, watch faces, get to know the town and the land. It's slow going, like you."

"I don't know the judge and the others will like that. They're looking for results and fast."

The Texan stood and dusted off his breeches: "My experience, good results can't be rushed."

Back at the motel, they had just dismounted when a truckload of a half dozen locals pulled up beside them, men from the Bottom, liquored up. HB recognized Everett Smalls, the father of the boy whose arm Chill cracked.

The Bottom boys rolled out of the truck, gathered around, rifles and shot guns in hand and their faces shone with sweat and excitement.

Smalls was a barrel-chested man in overalls. Thick, tan biceps, but a gut that arced out his shirt. Black hair, receding hairline and sunglasses. He pointed at Chill.

"This here's the one we after, chief. No need you getting involved."

Talking over his shoulder, HB uncinched Zach. "Everett, this gentleman is a guest of the chief's office. Anything he's involved with, I'm involved with."

"If that's the way you wanna play it," Smalls said, nodding. "Get him boys!"

Chill drew and leveled his weapon at Smalls' stomach.

"Mister," Chill said, "anybody touches me, I'm 'on blow your guts all over this here parking lot."

Smalls removed his sunglasses. He moistened his bottom lip with his tongue, then pointed at the gun. "That pistol put a hairline fracture in my boy's arm. Cost me fifteen hundred dollars!"

"He tell you about his Schwartz Gambit."

"What?" Smalls said.

"Your boy was about to gut somebody with a Schwartz Gambit. That's marine issue. Saw a lot of 'em at Parris Island."

Smalls made a puzzled face. He turned and looked back at his crowd. He squinted at the Texan. "When were you at Parris Island?"

"1990."

"You not by any chance from Lubbock, Texas?"

"Born and bred."

"And when you were at Parris did you win the base prize for marksmanship?"

"I did," Chill said, "You a marine?"

"How you think I had that Schwartz Gambit."

Smalls lowered his head. Slow chuckles rose up his fat-armored body until he shook all over. "Hot-ta-migh-ty, you gotta be Chill Wilkerson!"

"How you know my name?"

"Cause I was in the class of '91 and all we ever heard about from our DI was what a helluva shot you were and how if you ever got in combat you was gon' make somebody pay!"

Chill put his gun back in his holster. "Well, I'll be sow beat and butter churned."

The two men shook hands.

HB hauled Zach's saddle up the ramp into the horse trailer while the two men swapped tales and lies and the rest of the Bottom boys, disappointed, wandered over to the Motel Six restaurant to continue drinking. After getting Zach settled in his trailer, he joined the two men.

"HB, this has been an eye opener."

"How so Everett?"

"Well, the wife says I spoil the boy. Always take his side in everything. Now here I find out the little pissant stole my knife and attacked a boy on school grounds. And didn't tell me a thing about it so I come out here and make a complete and utter fool outta myself!"

The two lawmen said nothing. The man had hit one of those parenting brick walls.

HB put his hand on Smalls' shoulder. "Time for a come to Jesus meeting, Everett. I have 'em once a month with my thirteen year old."

Smalls slipped his glasses back on.

Chill offered his hand. "Semper fi, old buddy. It'll work out."

The two Marines hugged, and tears formed at Small's eyes.

He followed his Bottom boys into the restaurant where he joined them at the bar.

* * * *

It was Saturday afternoon, time for the Alpata's weekly shoot out. Today, HB invited Chill to join them and he and Rosie had already locked head to head in pistol combat that left everybody else in the dust. The German vs. the Cowboy. It was a good match. Finally, HB and Mico and Davy sat down in the fold out chairs and watched. Chill was good, as Everett Smalls said, but HB noticed that as the morning passed, being challenged by a woman did not suit the laid back Texan. His easy grin grew strained and his chuckle dried up. Even Davy noticed it.

"Your buddy's lookin' a little rough around the edges," he whispered from behind his bottle of Gatorade.

HB pulled a long neck PBR out of the cooler. "Chill, how about a beer?"

The Texan turned, reloading while Rosie put Coke cans on top of fence posts. "No thanks," he said. "Can't shoot and drink. But I think I will take a hit of my antihistamine. I get sinus headaches sometimes when I'm shootin' for serious."

He yelled out to Rosie. "Back in a jiff!"

She waved okay and he headed to his truck parked behind Zach's van where the horse's tail was visible.

HB considered the last few months. Murietta, Bucky la Motte and now Chill: the market for first rate lawmen was thin. Maybe Chill would be the guy; but without that forensics team how would they ever turn up the necessary clues to nail Big Rig's killer. Chill said he worked slow, behind the scenes. When HB told the judge, his laconic comment was: "Can't get no slower."

That week Iggy had e mailed him a name: Gator Bates, a friend who ran a scuba/forensics school on The Mackahatchee River off the south Florida coast. Bates taught his students, one on one, how to river dive and find clues in the water. It was grueling and expensive. The man's web site claimed he lived on gator meat and mango, and the Robinson Crusoe lodgings seemed almost calculated to turn clients off. But Iggy assured him Gator was the real deal. He'd worked with Clea Koff (The Bone Woman) in Rwanda and Bosnia. Iggy's improbable suggestion: HB should go down himself, spend six weeks and learn the trade.

Rosie's reaction surprised him. "It would look good on your CV. I doubt many chiefs in the Bubba Belt can do forensic diving."

After ten minutes, Rosie was getting antsy. She cupped her hands to her mouth. "C'mon, dead eye, not scared of a woman, are you?"

"Easy, girl," HB whispered. "Wounded male egos can get nasty."

Chill emerged from behind the trailer. He kicked up his heels and pointed at Rosie. "Set 'em up, gal. The battle's on!"

But instead of following Rosie's plan, the Texan hurled a full can of Coke and blasted it and kept blasting it, popping, twisting, bobbing it over and over until he ran out of ammo.

"Awesome!" Davy and Mico chimed together.

"What are you doing?" Rosie asked, hands on her hips.

"Just having fun!"

HB slipped away to the Texan's truck where he found a dark medicine bottle on the seat with a nose nozzle. He spritzed his hand, tasted it and his pulse jumped.

He hurried back.

Chill had decided the controlled, meticulous methods of Roswitha Alpata cramped his style. He was blasting trees, paint cans, old shoes, pine cones. Whooping and cackling.

"Stop it!" Rosie yelled. Her face red, her fists on her hips. "You're wasting good ammo!"

She was too engrossed in the competition to notice the man, his eyes.

"Ex-cu-u-u-s-e me, ma'am," he said, bowing and removing his hat. "Just my natural rambunctious taking over."

"Now," she said, plucking at her hair, "that's better. Mico, draw a tiny circle on this empty Coke can and throw it high as you can."

Mico drew a circle with a sharpie hurled the can up, but as Chill aimed, HB grabbed his arm.

"Your pupils are big as baseballs," he said.

Chill sneered. "So?"

"So, you just took a hit of speed. That medicine bottle in your truck."

The Texan snatched away, bared his teeth. "You been snoopin' in my truck?" he backed up, holstering his pistol, letting his right arm unfold into that iconic pose over it.

"Dad!" Mico yelled.

"Shut the hell up, kid!" To HB, he pointed with his left arm. "No-body goes sneakin' in my truck, no-body!"

HB's heart pounded. He was unarmed, but he'd dealt with enough speed freaks to know they don't acknowledge such minor points.

"I'm 'on count down from five," Chill said.

"My Dad's unarmed," Mico shouted. He and Davy were on their feet now. Mico moved toward the Texan but the Texan fired into the ground inches from the boy's feet.

"Five!" Chill shouted.

He never made four.

With the butt of her pistol, Rosie clocked him.

* * * *

The town council and several other guests sat gloomy and silent in Ann Glynn's office. The judge had begun the called meeting by reading a summary of their failed chief search. When he finished, he asked if there were any comments.

HB savored the moment. For the past six months, he had suffered. Oh, he put on a good show. Outwardly, he grinned, he was friendly, ready and willing to help, wrote the usual parking tickets, ran off the teen age boys who liked to smoke back of the church, hosed out the jail cell and put in a vase of flowers at Rosie's suggestion.

But he was withering away within. His sun had dimmed, and in the evening, as he rocked on his porch with Rosie and sipped his PBR, his moon waned diurnally because the town council inch by inch was cutting him like a cancerous growth out of his longtime home.

Now . . .

A woman stood to address the group. She informed them that not only was HB Alpata a fine law man, better than Ocopeeco deserved, but he was also a man with a conscience, which was more than she could say for the town council.

"You have expected him to be a CSI whirlwind," Rosie went on, "without even providing him with a weapon, a computer or a vehicle. Not to mention any forensic equipment. I realize you don't have any money, but you have foolishly assumed my husband could perform a miracle. And when he didn't, you fired him. You fired him! You know this man was born and raised here. This is not just a job for him. It's a way of life! He treats every situation personally, too much so. Now, finally, after seeing what is out there for the skimpy, insulting salary—a Harley-riding canine gourmand, a right wing devotee of Bishop Usher and a slow-walking speed freak—maybe now you will realize what you have lost, an irreplaceable gem of a police chief, HB Alpata."

Eyes blinking, her pale skin red with anger, she took her seat next to her husband, who stared straight ahead, struggling not to grin, although he wanted to shout: Hallelujah! and hug her. Neither Cicero nor Demosthenes could have spoken with more passion or eloquence. For the first time in months his spirits lifted, and he began to see a way out of this dark forest in the middle of life's way where he had run up on his own leopard, lion and wolf waiting to devour him.

Ann Glynn sat on the row in front of HB and Rosie. She turned around with tears in her eyes.

"Rosie, HB, I feel so bad about this. We have failed miserably. We failed the town, ourselves, but most of all, we failed you two."

Wiping her eyes with the back of her hand, she looked around at the others. "Y'all, admit it. Be honest with yourselves now. We didn't do right here. We didn't."

Jim Jeffords thrust his thumbs under his suspenders and pulled them out. "Well, gosh, I don't know as how I agree, Ann. I think the chief's job is to catch the killer. HB's the chief and he ain't caught the killer. Seems pretty simple to me."

As the debate wore on, Jim Jeffords and Mrs. Beasley on one side, Grace Daniels, Ann Glynn and the judge on the other, HB chuckled. But not for long. They still had no killer and worse, by now, given all the signs and posters around town condemning him, certain elements in the community were sure he was not fit to do the job.

Chapter Twelve

Taking a knee, Mico gulped the Gatorade the trainer brought around. An egg-shaped bump swelled on his left elbow and the tan flesh on his right forearm was ripped and showing white. His knuckles were raw, as well, and his ribs were sore from the last blitz, but he felt great. In his mind's eye he relived the tight spiral he had just thrown Davy in the end zone. His buddy had developed a pair of powerful hands and was taller and slimmer than last year. Together they were the offensive heart of the ninth grade team. Hours of backyard practice had honed their instincts so Mico knew how his friend juked left or right, knew he could reach over defenders and was confident Davy's long legs could outrun the safety. School practices seemed an extension of their backyard pass patterns. And he had finally learned to stand firm in the pocket, even with rushers barreling at him like two legged freight trains. The two inches he had grown since last year helped. Now he could see over the rushers and read the defense better. He glanced over at Davy, those big hands and long fingers dangling down like twin animals hungry for another grab. The two friends grinned and nodded.

But on the next play another blitz put him flat on his back and knocked the breath out of him. Junior Sweatman, a two hundred ten pounder, missing two front teeth, stood over him, laughing.

"If you gon' make the pro's, Injun, you got to move faster. Hey, you gotta support that sorry-ass old man of yours, too. Gon' take a lot of green."

Mico leapt up and pounced on the boy and they rolled over in the dirt. Coach broke it up quickly, but the fight continued in the locker room because Sweatman couldn't control his tongue. This time Mico got in some good shots, bloodied the boy's face so badly Coach had to drive him into the Immediate Med in Macon for stitches above his left eye.

Later Mico and Davy walked home down the well-worn path from the school through the field to Mico's house. The sky was darkening, blue black cirrus clouds streaking across it. Bruised and sore, they didn't feel the cold as they ambled along, reliving the day, the practice.

"The brothers' ll come after you," Davy said. "Once they get a look at those stitches around their baby brother's eye."

"Hard to think of Junior as a baby anything," Mico said. He tossed his shiny, deep black hair.

"Need to lay low, not long, couple of days."

Mico stopped. "What?"

"Hey, the Sweatman's don't fight fair. Bats did time in prison, nearly killed a dude!"

Mico grabbed his buddy around the neck. "Think I can't take 'em, huh?"

They tussled like puppies, then straightened up. "They'll jump you. Won't be a fair fight," Davy said.

That night Mico took stock. He pretended to be unconcerned, but he'd encountered the brothers once before, and he hadn't told Davy or his folks about it.

Against his Dad's orders to stay away from the 7/11 up on the highway, he was there, Saturday, a month before, stocking up on Skittles and shooting the breeze with Lizard who was trying to convince him smoking wasn't bad for you. To prove his point Lizard cited his ninety year old cousin who still consumed two packs a day, even in his nursing home. Lizard cut his eyes to the side entrance where the three brothers, Clete, Bats and Ike were getting out of a BMW. They had made known in town how little respect they had for HB Alpata. If he didn't leave town on his own, they claimed, they would be glad to assist.

Lizard motioned for Mico to slip out the back, but it was too late. They had spotted him. Clete blocked the door and said:

"Your daddy's gone, little Injun,"

Mico darted out the main entrance and sprinted all the way home and never told his Mom and Dad.

A week after the fight in the locker room, and nothing had happened. At practice, Junior seemed almost ashamed, would not look at him. Another week passed without incident. He decided the whole thing had blown over and a burden was lifted from his shoulder. His folks still didn't know.

Three weeks after the fight it was his turn to walk down to Jim Jeffords's store for Gatorade, so before practice, still wearing his school clothes, he pulled the red kiddie wagon with the empty blue cooler through the grass. Dark clouds rolling in from the east meant practice might be canceled. He hoped not. The day before, he'd thrown his first no-look pass and wanted to try it again. But when he knocked on the back door of Jeffords's store, there was no answer. Puzzled, he started around front, but just as he rounded the corner, the brothers grabbed him.

When they were finished with him, he lay curled up in the mud puddle the air conditioning unit made, bleeding from his ears into the water. Breathing hurt. Moving hurt. His legs would not work. Eyes at ground level, he watched as the rain fell, drops spattering mud in his face, and thought about Davy saying they didn't fight fair. Clete and Ike had held his arms behind him, while Bats beat him unconscious. After he finally dropped, they kicked him, steel toed boots in the ribs.

He lost track of time.

When the sun set and he lay in the dark, he heard his Dad and Coach talking: "The boys always come this way . . . " the Coach said.

Then, his Dad: "There's the little red wagon! Mico!" But Mico couldn't answer. When HB found him, he groaned, and his eyes rolled back in his head.

* * * *

Ann Glynn vaped blue, luminous smoke into the evening air where it hung, a thick cloud, like a signal warning a war party's on the ridge ahead.

They sat drinking wine and beer on HB's porch, their feet up on the railing, Rosie, HB and Ann. Overlooking the town, the porch was built from stones quarried in north Georgia and transported to Ocopeeco by Pain Alpata. Ferns hung from the ceiling; a Chinese wind chime glittered in the moonlight, unmoved in the windless evening.

Ann set her vaping device on the wicker table beside her. After removing her black pumps, she massaged her feet.

"Hurt?" Rosie asked.

"Like Hell. I try to walk instead of sitting. So, it's a fight: numb butt vs. sore feet. Today, my butt won."

Just that afternoon, sitting on his red John Deer mower, HB had cut the large field that stretched out in front of them as far as a line of pines. This evening a fat moon was perched atop the trees. Its light made the dew on the freshly mown grass sparkle.

He took a long pull from his PBR. As he rolled the icy can on his face, he lay his head back against the wicker rocker and his thick neck muscles bulged. He seemed to be talking to the moon.

"If I arrest the Sweatman boys, it'll be rough for Mico at school."

"It'll be hell," Ann said, nodding at him. She assumed the whiny, sarcastic tone of a sixteen year old: "'Hey, Daddy boy. Feeling better, Daddy boy?'"

Rosie took one drag from HB's cigarette, savored the smoke with the erotic pleasure of the reformed addict, and gave it back. "That's ridiculous. My son was assaulted! It's a crime!"

"Technically," Ann said, reaching forward to massage her toes. She looked back at Rosie. "But I guarantee you one thing: your son wants Daddy to stay out of it." She leaned back again. "When's he returning?"

HB and Rosie looked at each other.

"What'd the doc say?" he asked.

"Well, he says next week. But I think it's too soon. His ribs are still taped."

"I'll assign our hottest cheerleader to keep an eye on him," Ann said, winking at HB.

Rosie's eyes rolled; HB chuckled and squeezed her arm.

He crushed his can, then tossed it into the garbage.

"The oldest Sweatman brother served time in prison for cracking a man's skull in a bar fight."

Rosie's face twisted. "Prison? And he assaulted my son?"

The three allowed the gravity of that thought to sink in. Mico was no longer a child. More than anything, HB wanted to bring the full weight of the law down on these thugs, but he realized what that would mean for his son. The boy was popular, a fine athlete, top grades. By charging the Sweatman brothers, he would drag his son into the courts which would turn the boy's world upside down—at the beginning of his high school years.

But that wasn't all. Sonny Sweatman, the brothers' Dad, owned the biggest Ford dealership in the area, an expansive, flag-flying circus of glistening new machines that shone far and wide, a beacon to the truck-obsessed men and women of the area. The father would hire a swat team of lawyers from Atlanta.

"I gotta go," Ann said, as she stood.

She looked down at her friends, sitting. "You press charges, it'll kill Mico," she said. "I'm not saying you shouldn't, but I just want you to understand what it'll mean for your family."

"What are you getting at?" Rosie asked.

Ann paused, gnawed her lower lip, looked out into the night, gathering her thoughts. She spoke precisely, the professional.

"I've seen parents act in such a way as to protect their son or daughter, to follow the law, but wind up, in the end, alienating their child. Well-behaved outstanding students can go bad."

Rosie teared up. "Oh, Ann . . . "

HB leaned over and took her in his arms.

"I know. It kills me to tell you this. But I love you guys. I want you to know what could happen."

Ann bent down, kissed Rosie on the cheek and smiled at HB, a friend's smile.

This woman was as moved by this as they were; she was trying to do the right thing.

The two parents, holding one another, watched as their friend descended the stone steps and set out across the field on the well-worn, visible path like a thread through the darkness so even a lost and hapless soul could somehow find its way.

* * * *

HB's red pick-up eased in among the shiny Fords of all stripes parked in the expanse of white gravel in front of the Sweatman mansion, a three-story Georgian style house of red brick, dormers, end chimneys and quoins. The massive University of Georgia flag, red, black and white, unfurled majestically above the entrance until it was full and then it fell. HB grinned. He recalled similar flags in The *Triumph of the Will*, a thirties black and white film that portrayed Adolph Hitler as a Norse deity. The most avid bulldog fans were often wannabee locals like Sweatman, who never set foot on the Athens campus.

He thumbed through the notes and newspaper articles he'd gleaned from back issues of the Gordon Gazette, and prison records. Derwood, "Bats", the oldest son, assaulted a bartender because the man refused him a drink. Using a pool cue, he fractured the man's skull. Astronomical hospital bills the bartender couldn't pay. Daddy Sweatman paid everything, but his son still did two years in Coastal State Prison in Savannah.

Since he was in a different county, HB had paid a call on his buddy, Dietz Peeler, the sheriff of Gordon. Six six and still fit, Dietz had regularly beaten HB and Ocopeeco High with his uncanny throwing arm. Once HB explained the situation to his old cross county rival, he was given permission to serve the warrants himself, even though he was out of jurisdiction.

"And be sure and get pictures, HB. I wanna see Sonny Sweatman's face when somebody finally brings the hammer down on those three. They ain't fit to spit on."

Standing at the door, HB fingered the three warrants and lifted the large, metal knocker, a replica of a bulldog's massive maw.

The door was opened by a tan, tennis-togged woman, about sixty, long arms and muscled calves. Eyes slightly oriental, short silver hair, full lips whose silver lipstick needed touching up.

"Chief!" she said, almost squealing. She offered her hand, a strong grip and a bright smile as if greeting a party guest.

"Mrs. Sweatman, this isn't a social call."

"Oh, shush, I know that. But we can still be civil, can't we? I mean we're all members of the bulldog nation."

He nodded.

She shielded her eyes from the sun. "You played middle linebacker, didn't you?"

"I did."

"Sonny and I saw all your games that year. They called you the Crazy Creek."

He nodded, trying not to smile at a name he hadn't heard in years. "Yes, ma'am."

This small talk made him nervous. Either the woman didn't care her sons were about to be arrested or she was trying to stall him or put him off his game.

He followed her through cool hallways until she led him into a room with a long oak table and walls lined with books, mostly encyclopedias.

"Here he is, honey," Mrs. Sweatman said, squeezing HB's bi-ceps. "M-m-m-m," she murmured.

Sonny Sweatman sat at head of the table, beside him a clean-shaven, well-coiffed lawyer in a three piece charcoal gray suit. The room was used only for legal matters. It had an antiseptic feel and a slight lemony scent.

Sonny stepped out to greet him. Tall, lanky and tan, the Sweatman pater familias was dressed for golf: red and white oxfords, tropical fruit golf pants, a silver ID bracelet on one hand, on the other, a Rolex. The only flaw: a glass eye.

The eye carried on its own conversation with an invisible guest. HB tried not to stare, but when the live eye moved, the dead one sat, implacable and angry, two souls struggling to control a single body.

When the man smiled, he revealed a shiny, gold tooth.

"Got us a real mess, don't we chief?" he said.

"That depends," HB said, glancing at the lawyer and easing away from Mrs. Sweatman.

Sonny frowned at his wife and ushered her out; she protested. As the door closed, she threw HB a wave.

After they sat down, he removed his hat and handed the lawyer the warrant. "Are the boys here?" he asked.

Nodding his head from side to side, Sonny muttered something unintelligible.

The lawyer chuckled.

But HB bristled. He leaned forward, looking straight into Sweatman's good eye. "I didn't drive all the way over to Gordon to play games. Are the boys in the house or aren't they?"

"Now don't go gettin' your panties in a twist, chief," Sonny said, wiping the grin off his face. "They're around somewhere. Let me text 'em."

The lawyer examined the warrant.

He pointed to the signature. "Gussy B?" he asked.

"Judge Breckenridge," HB said.

"And this witness, this Jim Jeffords?"

"He saw the three Sweatman boys assault my son."

The lawyer's eyes shot up. "Your son?" He glanced at Sonny, then looked back at the warrant.

"They're at the Dairy Queen," Sonny said, beaming. "They'll be here in a jiff."

"Did you know the victim was the chief's son?" the lawyer asked.

It took Sweatman a second. He tilted his head, lowered his voice and leaned toward HB. "Chief, that was . . . your boy?"

"Yes."

The two men straightened up.

HB wondered how the lawyer had not known. He dealt with all local complaints about the wild Sweatman boys and learned about the details from gossip; but this time, the incident took place in another county. He'd heard little about it.

Sweatman and his lawyer excused themselves.

HB sat alone while they stepped outside to confer. When they returned, the tone of the meeting altered. The we're-just-good-old-boys mood vanished and was replaced by solemn faces and measured speech.

"Chief," Sweatman said, "the law has caused a lot of pain in my family. Two years in that prison—my boy saw things, God, things no Christian child should ever see."

The dead eye had taken over. Whatever good will the live eye had shown, was gone. Its inert glass twin meant business.

"That's not going to happen again," Sweatman said, "ever. Not as long as I'm alive."

"Mr. Sweatman," HB said, "I'm an officer of the court. I'm here to arrest your three sons for a crime which took place in Ocopeeco, GA on the fourteenth of January 2018. I want to assure you of one thing. Today, your sons will leave this house in handcuffs."

Sonny Sweatman stormed out, leaving the lawyer and the chief alone for fifteen minutes of strained silence.

He wasn't comfortable around the rich, a character flaw that rarely came to the fore in Ocopeeco where there weren't many folks who fit that description. Rosie claimed it would get him in trouble someday. He'd seen her at university functions where fat donors and trustees were enchanted by her grace and small talk while he usually wound up hunkered down in the corner with some ancient AD talking steroid enhancement or an effective blitz.

Even in the insulated conference room, he heard the front door fly open and the three boys tumble in like puppy dogs. The oldest and smallest, Bats, sported a Prada leather jacket, a freshly shaved bald head, earrings and dark circles under his eyes. Ike and Clete stood a foot taller than their big brother. Their matching white polo shirts engulfed their large bellies and were spotted with mustard and chips. Both had stringy brown hair.

When HB arrived, he hung back and watched the father trying to calm the boys.

The three circled their daddy and glared at him.

"A warrant!" Bats said. He moved his toothpick from one side of his mouth to the other.

"Now don't get all goosy loosy, boys. Sam Sharp is here, he'll have you out in a jiff and we can set down and strategize'"

Ike and Clete continued to grin. "How many cops?"

"Just one," Sonny said, "but it's HB Alpata."

"That Mico's Daddy?" Clete said.

"It is."

"One measly cop?" Clete said.

Ike shoved him. "Dude, that's the crazy Creek!"

The two sons bounced up and down, energized, and oblivious.

"Boys," their father said, "I'm telling y'all, now. Let Sam take care of this. We gotcha covered."

"Yeah, Pops," Bats said, pulling out a pair of brass knuckles. "That's what you said last time." He slipped them on, squeezed his fist and admired their dull, gold-colored coating.

Clete and Ike took the brass knuckles and tried them on and pretended to sock each other.

When they spotted HB, the three sons bolted.

He tackled and cuffed the two fat ones even before they got out the front door.

Bats made it to his BMW convertible, but the clump of cars blocked him.

HB shot out his back left tire.

"You son of a bitch!" Bats yelled, leaping out to inspect the damage. "That's a brand new Pirelli, that's a Ferrari tire, imported from Milan, Italy!"

HB cuffed him from behind, yelling in his ear-ringed ear: "Yeah? These are twenty-year old cracker cuffs from Sally's Cop Shop in Brunswick, GA!"

He snatched Bats off his feet and dragged him over the gravel, ripping his Prada jacket.

"Police brutality!" the mother screamed, pointing a shaky finger.

"Yeah!" Sonny yelled, behind his wife. "That's excessive use of force!"

HB hurled the man's son into the back of his truck like a sack of chicken feed. Then as he hauled the other two out of the foyer, the mother nagged him, pointing and screaming:

"Excessive use of force!"

The boys yelled, as HB kicked them up onto his tailgate and into the truck bed to join their crumpled older brother..

"O-w-w-w-w!"

With their sons moaning as a backdrop, the parents huddled.

He stormed at them, fists balled at his side.

They backed away, shocked, as the Ocopeeco chief, a bull of a man and beside himself with rage, approached to within inches of the mother's face.

"They cut Maximus the Confessor's hands off!" he shouted. "And not for assaulting a thirteen year old boy. But just because he spoke the gospel truth. That, Mrs. Sweatman, is excessive use of force!"

He jammed the pedal of his big Ford and wheeled out of the yard spewing gravel on the fleet of marvelous sparkling cars.

* * * *

As HB climbed the steps up to the high school, the kids raced by him going in the other direction.

"Hi, Chief!"

"How's Mico?"

He nodded and smiled, but none stopped long enough for him to tell them how his son was doing.

Ann Glynn waited at the top with the glass door open.

As he approached, she nodded toward the flagpole. "Check out Davy and his new girlfriend. She's a sophomore and he's still a ninth grader. This is the star power football players have in this school."

HB turned to see Mico's pass catching buddy leaned over a tall, blond who rested her back against the flagpole. Their faces were an inch apart.

"She's cute," he said, as he waved to Mrs. Coleman, who waved back.

He followed Ann into her office.

"I never understood why they call 'em 'sweet nothings,'" she said, over her shoulder. "Those 'nothings' may become an 8 lb. something that poops and squeals."

"He's just fifteen, Ann," he said, as he sat down beside her desk.

"Maybe so, but did you see his hands. Huge."

HB chuckled. "I think you had too much fun in high school."

She opened her mini fridge, pulled out two Diet Cokes, tossed one to him. He caught it, popped the can and took a long swallow.

She threw her shoeless feet onto the desk.

"So, you locked 'em up."

"I did. They're in a cell in Irwinton."

"I'll bet Sonny was not happy."

He cocked his head. "Yeah, tell me about Sonny Sweatman."

"Me? What should I know?"

"You and he have a history."

She bobbed her head back and forth. "If we do, it's more because of gossip than fact. In high school, he got the hots for me, even though he knew I played for the other team. Took me to the river in one of his daddy's big new cars. But I didn't cooperate . . . well, I got the giggles and ran through the woods, playing hard to get. Sonny came after me, sort of a game, and he ran into a pine limb. The surgeons in Macon performed three operations but couldn't save the eye."

"So, you're the cause of the glass eye?"

"You could say that."

"The doc says Mico needs another week for the stitches to dissolve. Then, it's up to you."

Ann brought her feet down. She put her elbows on the desk and leaned forward.

"Actually, it's not," she said, her voice lowered.

"What do you mean?"

"The superintendent called this morning. He's been following this from day one."

"What does he care?"

"Favoritism. He's giving Mico ten more days. After that, since Mico's been out so long, he's talking about holding him back a year."

"What!"

"Don't worry. Just get the boy back in class. It'll work out."

* * * *

At Pain's cabin, Rosie herded a dozen of her father-in-law's former students onto the pine wood porch and the row of wicker rockers. Even the popcorn balls of white clouds hovering above them seemed to feel the heat. The men sported coats and ties, lawyers, teachers or businessmen, some from Macon, some Atlanta, and one all the way from Cleveland. The women wore skirts or business suits. They were all dabbing their necks and foreheads and faces with Kleenex.

Golden rod glowed around the cabin, pansies, too, and a panoply of other colorful flowers Pain cultivated.

The men leaned against the pine rail on the porch while the women sat in the wicker rockers. Rosie's e mail explained Pain's condition and asked if they would be willing to show him some moral support, take a day off and gather at his cabin. She knew this was a lot to ask; she hated missing even one day a year from her teaching schedule, but she hoped the old ties between a fine teacher and good students were still strong.

Her index finger over her mouth, she caught their eye and slipped the front door open. The others nodded, acknowledging the need to be quiet. She had tried to convey in the email there was a possibility they might never see their old teacher again. She hoped she hadn't been over the top dramatic, but she wanted to insure they would show up.

Inside, she cracked the door to his bedroom where the old Creek lay stiff, arms at his side, fully dressed in starched jeans, moccasins, and a fresh work shirt, his long gray hair in a buckeye clasp and single pig tail that came down to his waist. His bright black eyes shone as he saw her.

"You're awake," she said.

"I am and I have one question: did you bring marzipan?"

She giggled

He was in good spirits. She wondered if he knew what she had planned. He always knew things before anybody else. But that was why he was an empath.

"As a matter of fact, I did, but first I have a surprise." She pointed to him. "You stay right there."

She slipped back out, assembled the group the way she explained to them in the email. Everybody knew their parts. In Pain's class they performed this number many times, his favorite poem.

She raised her hands, and they sang in parts:

> Down by the salley gardens
> my love and I did meet.
> She passed the salley gardens
> with little snow-white feet.

> She bid me take love easy,
> as the leaves grow on the tree.
> But I, being young and foolish,
> with her would not agree.

Inside, lying stiff on his bed, the old teacher blinked. Tears pooled in his eyes until rivulets broke out and ran down his cheeks as his lips mouthed the words and his face shone.

Rosie peeked in. Watching him made her cry, as well.

In the second stanza the group rose toward the meaning.

> In a field by the river
> my love and I did stand,
> And on my leaning shoulder
> she laid her snow-white hand.
> She bid me take life easy,
> as the grass grows on the weirs.
> But I was young and foolish,
> and now am full of tears.

Having lived for two decades, having been broken and discouraged by life, the group of ex-students understood the words and comprehended the story, so their voices lifted in the fullness of their hearts to show it: the pain of a young love gone wrong, the universal suffering that few manage to elude along the race's juvescent journey.

When the song was over, for a moment, the singers stood, slightly dazed at the power of memory and of music, and the way those two lifted them out of their everyday lives into their former selves.

Rosie summoned them to his bed. They gathered around him, beaming, as he whispered their names, one by one. Several of the women bent down to hug him until, finally, one of the males, smartly dressed with a brightly colored bow tie and thick black glasses, leaned over and Pain sobbed as they embraced.

The emotional moment exhausted him. He tried to sit up, but he was so weak, and his head was trembling; Rosie eased him back down, whispering and comforting him. She knew how much he wanted to say, but she could also see he was too feeble. He lay, head on the pillow, staring up and muttering to himself.

She ushered the group back out on the porch where she had arranged Marzipan cookies and coffee.

The group ate, somber, but puzzled.

"What happened?" the bow tie asked. "We heard something about him starving himself? Is that true?"

She told them about the people in the community he had saved over the past few years. The town adored him. Families offered him money, which he refused. Cakes, pies, even a big, new LED TV, which he didn't refuse, but gave to HB and Rosie.

"Then, Dec. 25, 2014," she said, "he was summoned to the shack thinking someone needed help."

"What do you mean, summoned?" the bow tie asked.

"Hesegadamasse, the Creek messenger spirit comes to him and informs him who is in distress."

"Sort of like the Holy Spirit?" the bow tie asked.

"Yes!" Rosie said. "But when he got there, he found no one, nothing. He searched and searched. No sign of blood or a struggle. Went back for days. Eventually, he became convinced he had failed. Someone had needed him, and he wasn't there. A great guilt settled in. He fasted to prepare for punishment, which he knew was coming. In the Creek world, when you fail, there are consequences. You don't get a smiley face."

The group remembered how Pain was known as a healer, even among the students and teachers. He saved two puppies and a cat during their eighth grade year. Brought them into the school and fed them, nurtured them, and let the kids play with them and taught them how important it was to be gentle to the injured and the disabled. The principal objected on hygienic grounds and threatened to fire Mr. Alpata, but the whole school got up a petition to support him and the principal backed down. Three of the group, two women, a redhead and a blond, and a tall, already graying doctor in wire rimmed glasses, said they had become medical professionals because of that class. Even then, Pain shared with them how he had been marked as a Native American child in Ocmulgee, OK to be an empath and a healer. He conveyed to them how his calling was sacred.

The bow tie turned to the others: "Remember that look that came over him when he talked about his sacred calling."

The others agreed.

"Oh, boy, do I remember," the red head said, "He would stare out at us, but we knew he was in another world, that was when I realized healing others is more than merely collecting a paycheck."

"But why doesn't he stop?" the doctor asked in a soft pleading voice.

The others turned to him.

"Remember Holy Alice?" the red head said.

The others nodded and whispered.

Rosie sat down in a wicker rocker. "Here is where I lose the thread or rather the thread loses me."

The group gathered round her. "It's as if they made some kind of a fasting to the death pact," the red head said.

"Oh, don't be melodramatic," the doc said.

"I don't think I'm being melodramatic. We know how much he loved her."

"He told us often enough," the bow tie said. "She died five years before our class, and yet he was still talking about her as if she were in the next room."

The doctor rolled his eyes.

Rosie realized she had allowed the conversation to take an unhealthy turn. She and HB had already covered all this spooky gothic ground and were long past it. No, the only way to save her father-in law was to find out what happened the night of December 25,2014, so Pain Alpata could find some peace of mind and save himself.

Chapter Thirteen

Mico ripped off a bite of beef jerky. He liked the tough chewing, the workout it gave his mouth. Lately, he'd eaten too much soft, sugary junk, Davy's doin's. His favorite wide receiver always brought him a sack of candy, Butterfingers, M & M's, Skittles, and Peanut Butter Cups.

He snapped off a bit and threw it to Nate who snagged it in his beak, tossed it up and gulped it down. No chewing.

"I prefer Skittles," the crow said.

"Sugar's bad for you."

"Bad for you Mammals, not so much for us Aves."

"What?"

"Sugar drives a mammal's insulin up. Makes you fat and diabetic. Me, it just tastes good."

The half-full moon looked down at them, amused from its perch above the bear caves. Around them, the high grass by the Ocopeeco still glistened with dew and the air was cool and moist.

As they made their way from the house down to the river, several times Mico stopped to run his long fingers down his side, the layer of thick tape and under it the gauze. The stitches were holding, but he had no idea what to expect. If they broke, would he bleed out right there by the river? Would the pain be excruciating? After he first woke up in the hospital, agony seared through him. He clutched his Mom's hand as the nurse gave him a shot in his IV and within seconds it went away, and he marveled at how any chemical could take away such hurt so fast. That's when he understood he was in a new world. He didn't know the rules and he didn't even know what the game was. On the football field he felt confident. Sure, it was brutal; but he knew what to expect. The moment he felt that pain disappear, and the syrupy flow of pleasure replace it as the drug took hold, he realized there were things in this world so far beyond his thirteen year old brain, it frightened him. The pain passed; but anxiety replaced it.

He was already condemning himself for running away.

"How long will we stay in the caves?" Nate asked.

"A week, maybe more."

"Do you have a week's worth of food in your backpack?"

Mico blinked. He hadn't thought of that. He hadn't thought of anything except running away from the inner voices calling him a daddy's boy, can't fight his own fights. Davy's visits made it worse. He told him the truth, what the kids at school were saying. He'd always been proud of his Dad. He knew lots of kids who weren't. Since the first grade this good-Dad-wall kept out of his mind so many thoughts and feelings others kids dealt with every day. It gave him strength. But the wall crumbled once he saw the posters and heard kids gossiping at school about that sorry chief.

His parents tried to put his mind at ease about it, but he knew Davy was right. He couldn't set foot in school again.

"We'll make it," he said to Nate.

They started up the hill towards the bear caves. The rise was steep, boulders and scrubs and hard clay.

After a half hour Mico stopped and sat down. Two weeks in bed—he was weak; his legs were shaking.

"Are the stitches gonna hold?" Nate asked. He perched on a rock opposite and preened his feathers. In the moonlight his black coat took on a bluish tint.

"I can do it. But I'm a little weak."

The crow hopped down and moved closer. He looked up at his friend as he lowered his voice. "You know, it's not too late to go back. I doubt your Mom and Dad have discovered we've gone yet."

The boy tried to think clearly, but it was getting harder.

"I don't know . . . "

"Think about it. You wake up and your Mom has made one of those giant German pancakes with maple syrup and a ton of butter and your dad has cooked bacon and sausage. I can smell 'em now."

Mico shook his head. "Stop trying to talk me out of this!"

"I'm just saying maybe with all the time in bed, you're not ready yet."

Mico leaped up. He took a deep breath and felt dizzy, but it passed. "Let's go! It's getting late. The sun' ll be coming up soon and we need to be in the bear caves by then."

Nate flew up onto his shoulder as they soldiered upward, up the steep, rocky incline.

When Mico looked down, there was the river, sparkling in the moonlight, but covered in fog in other spots. Beyond lay River Street, Clean Jeans, and further up his Dad's church, a single spire with a small bell inside.

Since he'd never been sick or laid up for any reason, he had no gauge. How much could his body stand? The stitches were stinging now, and the broken ribs throbbed, but that was the blood flowing. His Dad said the blood needed to get into those wounds for them to heal so the throbbing was good. His body was feeling pain again after weeks of drug induced numbness.

"Slow down!" Nate said.

"Can't! Got to get to the caves."

Higher and higher. The river grew smaller and they could see farther up River Street all the way to the high school. Beyond lay the Alpata house and beyond that the cabin where his grandad lay dying from fasting.

His screwed up family. A grandmother who starved herself to death and now a grandfather doing the same. He couldn't imagine skipping one meal, let alone a day. Thinking about his granddad brought tears to his eyes. Lying by his fire as a little boy listening to tales of Creek warriors. The great battles. And his grandad's grinning face, that intense look always so full of love. That eye circled with red dye, his healer's sign. Like a second Dad. Tears ran down his cheeks. Running, too, from taunting in grammar school. "Don't scalp me, Mico!" "Injun boy!" "Where's your bow and arrow?" Put it all behind him.

Something in his side un-zipped!

He dropped to one knee, fell over in the dirt.

"What!" Nate squawked. He lit on the ground beside Mico's face.

Blood trickled through the bandages.

Mico pointed up. "The caves!"

He hobbled inside the first one with Nate on his shoulder.

The stench! Boxes of fast food, trash, bones, chewed up shoes, and an animal smell.

Nate flitted around from wall to wall. He cocked his head and inspected everything. When he returned, Mico leaned against a boulder, sweat dripping off the tip of his chin, breathing hard.

"This room is occupied," Nate said. "And they were here today, not hours ago."

Mico struggled up. "Can't stay here. There's another one further up."

His legs trembled. Since they stopped climbing, the pain had gripped him like a vise. It ground into his bones, crushing, shooting up into his head like lightning bolts.

"No, you don't look good . . . "

"I'm fine . . . " he said, but twisted around, grabbing at air, his eyelids fluttering as he went down.

"Mico!"

His mouth half open in the dirt, he felt his confidence throw up its hands and walk away. Now nothing but the pain, like steel, implacable. It would never release him. Even the hospital shot, the miracle drug, powerless.

The commotion aroused the cave's occupants. Two black cubs tumbled out of the darkness.

They wanted to play.

Nate fled to the top of the cave as the bears nudged Mico like puppies, their noses cold but their stink unmistakable.

Any distraction from the pain felt good! "Hey, little fellas . . . "

They licked the salty sweat from his arms and face with their long, sloppy tongues.

"Nate!" Mico moaned. "Where are you?"

One cub slurped his face.

"Up here!" Nate yelled.

"Get Dad!"

The crow didn't need to be told a second time, but just as he flew out of the cave, he recalled that bear cubs never travel alone.

* * * *

Rosie set down the platter lumpy with scrambled eggs, the grease-glistening bacon dangling off the side. HB read the Macon paper as sunlight flooded the kitchen and brought out the red fire in his beard.

As she passed by, he grabbed her and planted a wet, sloppy kiss.

She giggled but struggled up. "Eat your bacon, Rotbart, the bad guys are prowling around like a roaring lion."

"Hey, I like that, giving me some St. Peter protection. You think Mico'll have a red beard?"

She pouted. "Could we not fast forward to a beard just yet. I still remember changing diapers."

He touched her arm. "I know . . . " he said, softly.

He set to spreading butter and jelly on his toast.

She sat down to her muesli.

"Let's tell him this morning," she said, as she took a spoonful and dabbed at the corners of her mouth with a napkin.

"Good idea. The fifteenth gives him ten days to get used to the idea."

After they finished, they knocked on his door.

No answer.

"Spud," HB said, leaning in and whispering, "Mom and I need to talk with you."

He eased the door open to an empty bed and an open window.

Panic took shape as a rock in their stomachs. "What if" images hail storming their brains.

They called or texted everyone. No one had seen Mico.

Rosie canceled her classes.

At ten AM she sat at the kitchen table scrolling through her contacts list. HB stood at the sink, hat on, gazing out the window onto the big field. He'd been out searching in his truck.

"He figured out the holiday couldn't last," he said. "I just never thought he'd run away. What about the stitches?"

She paused and looked up at her husband. "I don't know."

A cloud of fear was forming over them, one they weren't acquainted with. Usually, Mico pushed too hard, competed for top grades, stayed up late on the science project or the essay for English. They cajoled: son, you've got to eat and sleep. And they accepted the painful truth: part of his drive derived from the racist taunts of his youth. Thankfully, those were a fading memory, and high school beckoned with a world of healthy growth, physically, intellectually—until the Sweatman brothers. Now, for the first time, Mico was rebelling against everything he stood for, undone by a pack of oppressive teens, some jealous, some resurrecting the taunts from elementary school, some even egged on by petty parents who resented his Dad.

For his part, HB was more than ever convinced he was at fault. His failure to find Big Rig's killer lay at the root of his son's problem. From the moment Junior Sweatman called Mico out on the football field, mocking his Dad, mocking his family, the line of causes led back to him, HB Alpata.

Rosie blamed her job. She loved it, but she was too devoted to it and neglected her son at a time when he needed her the most. Afternoons, when she got home from a day of full classes and meetings, counselling students about their grades, even helping them to write papers, she lacked the time and energy to nourish and nurture her own son.

Both gave in to the accusatory sound track playing in their heads as they sat lost in themselves.

"Ex-cu-u-u-use me!"

The familiar voice came from Mico's room.

"Is there an adult in this house?"

They found Nate perched on the still open window sill, head cocked to the aside. "I hate to be the bearer of bad bear news, but Mico needs help—in the caves!"

* * * *

When they arrived at the caves it was noon, the air clear and but hot. They had come up on the backside on a rocky dirt road, little used. HB hopped out, talking a mile a minute.

"I called the bear guy at the university," he said as he pushed shells down into his clip. "He said there would be some groups hibernating. So be careful, but when black bears go into winter sleep, it's a lot lighter sleep than people imagine. They'll hear us and wake up and might be mad. But mostly they're more afraid of us than we are of them. And if one stands, don't panic. The myth is that's when they charge. Not true. Usually, they're just trying to get a better look at the lay of the land just the way you or I would do."

He paused. "Hey, let's go! Nate said he'd be waiting outside the cave"

Rosie didn't budge. She sat staring ahead. He could see she was upset. He walked around to her side.

"Babe, what's the matter?"

His wife was trembling. Tears ran down her cheeks.

"We're here," he said, his voice lowered. "I think it's almost over."

Like a child, she shook her head.

When he reached his hand in the window, she jumped.

"What?"

Her face when she turned shocked him. It wasn't the expression of a woman whose child has just been found. It was a look of stark terror.

"I . . . can't . . . go . . . in . . . "

"Why not?'

"I just can't . . . "

He opened the truck door and reached out, but she shoved him away.

"Rosie! What's going on?"

At the age of seven she and one other girl got lost in the Kluterhöhle (Kluter Caves) near Dortmund, underground lakes, bizarre rock formations and a maze of 380 tunnels. Their teacher was a young active man only twenty-five who sprinted through the caves, excited, jabbering a mile a minute in a Bavarian accent, hard to understand.

"We both had flashlights. And some passageways were well lit, but others . . . oh, God, it was awful. Pitch black. Rocks looked human, like ghouls. Or masks. My friend, Gisela, couldn't stop crying. I slapped her. I slapped her hard."

"Did she stop then?"

"No! She screamed, over and over. That was worse than anything. I was doing alright until then. When she screamed something in me broke. I thought we were going to die."

Several times the girl fell, and Rosie had to pick her up. Afterwards Rosie's father, a disciplinarian, held his daughter and her friend responsible. "der Lehrer ist nie schuldig!" (the teacher's never guilty) her Dad's favorite saying. She had nightmares for months always the same: helpless, abandoned, hopeless.

"I never told anyone else about it. The other girl moved away. So, I have never spoken to anyone."

"Your folks didn't want you to see a therapist?"

"A therapist!" she said. "My father?" She lowered her voice and spoke gruffly: "No child of mine is so weak willed that she can't handle her own emotions."

They hugged. Slowly, she slipped out of the truck. Embracing, they stood beside the truck. Behind them rose a mound of kaolin covered over by clay. A gaping hole caught Rosie's eye.

"Is . . . that it?"

"I think so," he said, leading her gently toward the hole.

The ground was level, but they had to climb an incline to the entrance. From there they could see down into the cavern, the size of their living room. The sunlight from outside lit half the space. The back side was dark, the floor covered with trash, the stench feral, fecal and rich with half-eaten food.

Nate perched on a rock. "C'mon, I'll show you," he said.

He flew into another room where they found Mico propped up on one elbow, munching a candy bar. He was shaky, but grinning.

Rosie moved tentatively. HB walked behind her. In a half squat she gawked around, her right hand raised as if to protect her face. But there wasn't much to be protected from. The bear family vanished after Mico fed the babies some jerky. He never saw the mama bear.

"Mom! Dad!"

Thoughts of punishment and anger vanished in a group hug with tears from all three. As they made their way back to the truck, Rosie promised to take the next semester off and home school Mico. Mico loved the idea and HB said he had an announcement:

"I'm going to dive the river myself," he said. "But first I'm headed to Florida's Ten Thousand Islands for a six week course with Gator Bates to learn forensic diving."

Chapter Fourteen

Iggy's description of his buddy Gator Bates proved accurate: "B, he's a small gorilla, slope shouldered, hairy and fast. Lives with an ex-hippy who makes boots and belts from python skins. They're well-off, but they live like Tarzan in some southwest Florida jungle. Somehow folks all over the world find out about Gator's forensic diving skills. He's been river diving in China, Africa, Bosnia. Told me he'd teach you for a reduced fee since you're dirt poor and are fighting for your job."

Iggy's description left out the black hair that grew out of Gator's ears and the knotty rope-like veins and muscle across his upper body. The cigars he constantly smoked he squashed with his soles.

HB stood in the hot sand looking up at his quarters, constructed inside a huge, live oak. The air staggered under the sun.

Gator clambered up the tree—there were steps; HB struggled, missing limbs and steps.

Gator slapped him on the back, which he had to reach up to do. "You'll get the hang of it. All our ancestors came outta the trees!"

The tree house room was built mostly of plywood, some corrugated aluminum and chicken wire. Lots of skins and pillows and reading matter, mostly about diving and divers. It was comfortable and the breeze blowing off the river was sweet.

The only thing that made him uneasy sat about fifty yards from the tree. He could see it clearly, so he asked Gator about it.

"That's Skade's rescue pen. Let's go down."

They climbed back down and walked through bromelain and palm trees to a large wire and bamboo pen where Gator's wife kept her babies, Burmese pythons, a sea of coils in which three dozen serpents dozed or dallied.

HB gaped.

Gator slapped him on the shoulder. "HB, you are flat shocked!"

"Never seen so many in one place."

"After hurricane Andrew wiped out a breeding station in the Glades, a bunch of these boys escaped and proliferated. They breed like rabbits. One female can carry ninety eggs. Imagine your wife with ninety babies. The state of Florida is overrun with them."

"Any way to stop them?"

"The scientists implant chips in selected males to locate breeding aggregates. That's where a lone female surrounds herself with a half dozen hot to trot males and they party out in the weeds. The rangers catch 'em at it now and then, but it doesn't do much good. We had a freeze one winter, killed a lot, but the next summer they popped right back up."

Some snakes crawled over bamboo, make-shift gym sets. Others curled up snoozing. One, larger than the rest, had a large lump in its belly.

"Pregnant?" HB asked.

"That's Beverly. She's digesting a small goat. She's a reticulated python. Biggest on the planet. Skade got her in a swap with a guy who raises goats up in south Georgia. Thought having a python would be neat until she kept breaking out of her pen and eating his means of making a living."

The walked around the cage to the back side where Skade sat at work on a bench. She was tall, barefoot and muscular, long black hair and a big grin, tan and welcoming.

"Hey, HB!" she waved.

She was leaning over a bench with what looked like a stone adz scraping the inside of a large python skin. Curls of a filmy white substance emerged from the blade slot.

"What's that going to be?" Gator asked.

She raised up, wiped sweat from her brow with the back of her hand. Her teeth were large and white. "Python covered paddle guards. Some pickleballers up at Naples like hand crafted native souvenirs. Like all the great warriors, they want an animal spirit in their corner. How 'bout you, Mr. Lawman? Like a python covered holster for your Glock?"

"Is that a thing?" HB asked.

"Sure is. I fitted out a whole precinct in Tampa."

That night they ate mahi mahi and squash with garlic and mango tarts, all fried over Gator's rock grill. Around the big fire pit afterwards they drank Coors and PBR which Gator had stocked in for HB's benefit. Though the palms and palmetto they could watch the Mackahatchee, gliding in the moonlight like silvery piece of modern furniture that moved and threw off lunar illumination.

"Tomorrow we get you in the water, see how you handle the river mud." Gator said. He was grinning at HB and leaning back on his elbows, holding a Coors in one hand.

"River mud is hard to negotiate in?"

"Can be. Right now, the Mackahatchee's runnin' middlin' high 'cause of the rain last week. But when the water level goes low the mud gets thick."

HB noted a long scar on his leg.

"That's a souvenir from a bull gator on Fahakhatchee Bay," Gator said, holding up his hairy leg. "Diving for some tech mogul's Rolex. Fifty thousand reward. I don't like rewards, usually. But usually, they're not fifty thousand. I got the watch but got that, too."

His wife slipped over and kissed his head. "Usually, he doesn't take chances. Heck, it was partly my fault. I told him to go for it. He knew there were bulls in the neighborhood, but he'd dove in the Bay before, but this time . . . "

HB knew what it was like to worry about the one who worries about you. It made the bond strong, but sometimes the bond threatened to break altogether.

"You're a preacher, too, right?" Skade said.

"I am."

"That's so spiritual," Skade said. "Gator and I are very spiritual, too. Aren't we?"

"Yeah," Gator said. He pointed with his beer can toward the river. "The water's my church. It's like a cathedral under there. I can feel God's presence."

HB had heard the I'm spiritual, but not religious pitch before, but he didn't want an argument.

"So, you preach and do funerals and weddings and all that?" Skade asked.

Wincing, HB nodded. "I do—I do all-l-ll that."

"Man," Skade said, "don't you have to go to school a long time and read a lot of books?"

"It's not so bad. I like to read, anyway."

"Hey," Skade said. "Show him Semmes's video!"

Gator pulled up a You Tube video on his phone of a wiry sixtyish Seminole decapitating a twenty foot python. Within minutes he had the creature, whacked, packed and racked into his Ford pickup.

"Who is that?" HB asked.

"Seminole Semmes," Skade said. "Gets calls from all over the state to get rid of snakes. Sometimes he brings 'em wounded to me. I don't pay as much as the folks who hire him in the burbs, but he thinks I'm cute. I feed 'em and nurse 'em back to good health."

"I don't get it," HB said. "Why not just take the skin when Semmes brings 'em in? Why go to all the trouble of feeding and nursing them? That must cost money and resources."

"No, gotta get 'em healthy," she said. "I like a skin glossy and supple. On a boot or a vest, you want a vibrant skin. I feed 'em Vitamins B and C to make 'em glow."

She paused, about to say something else.

"What is it?" HB said.

"Do you work out? I mean we get some buff guys around here, but you . . ."

He grinned. "I played football at Georgia."

Gator nodded and threw his empty into the oil drum trash barrel. "I told you, HB was an awesome linebacker. The Crazy Creek, right?"

"Well, I never liked that name."

"I understand," Skade said. "I'm one quarter Seminole. Used to get kidded in school."

"I have a question," HB said. "What is it about water that attracts us? It's mysterious, isn't it?"

Gator chuckled. "The water echoes our earlier lives before we flippered ourselves ashore."

HB nodded. "Well said."

After a week of tree sleep, he settled into a nocturnal peace. The symphony of night noises mesmerized him and led him gently into dreams and refreshing mornings, waking up energized. But some nights, when the breeze was strong, the twist wind wrung ten years of tangled echoes out of air and he wondered if he was hearing the wailing and moans of women and men, natives and newcomers from centuries gone by.

In his nightly calls to Rosie he suggested they vacation in south Florida.

Rosie: I burn. Teutonic skin.

HB: Wear a shirt.

Rosie: Has Skade hit on you yet?

HB: Not one hit.

Rosie: She will.

HB: I'll be home soon to catch Big Rig's killer.

Rosie: She'll strike when you least expect it. Anybody who raises snakes . . .

HB: Are we being judgmental?

Rosie: As only a German can be.

Chuckling, he switched off his phone. When he rolled over into the perfumed breeze coming off the river, the night music accompanying the wind serenaded him to sleep.

Around two AM he was aroused by a whispering, a tongue tip titillating his ear.

When he sat up, Skade gave him a Cheshire cat grin.

She was sitting on her haunches, wearing a bit of this, a bit of that.

Her long black hair swept across his face along with a lemon/coconut scent as she threw her elegant leg over him and sat astride his chest.

"You might at least knock," he said.

"Our services do not include doors."

"But they do include carnal relations with the boss's wife?"

She pouted, languid eyes, her long arms raised as she ran her fingers through her hair. "We're not married."

He rose.

She looked up at him. "You are one hunk of a man."

"Well, this hunk has a hang up."

"You're gay?"

"No, but it's against my faith to indulge in carnal relations with any woman who has not been baptized and you mentioned at the campfire last night your parents we're atheists."

She flipped over on her back and toyed with her hair. "So, if I get baptized, then. . .you and me?"

"Absolutely, sweetheart."

He got dressed, fetched his prayer book, and purple stole and they headed for the river.

As they descended the well-trod path to the water, above them like the discarded mantels of gods, skeins of moss swayed from the riparian water oak and poplars. The river whooshed, moon-lit and moving more ways than one.

Standing with his stole around his neck, he flipped through the Book of Common Prayer to the baptismal rite, the smell of the river like a strangely refreshing tomb.

"Do I kneel?" she asked.

"Yes."

Her knees sank into the squishy bank.

That she had received no prior catechetical instruction gnawed at him, but there were times to trust the Holy Spirit. He would provide whatever was needed, visible or invisible.

"Do you renounce the devil and all the spiritual forces of wickedness that rebel against God?"

She twisted her face. "What's the devil got to do with this? I thought I was getting baptized."

"We're casting the devil out of you."

Her eyes flashed. "The devil's not inside of me! Heck, before I met Gator I was a vegan. For twenty years I didn't eat meat!"

"I don't mean that you actually consumed the Devil. He's a spirit."

"And this spirit—according to you—is alive inside me?"

"He is. Before you're baptized."

"I think I'd know if I had a horned spirit with a tail and a red suit inside me!"

"You don't recognize him."

The wind blew her hair away from her body. She glared out across the water, drumming her fingers against her bicep.

"We can't go on," he said, with his finger in the prayer book, "until you renounce the devil."

Shaking her head back and forth, she muttered. "All right. I renounce him, even though I have never once laid eyes on him."

"Do you renounce the empty promises and deadly deceits of this world that corrupt and destroy the creatures of God?"

"You mean like Social Security?"

"No. Material things like big cars, expensive houses, that sort of thing."

"Hey, look around you. See any big cars or expensive houses?"

"Yeah, you and Gator are ahead of the curve on that one. So—the last one. Do you renounce the sinful desires of the flesh that draw you from the love of God?"

Her face twisted. She shook her head and stood up.

"What is it?" he said.

She reached for him.

He backed away.

"C'mon, baby," she cooed. "This is as good a place as any. Heck, Gator and I have done it in the mud plenty of times. C'mon, just you and me and the moon and the stars . . . " Her lips parted, revealing her beautiful teeth.

Again, he backed away.

Hands on her hips, she stared out at the river and gnawed at her lower lip. "Man," she said, "You are one stuck up son of a bitch."

She stormed up the bank.

As he watched her running back to the camp, the wind whipped the pages of his prayer book.

He would sleep well tonight.

He recounted the event to Rosie.

Silence.

HB: You still there?

Rosie: What would you have done if she had renounced the sinful desires of the flesh and allowed you to go through with the baptism?

HB: I would have pointed out to her that fornication falls into the category of sinful desires. Her baptism, by definition, would have stopped her.

Rosie: You were counting on the prayer book to shock her into a recognition of her wayward ways.

HB: I've seen it happen before.

Rosie: Adam, you are so naïve.

HB: No, Eve, I am not naïve. I merely believe in the power of the spirit.

* * * *

After three weeks, his wild disordered beard combined with his tan turned him into a cross between Robinson Crusoe and one of his Creek ancestors. And without the stress of job loss and rejection by his community his mind cleared like a crystal pool and his body grew green vine strong.

But the diving was tough. In the water, his unruly teacher became a rules tyrant. "Items must remain undisturbed, so you cannot touch that knife, even after you find it. Do you understand?"

"Got it."

"It's a crime scene. Every move you make has to stand up in court. When you find the knife that killed Big Rig, you want to make sure you don't screw the case up by doing something stupid in the water. Understand?"

"Got it!"

Gator also proved a stickler for safety. "There is danger in undertow, currents, water pressure on the body, hypothermia. Sometimes," he said, "the conditions make it too dangerous to dive at all. Are you willing to just sit the day out, do nothing until conditions improve?"

"I'm willing."

Gator taught him two forensic systems: the arc and the jackstay. The former required less equipment and was easy to learn. The latter, though more complicated and more difficult, offered the better chance of success. Jackstay involved two weights with a long rope between them. The diver keeps one hand on the rope and moves from one weight to the other, groping with his other hand along the bottom. When he gets to the end of the rope, he moves the weight two feet over and starts back the way he came.

Groping blind on the muddy bottom of the Mackahatchee, he marked where he had searched and where not. Gripping the rope with one hand he felt through the mud; with the other he communicated with Gator by tugging. Some days, especially after a rain, the current carried him away and he had to struggle against it to keep track of his search area.

At the end of the day, he crawled up into his tree, exhausted, which led to luxurious sleep and for the first time in years, dreams that energized and didn't drain him. Best of all, he envisioned the end, finding the evidence to catch Big Rig's killer. Gator encouraged and convinced him he had made the right choice.

One night around three, something brushed his leg, then his mid-section.

Drowsy, he spoke without opening his eyes. "Skade, I thought we . . ."

A vise squeezed out his breath and squelched his voice.

"A-a-argh!"

Twenty-eight feet of reticulated python coiled around him, pulses rippling through it, a steady, sequential, contiguous wave, cinching tighter and tighter. He sucked in breath, but none came. Pushing with his hand, he forced a tiny breathing space, but the snake squeezed again, pinned and crushed his arms. He struggled, pulled them out. Pounding had no effect. It was a flesh-plastered brown and orange barber's pole, a helix twisting up-ward, a muscled golden body burning in a sea of night.

He recalled Gator telling him: "It doesn't suffocate you. It cuts off the blood supply. The heart literally doesn't have enough strength to push against the pressure."

His vision blurred as his head drooped and consciousness dripped out of him like leaky faucet.

He tried to scream, but his voice was too weak.

Flailing around, his hand struck metal.

His Glock!

Getting it out of his holster was a struggle. He couldn't aim it, so he just began firing.

Within seconds the camp exploded, shouting and screaming.

Gator and Skade climbed into his tree.

"It's Bev!" Skade shouted. "Gator, my machete! He doesn't have much time!"

Gator leapt down, sprinted back to their cabin, returned with a machete.

Skade found the head. "Sorry, Bev," she said, as she laid the blade just back of the neck. When she struck, blood spurted out across a stack of Greek books in the corner.

Gradually, the pressure subsided.

Blue-faced, he struggled out, stumbled, and fell. Gator helped him sit down.

His chin trembled as waves of nervous pulses passed through his body, head to foot, breath returning in hesitant waves like an estranged old friend.

Skade gave him a bottle of mango juice and the two local teens Gator employed as gofers struggled to drag the snake out of the tree. After fifteen minutes the beast thumped in the sand.

Gator squatted over him and ran his fingers over his rib cage.

"I don't think any are broken, but let's head into town tomorrow and have 'em looked at. Plus, we need to check for salmonella. Watch your poop the next couple of days."

"I get a salmonella check once a month," Skade said, squatting, as she screwed the cap back on the mango juice.

Gator bounced around his room spraying with disinfectant, wearing only skin-tight spandex shorts, barefoot, his long hair bound in a man bun.

"How're you feeling?" Skade asked, moving closer and lowering her voice.

"There's skip and nimble in me yet, but my ribs are throbbing."

"Hon, you're spraying too much," she said, waving her hand in front of her face.

Gator stopped, looked around. "Too much?"

She nodded, pinching her nose to show how bad it smelled.

One of the teen gofers popped his head in. "They were aimin' to get at them coons," he said to Skade.

"Who?" HB asked.

"Wild dogs," Gator said. "Skade keeps raccoons in cages to feed the snakes. Every so often we get a pack of dogs that rip into the cages. That's how Bev got out. The dogs tore through the bamboo and left a hole. It happened once before about two years ago."

Skade made a face. "Plus, it's shedding season. Snakes get aggressive when they lose skin."

"I guess it's time to think about a Rio Grande," Gator said, looking at his wife. "I hate it. They cost like the dickens. Plus, they look like a penitentiary."

Skade handed HB a stack of books, spattered in snake blood. "Sorry, I should have moved her head."

He tried to smile, but his face muscles weren't working yet.

"Yeah," Gator said, watching him struggle. "Get a good night's sleep. Your face will be working tomorrow."

He opened the book on top of the stack.

"What language is that?" Gator asked.

"Greek. Maximus the Confessor. It's appropriate. Bev had her head chopped off and Maximus had his hands and tongue chopped off."

Later he phoned Rosie:

Rosie: I'm driving down, now!"

HB: No, you're not. I've got a few sore ribs and maybe the runs for a day or two. Nothing more.

Rosie: If a Mack truck hit you, you'd say it was just a scratch.

HB: Look, I'm close to the end of the course. In a week we head up to the Caloosahatchee which Gator says is my Final Exam. Then, I'm coming home.

Rosie: And when you dive in the Ocopeeco, suppose you don't find anything?

HB: Guess I'll take Sheriff Brown up on his offer. There is one thing, though . . .

Rosie: What?

HB: Gator said wild dogs were after the racoons Skade keeps in the python pen. The dogs tore a hole in the bamboo web the pen is made of. That's how Bev got out.

Rosie: So?

HB: I was in their barn a few days ago. It's decked out with security cameras, ADT and all kinds of critters in cages, including racoons. Yet, she left one cage with three racoons in it inside the python pen.

Rosie: Oh, boy. She was luring the dogs in. A woman scorned. I doubt she's been turned down—ever.

HB: I don't know . . .

Rosie: Up until now I haven't been worried. Not worried worried.

HB: And now?

Rosie: Finish the course. Then come home.

* * * *

The last night before the river trip he was roused from sleep by shouting in between dish ware breaking. Two silhouettes against the shade over the window of their bedroom. Arms flailing and heads bobbing. A few phrases. "the last time," and "irresponsible" and "your mother's money".

Apart from God who knew what was really going on between those two? The dormant violence in camp was thick as gnats and since the couple wasn't married, what held them together other than the by-now-diminishing pleasures of the flesh? Like the old hippie communes the camp offered a paradise for any free spirit yearning to throw off the shackles of conventional morality. Remote, wild, sensual breeze nightly, moonlit camping in scanty clothes. Who knew how many lovers Skade had brought into camp while Gator stayed away for weeks, leaving his woman with Beverly and the pythons as chaperons? Worse, he was certain Gator realized his woman had "a thing" for him, the out-of-work chief from Ocopeeco.

After the couple quieted down, he drifted off, but he could still feel the shadow life of the place floating above it like a dying queen carried away to her final rest on a slow, solemn funerary barge.

Chapter Fifteen

The evening before the Caloosahatchee trip he and Gator travelled in separate trucks into Naples, where they hit a watering hole, the Caloosa Booze Barn, and a sea of vehicles, everything from glittering Corvettes to ancient VW surfer vans with rusted out tags and fishing poles strapped to the side. The barn itself was a large antique structure made from cypress log, a remodeled train depot, high, ribbed ceiling, hardwood floor and crude tables teaming with students, workmen, lawyers. The name 'Caloosa,' came from a tribe of war-mongering Native Americans, long since erased from history's blackboard.

The room was layered with smoke. Gator found a table, oily, pony-tailed men and sun-grizzled women with everything from silver rings to sea shells over their belly buttons, some toting holstered pistols.

HB was left alone to drink and read his Maximus, blood splotched over the bright red title: Quaestiones ad Thalassium.

His waitress brought him a pitcher of beer; he requested PBR, ice cold.

When she set down the beer, she pointed to his book:"Is that blood?"

"Sure is."

"Interesting. Maximus was tortured for opposing the heretical Monothelites."

The music was so loud he thought he'd misheard.

She shouted, "I said, Maximus the Confessor was tortured for opposing the heretical Monothelites!"

She was medium height, long blond hair, tinted Ben Franklin glasses, a winsome smile, but crumbs of icing in the corner of her mouth.

"Birthday cake," she said, wiping, embarrassed. "One of the dishwashers turned eighteen."

"How do you know Maximus?"

"I teach classics at Miami U."

They chatted until she began glancing around. "Look, I'm off in half an hour. Can you stick around until then?"

When she returned, she had put her hair up and wore a rumpled black pants suit and carrying a bag of books.

After she sat down, she lit up. "You mind?"

"No."

She leaned her head back against the high head rest. Her eyes grew languid as she blew a few smoke rings.

"Yeah, the byzantine world of academia holds me in fee. I'm an Instructor, translate 'chattel slave,' chained to intro Latin and Greek, hungover, illiterate freshmen. Occa-a-a-sionally, the eunuch oligarchs that sit on their burnished thrones on the third floor, toss me a crumb from linguistics or art history to keep me from bolting to another school. They keep telling me how much potential I have and how well I engage the students. Bull. They just don't want to go to the trouble of another search for another slave to replace me.

"Most of my customers here read Hustler. You may be the first who reads a pre-Reformation church father."

HB summarized his situation.

"Wow," she said, "a police chief/preacher. Do you pray for the bad guys?"

"I do."

She pounded her cigarette in a glass ash tray. "So, when you find this bit of evidence, this weapon on the river bottom, that will solve your crime, and everything will return to normal?"

He finished his beer and she hopped up to fetch him a fresh cold one.

"Yeah, I do hope things return to normal."

Her lips drooped. "Hope that works out for you. Hasn't for me."

"How so?"

"My doctorate was supposed to open up doors; instead, it opened up one, endlessly revolving door, two years teaching here, two years teaching there and so on for the last ten years."

"I'm sorry," he said. "I bet you're a fabulous teacher."

"Thanks."

She touched his Maximus. "So, you prefer later Greek to Plato, and Aeschylus."

"I do."

"But the real gold's in early Attic."

"I'm not prospecting. What I'm looking for is more precious than silver."

She wrenched her face. "Uh oh, I smell the rank odor of a sermon slouching toward our booth. My cue to exit."

"No sermon." He held up his hands. "I promise."

"So, for you, when Maximus is talking about becoming one with God—that's not just an antiquated idea somebody has worked into a dissertation. You actually believe it?"

"Yes."

She stared at him, shaking her head, as if she were seeing him for the first time. It made him squirm. Here he was sitting in a bacchanal in the Booze Barn and a strange woman approaches him from nowhere and peeks into his private, esoteric word of Greek thought and faith.

"What?" he said.

"Sorry, I have never met a scholar of ancient Greek who actually believed something. Most of the Greek profs I know are prissy, narrow-shouldered geeks who wear clownish bow ties below plaster of Paris smirks. They wouldn't set foot in a Unitarian Church, not to mention a Baptist."

"Well, let's take Maximus, here. You may think his ideas are antique, but he refused to renounce his faith and he lost his tongue and his hands. Anyone, atheist or believer, has to admire that. What would you give up your tongue and hands for?"

She stamped out her cigarette and swallowed a half dozen mints. "Not much."

"Is there nothing in your life you care deeply about?"

Her face contorted as she rolled her head around. "I worry a lot. Don't eat for days."

"Well, that's not exactly what I meant, but why do you worry?"

"Afraid I'm going to get fatter."

"Fatter? You have a fine figure. Didn't you notice the guys in here giving you the once over?" He omitted her blood shot eyes.

"My Dachshund has a higher IQ than this crowd. Thanks for trying, but I'm a fat slob."

He bit his tongue, trying to remember what he'd learned in counseling classes.

"What's wrong, preacher," she said, "out of pastoral cliches? I'll help: I'm OK and You're OK."

"Oh, come on!"

"Or how about 'Let's get in touch with your inner child'"

"My inner child's a brat."

"Or: how does that make you feel?"

"Please," he said, holding up both hands in a No Mas gesture.

He related his battle with PTSD after Afghanistan.

Her face slipped out of its sarcastic sneer. "Wow," she leaned forward and lowered her voice, "have the flashbacks stopped?" She was genuinely interested.

"They still stalk me now and then, especially when I'm stressed."

"Yeah, stress gets my bulimia working overtime. Brittle skin, nails. Even teeth trouble. I see a therapist, after my dentist. One day I'm going to switch that and see if it helps my mood and my teeth. My therapist is good. But my heart's not in it."

Her lids sagged.

"Don't get much sleep working two jobs?" he asked.

She smiled, feebly.

"It's tough. Three days ago, after a faculty meeting where the non-tenured instructors were made to feel lower than Job's slug, I scarfed down a dozen Krispy Kremes and a gallon of Ben and Jerry's Chubby Hubby. Afterwards I puked my inner child out in our unisex bathroom."

"What did your therapist say?"

"Out of town. Every six months she's off to Kiawah Island or Hot Springs. But she can't fool ol' Cassie. She's hooking up with some raunchy rich CEO. I . . . right now . . . I feel . . . kind . . . of . . .

Her head hit the table THUNK!

He leapt up to lift her head, bringing her gently to his shoulder.

"Cassie!"

"Ungh . . . " Her lips parted, and her eyes rolled back in her head. He slapped her cheek.

Nothing.

Gator saw what happened. With a cigar stub in the corner of his mouth, he rushed over. "You slip her a roofie?"

"No. She's anorexic. Is there a hospital nearby?"

"NCH Baker in Naples."

* * * *

An EMS unit's red light rotated in the porte cochere as HB carried Cassie into the emergency entrance where he paused to decipher the cluttered marquee.

A pale, rail-thin orderly, flicked his ash into the cigarette bin.

"Hey, cowboy, follow me."

They were given a small room.

HB stepped out while nurses came in and out to undress the patient and get her into bed.

When he stepped back in, Cassie's long, blond hair flared out on the bed as she rolled her head back and forth.

The cubby hole had room enough for a bed and one chair. On one wall hung a colorful laminated chart showing with arrows the route blood takes on its journey through the body. Boxes of rubber gloves, gauze, swabs. On another wall a bright blue and orange college poster depicted a U of Florida quarterback, set in the pocket, his arm cocked, his eyes lasered on a receiver.

He texted Rosie and Gator. Rosie would understand. She knew his heart for the broken never went off duty. But Gator? The man was giving him a big discount for his world-renowned diving course. And here he was, the student, missing his final exam. For what? To stay by the bedside of a tart-tongued, over-educated anorexic.

The doc parted the curtain secluding Cassie's nook. Lyle Lovett hair, brown beard, high forehead, sleep deprived eyes.

The man attached electrodes to her naked upper body without a hint of emotion.

Averting his eyes, HB grinned at the comments she would crack at the man were she conscious.

He was all business. Didn't even glance at HB. His lips tight and his hands working quickly.

As the EKG ran, she woke up.

"What the hell . . . "

"You're in NCH Baker, Ms. Martin. In Naples. You passed out and this gentleman brought you in. Has your anorexia resulted in a-fib episodes before?"

As she came to herself, she realized she was talking with someone who understood her illness.

"For the past few years."

She looked down at her chest and grimaced.

"Again, with the drab gray electrodes? Look I realize you medico's don't get out in the sunlight much, but why not spruce things up, lavender or pink? Or—oh, my God—go hog wild, two colors on the same pad."

The doc did not smile, but his eyes met hers.

Cassie screwed her face up and glanced at HB, leaning against the wall.

Grinning at her, he shook his head.

After the doc read the EKG printout, he turned back to HB. "Anorexia causes the heart to eat itself," he said, softly.

"Thanks, doc," she said. "Where'd you learn your bedside manner, Charles Manson U.?"

For the first time, he smiled. "Am I telling you anything you don't already know?"

"Nope," she said. "We toilet huggers are a well-informed lot."

"You're in a-fib now," the doc said.

"I can't tell."

"Some can't. I've ordered a bed for you for overnight. Just to be safe."

"Oh, boy, hospital food!" She turned her head to the side, teared up.

The doc looked down at her. A fatherly smile appeared.

"Does this mean . . . " she whispered, without looking at him.

"A pacemaker?" he said.

"Yeah."

"Maybe." He placed his hand on her shoulder. "We'll take good care of you."

Then he left.

"Tell you a sob story," she said and held her hand out to HB. He took it as he pulled up the chair.

"I'm from Norman, Oklahoma. Apart from worshiping Sooner football, my family attended church five times a week. When I was little, I loved the church, the lemonade and the cookies and the singing and all the talk about how Jesus loves the little children, but one day in Sunday school a girl called me "pudgy". Her dad was assistant coach for the Sooners' football team, so she had to be right. But nobody had ever called me that before. Went home, spent the whole day in front a mirror, turning, twisting, and trying to see myself as others saw me. I looked at school, at church, at the mall. All the pretty people, all the important people were thin.

"I began to hate fat people. One day in the summer before the eighth grade I starved myself for three days, didn't tell anybody. I lost five pounds. I thought: Wow! I can do this. Unfortunately, for the next three days I gobbled down everything in sight and gained it all back. That's when I saw a movie in PE about a girl who puked a lot. The film was warning us what not to do. But I figured it looked like a good way to lose weight, so I took the film to heart and started puking whenever and wherever I could. My senior year I concluded the people in my church were all hypocrites. They excluded gays, there were no blacks, and adultery was rampant. And I knew if my parents or their sanctified mannequin friends found out about my condition, they would stick me away in the Undesirable File, just like all the others. So, from then on, I felt like a spy. Watched what I said, watched who I talked to. And eventually, when I got to OU, I realized church folks think the Bible's a rule book. Do this, God loves you; do that, he hates you. Snip, snip, snip. I was done."

A nurse came in with a rolling IV cart.

Cassie closed her eyes. "Oh, God! Do I have to?"

The short black woman with orange-dyed hair and spunky swagger wrapped a rubber hose around Cassie's naked arm with the skill of a calf-rope artist. She thumped the arm hard with her middle finger.

"Naw, baby," she said, "you don't have to. You can get up and walk outta here right now, but when you pass out again and wind up right back here—guess what? We'll hook you right back up to an IV. Just close your eyes and dream about Brad Pitt."

"Do you dream about Brad Pitt?"

The nurse grinned. "I don't mind the white meat."

Cassie opened her mouth in fake shock. "Why, Miss Fahrquart, you are talking mis-ce-ge-na-tion! I'll have to notify my re-tard cousin in the Knights of the Albino Knuckledraggers and we'll just see about that!"

As the nurse shook her head, laughing, a gold tooth peeked out and she found a vein. She eased in the needle and taped up a portal before the patient knew it.

"Sister, you are good!" Cassie said, looking down at her arm.

"Piece of cake, baby. The real test comes when a three hundred pound ex-middle linebacker from Naples High battles his way in on ecstasy and it takes half a dozen orderlies to pin him down so I can stick him."

After the nurse left, Cassie's face went cold and blank as if the young woman with her IV cart had rolled away the joy.

"I'm so scared," she whispered to HB.

He took her hand. She squeezed it tight and put her other one on top. Her eyes grew larger as they filled with tears.

"Do they let you smoke in hospitals? I could use a smoke."

"I don't think so. Look, is there anyone I can call. A colleague in classics, a friend, another waitress?"

She took a deep breath. Her lips pursed showing dried flakes of red around the edge. "No colleagues in classics, no friends, but there is someone."

"Hand me my purse."

She scrolled through her contacts and showed him a number. "She's the manager at the Booze Barn. She was a gender studies major so we stand around when it's slow and consider who on the staff should undergo sex reassignment surgery."

After the orderly rolled her away, he made the call.

*   *   *   *

During the drive back to the Thousand Isles, he passed a Lutheran Church, an A frame structure with a glass front overshadowed by a concrete cross. Its silhouette against the star speckled sky called out to him. He turned around, parked and pulled a thick blanket from the back seat. A long, shell-studded walk crunched under his boots until he reached the cross. There, he knelt. The blanket cushioned his knees and he rested his elbows on the bench the church had thoughtfully provided for petitioners.

He prayed for Cassie, Skade, and Gator, three broken pilgrims entangled in spiritual traps, mostly of their own making. The DSM5 Handbook of 297 disorders doesn't included the unclean spirits the Lord drives out of men and women in the Gospels. Cassie and Skade and Gator were enthralled by such spirits, who intended to destroy their host. He launched his prayers against them.

After a half hour, his body ached, so he leaned back against the bench. The breeze rolling up from the not too distant gulf fluttered through his beard. Cars whizzed by on the highway, blurs of light speeding into the darkness, the big trucks grinding their gears and whining, the speedsters weaving in and out of traffic as if a six thousand pound vehicle were a toy. What did Rosie call them? "Spielzeug?" Sports car Spielzeugs.

Big Rig's murder had set up such a domino effect of events in his life. And not all were bad. Look at Lurleen Scruggs, donating money to Rosie's favorite cause and the high school and a refuge for abused children. As Augustine said: God makes good to come out of evil. The whole Christian world arose from the tragic fall of Rome.

He nodded and laid his head on the bench.

In his night vision Jesus passed among the pythons. He carried a lamb which he laid down in front of a twenty foot snake. The gargantuan creature, massive and slow, inched forward; its head hugged the sand.

"What do you see, brother serpent?" the Lord asked.

"A lamb, Lord. A fine meal."

"And will you dine today?"

"I thought I was hungry. But now . . . "

The Lord stroked the massive, elongated body. The creature was transformed into a lion that nudged the Master's leg before it lay down beside the lamb, crossed its furry paws and gazed with affection at its wooly, prophetic partner.

The Christ passed through the python fence into a bedroom where Skade and Gator stood, hands and arms down by their sides in a gesture of defeat. Pictures of bleakness, who had wandered long in a dry and bitter land where there is no water. Rags clothed their bodies, their hair was stringy and long, and it dangled to the waist.

Above them a bright ring appeared, embracing the room with its light. The couple looked up at it, blinking, the pain in their faces blurring as the ring shrank and slipped onto Skade's finger. Her come-hither eyes and libertine lips were transformed into those of an innocent girl. The Lord took his place before them. When he placed his palms on Gator's shoulders, the wild jungle look eased into a man at peace with himself, firm-jawed, and a freshly - razored face. As if for the first time, the pair kissed.

* * * *

He passed his final. Goofy Gator bounced around, pulled out a fresh box of cigars, beaming and proud.

He reached up to thump HB on his chest. "It's your athleticism. Your balance and the leg strength—most new divers take years to develop those skills."

"I had a fine teacher."

Gator grinned and nodded. "Yeah, that, too."

He wrapped a rope around his shoulder. With the Caloosahatchee behind them, broader and faster than the river at camp, a wavy V of pelicans winged its way overhead. Behind the birds the evening sky filtered a fanfare of red and gold, now bursting out unfettered, now shushing itself and fading as if toying with the clouds.

Gator heaved the rope into the back of his truck where it landed with a thunk. He put his hands on his hips and looked up at his student, squinting as if in pain. "You probably figured out the missus and I are diving some deep waters. Current's trying to pull us apart."

"I know a fine therapist in Tampa."

HB pulled out his wallet and handed Gator a card, a Catholic priest.

"He a real therapist? I don't want one of them flaky astrologer types Skade likes."

"Father Greg is the real deal. You'll like him. He plays a mean game of racquetball. But . . . "

"But what?"

"Skade may not like the fact that he's Catholic."

Gator scratched his face. "Maybe not. But, hell, it's worth a try."

* * * *

As he headed up I-75, he got a text from Cassie Martin. "Looks like I'm getting a pacemaker, but hey, a little help from a friend is good, right, even if it's a high tech inanimate friend. BTW, remember the doc from ER? Lyle Lovett hair? Guess what? He asked me out! I wore a dress! HB, he is old school. All dressed up, went to a private country club where he's a member (I'm thinking: Is he rolling in dough?) and we danced. I felt like I was in a forties flick. I was Bacall, and he was Bogie. So anyway, I got that going on, plus, the sexless oligarchs on third floor Classics have decided to give me their much-beloved Catullus class. La, dee dah! The old fart who taught it for decades can't climb the steps to the third floor anymore. And he's so old he probably turns ten shades of red when they read Catullus's bi-sexual bombs. Man, now I have to pretend to be a real professor, stop buying my duds at Walmart and curb my tongue and go for tenure and all that. It's all your fault, you know. No, seriously, thanks a bunch, my old Maximus man. You know, I'm gonna tell you this and I don't want you to get the big head, but I bought a copy of the Mystagogia on Amazon. This summer I'm gonna try to figure out what he means by becoming one with God. Sounds kinda loosy goosy to me. Talk like that back in Norman OK is more dangerous that sexting. I'm sure my old Baptist minister would think Maximus the Confessor is part of a communist plot. You did that, HB Alpata, you sneaky evangelist. Anyway, this'll be my last missal. Good luck with your dive. Love and kisses, Cass."

He said a prayer of thanksgiving. More good emerging from the bad. Now, if he could only uncover a bit of incriminating evidence on the bottom of the Ocopeeco.

Chapter Sixteen

While HB unloaded the ropes and weights from the truck—Gator had gifted him a complete set, old and frayed—Mico sank his bare toes into the river mud. Behind him, the water ran high and red and faster than normal from a week of afternoon rains.

"I love mud!" the boy yelled.

He poked his index finger between his toes, brought up a dripping gob he streaked his forehead and cheeks with.

On the bank, leaning against a pine, Davy looked up from his biography of Jerry Rice. "You look like one of your bellicose ancestors."

"Belli-what?"

"It's a Jerry Rice word. An NFL player has to have a bellicose heart or a bellicose mind. I figure it's something to do with fighting."

"Bellicose, from the Latin bellum, war," HB said as he stripped off his clothes. "Not to be confused with bellum meaning beautiful, which the French picked up, as in 'Elle est belle.'"

The boys exchanged knowing glances but knew better than to roll their eyes.

Mico grinned, showing off his biceps: "The bellicose blood of my ancestors flows in my veins."

Stripped down to cut off jeans, HB dragged the gear to the river's edge. "That blood include the half gallon of Rocky Road you devoured last night?"

"What!" Davy yelled as he sat up and pointed to his buddy. "You ate Rocky Road and didn't call me?"

"It was an emergency, bro." Mico reached up from the water for the ropes his Dad handed him. "Mom's on another diet. I had to save her from temptation."

HB grinned. "Davy, if you buy that, I'll have to tell coach about your weed habit."

The wide receiver threw up his hands. "Chief, I don't smoke weed!" The boy looked from Mico to HB, beside himself. "I've never smoked weed! Chief Alpata, please!"

Mico and HB sniggered. Playing football and following good dietary practices were serious for Davy. He ate, drank, and slept rules and regulations, good diet and adequate sleep.

"What!" he said. "Why are y'all laughing?"

When they finally bent over, cackling, Davy got it, but it took several minutes before the shock wore off, and he could settle back to the greatest wide receiver ever.

"Guess I'm too serious, sometimes," he said. "That's what mom says."

"Listen," HB said to Davy, "I'm sure when he was your age, Jerry Rice was just as serious. You keep on just the way you are, but it's good to see you can still take a joke."

Mico leapt out of the water and knelt in prayer in front of his buddy. "Oh, holy St. Davy, please show me how to be such a serious, straight shooter and how to get such a fine looking chick as Lisa."

"Put a sock in it, Bullet Boy," Davy said.

"Bullet boy?" HB said.

"'cause he throws so hard," Davy said. "Me and one other guy are the only two receivers can catch Mico's rockets."

HB squinted into the cloudless blue and two buzzards soaring in a slow circle. "We've got company."

"Some dead critter," Davy said, hand over his eyes.

"What was it?" Mico asked.

"'Coon or a dog. I passed it on the way in. It was mangled so bad, hard to tell what it was."

"It's a jungle out there," Mico said, half joking.

His Dad motioned for him to get in. "Okay, Tarzan, tell me what your game plan is."

Mico rattled off the jackstay sequence, step by step. For three days they worked the operation on land until HB felt certain the boy had it down pat.

As they eased into the water, swimming with the ropes and weights, the judge's white SUV eased up beside HB's truck. Dressed in madras Bermuda shorts, his pale, milk bottle calves, the judge waddled out to the water's edge, unfolded a chair and took a seat. He pulled out his cell camera.

"I figured we could use some documentary proof showing where and when you found whatever it is you gonna find."

HB noted a plastic hospital band on the judge's wrist.

"ER visit," the judge said. "My blood pressure decided to launch a moon shot last night. Took 'em two hours to get it back into the earth's gravitational pull."

"Maybe you should slow down," Mico said.

The judge gave HB a dead pan look. "Out of the mouth of ninth graders."

The divers went to work while the judge flipped through his phone and Davy read about Jerry Rice's grueling off season exercise and diet regimen: kale, skinless chicken, and protein shakes between painful sprints from the bottom of the stands to the top and back, over and over. Davy bit into his power bar as Mico was swept off his course and struggled like a puppy to get back into position.

Davy left, and the judge strolled to the water's edge, peered out at the pair, as they bobbed and dove and fought the frothy, red current. He made a call, then claimed Davy's still warm spot under the pine. Within minutes, he was snoozing, his breath fluttering his fluffy moustache and drool snaking down his chin.

After two hours, the divers dragged themselves out, beat from battling the current, and empty-handed.

* * * *

HB drove up to his Dad's where the full time nurse greeted him at the door, a chunky black woman, shy eyes, a gentle smile, and a growth of curly, black hair down her jaw line. She led him into the bedroom where, at Pain's request, a dozen candles burned to keep away the bothas.

He pulled up a straw-bottom chair, which he sat in backwards.

The earth was drawing his Dad's cheeks deeper into cadaverous depth.

The old man grinned up at his boy.

"You look anxious," he whispered.

"Just the usual," HB said. "Catching the bad guys."

He stroked the feeble hand, its knotty veins, and brown spots. It was like a fatigued animal, barely able to crawl. Coming here always made him feel like a child again, all the confusion about White vs. Creek, Christian vs. Pagan. Would these tugs of emotional war ever cease? He and Rosie had tried to shield Mico from this, but had they succeeded?

On the table sat a cold bowl of chicken noodle soup and a spotless spoon. HB glanced at them but chose not to comment.

"Ibofanga is calling a bi-i-ig council," Pain said. He looked into his son's eyes. "He's asked me to stand and be counted. It's quite an honor."

"They're recognizing your faith, over the years, to the whole nation."

Pain's eyes glistened. The corners of his lips lifted. "You think so?"

The son pressed his Dad's brown hand to his cheek. "I know so."

With his other hand, Pain strained to reach for his son, but his arm trembled, so the nurse helped. As the father touched his son's face and beard, the two men embraced and clung to one another.

Tears welled in HB's eyes.

Afterwards, on the porch, drinking coffee, the nurse put her hand on HB's arm. "Chief," she whispered, "your Dad is torn. He wants to join his wife, but he also wants to stay and see your name cleared."

"He knows?"

"Asks me about it every day."

He grinned. "Well, if my problems are what's keeping him alive, that's a good thing, isn't it?"

She nodded. "I think so."

The next day, he and Mico tried again. This time they counted ten yards from their point of entry the previous day, a point they marked with a pine wood stob, dated and pounded into the bank. They brought up: a mud-clogged Millennial Falcon, a weed eater, an ancient baseball glove from the days when the four fingers were not joined at the tips by a leather thong, and seventeen golf balls. Mico brought down an oil drum—there were so many beer cans. Standing in the shallows, he chunked them in.

They sat, dangling their legs off the tailgate, eating Rosie's tuna sandwiches, laced today with grape slices and almond slivers. The gray gloom of morning was under assault by the dayseye sun who peered through at intervals like celestial flashlight beams.

Mico had bound his hair in a man bun. HB noticed the new whiskers.

"Are you shaving?" he asked.

His son grinned. "Not yet. Davy's been at it a year. Says it's a pain."

"It is a pain, but it shows God is making you a man. Plus, a beard used to be a sign of strength and wisdom."

"That why you wear one?"

"Maybe, once. These days it's just a habit."

His son stared at him.

"What?" HB said.

"I'm trying to imagine you without it."

"Have to ask Rosie first," HB said.

"Really?"

"Of course, she's got a say in everything I do. Wouldn't have it any other way."

He hopped off the tailgate and the truck bounced up.

Mico looked off to the side, hesitant, wanted to ask something but didn't know how.

HB grinned. "Okay, what is it? You've got that look . . . "

"Dad, the older players on the varsity team talk a lot about guys who're controlled by their girlfriend, or wife, in your case. They use a word, it's a pretty bad word so I'm not gonna say it . . . "

"I know what it is," HB said. "Heard it all my life. Some men never grow out of thinking they can't be tamed."

"Really?"

"Your Mom and I live under a divine covenant."

"Is that what happened to Big Rig?"

"What do you mean?" HB asked.

"He broke his covenant?"

"Something like that."

* * * *

Rosie poured coffee into his mug at breakfast as he relayed Gator's conclusions.

He watched her move and marveled at the way her grace never left her, cooking, grading papers. There was about her an aura he could never define, nor did he want to. Defining it would defame it. He just reveled in it and gave thanks.

"Does Gator think you didn't do it right?"

"Just the opposite. But then . . . "

"But then . . . what?"

"He says . . . maybe there's nothing there."

He spoke softly, eyes lowered.

Rosie saw how down he was. Finding the evidence: that had been his goal. No, it wasn't just a goal. It was the weight of their common life there together, the way to keep from leaving Ocopeeco, his home, where he was born and where his family roots were, everything.

Before responding, she wanted to gather her thoughts. What she said now was critical.

She turned to wash her hands. These days, as home schoolteacher, she wore flip flops, jeans, and a blouse tied at the waist revealing her navel.

"You're the sexy teacher I never had," he said as she sat down.

She reached for his hand.

"I have a question," she said.

"What?"

"Have you prayed about it?"

Her words worked on him like an old familiar hymn. He raised his head, gazing at her and grinning from ear to ear, which caused the wrinkles at his eyes to leap out like fleshy sparklers.

"Physician, . . . " he began.

"Heal thyself."

* * * *

By the time he arrived that evening squibs of fading sunlight eked through the sanctuary windows, their intensity against the encroaching darkness like liquid gold portending all the blessings that royal metal embodied, nobility, honor, and wealth. Even in his tiny, attenuated church, all the riches of heaven came and gave counsel.

Some stores on River Street kept their neon on till nine: the flashing CLEAN JEANS, JEFFORDS HARDWARE, but then, darkness. It was a blessing to live in a place where folks shut down at night and there were no stores of any kind that defied the sun and moon and all the forces of nature by staying open.

He found his pew, the one by the pillar underneath the balcony, a reminder that the church was built before the Civil War. He suspected his congregation gave it little thought, but he did, every time he mounted the old, creaky pulpit. His 19th century predecessors faced a balcony of people who weren't allowed on the main floor: They were black.

Legs together, he leaned back against the hard wood, reining in his thoughts to prepare for silence. The soul that possesses it carries it everywhere. The soul that lacks it finds it nowhere. To enter silence, he explained to Rosie, it's not enough to stop the movement of lips and thoughts. That's only being quiet, which is a condition of silence. Silence itself is a word and a thought into which all words and thought are concentrated. When she told him she didn't understand, he realized that during his trauma in Afghanistan and his subsequent recovery, he'd received a gift. Maybe he would never be able to explain it. But it was important to try because he wanted his precious life companion to share it.

After an hour, he offered prayers of petition and left.

That evening after supper, Davy called on their land line.

"Davy, I'll get Mico. He's battling binomial equations."

"Chief, I really wanted to talk with you."

"With me? What about?"

"Well, I wanted to apologize. I know how hard you and Mico have been working, and I didn't mean to do it. It just sorta happened. I mean I just went down the river to that same tree, and I was reading my Jerry Rice book, and I was just at the section where he talks about what it felt like the first time he played a game in the NFL. I mean that's a big deal! He was so nervous and all. Shoot! I'd be nervous, too. Heck, I can't imagine what it must feel like . . . "

"Davy . . . "

"Yessir, of course. Well, it was hot. So, I'm sitting there thinking if I should do it . . . "

"Do what?" HB asked.

"Jump in."

"Did you?"

"I did! Got up, right there, stripped and jumped in. I've never done anything like that before, I mean real spontaneous and wild. I'm so sorry . . . "

"Davy!"

"Chief, I stepped on it!"

"What?"

"The knife, Sir. I found the knife!"

* * * *

He identified it on Amazon: Yarenh Best Chef knife, 5 piece set, Damascus stainless steel, Full Tang Galbergia wooden handle. $245.00. The steel was partially wimpled, giving that part of the blade a rough feel like a cheese grater. It looked to be the middle one in the set, but he needed to fit the knife into its wooden case to determine if he had a match.

Who in Ocopeeco would spend that much on a set of knives? Not any of the working class folks, which was ninety-five per cent of the town. Who was a foodie? Grace Daniels grew her own carrots and tomatoes, but she also economized like the most frugal child of The Great Depression. Made her own clothes. Made butter, bread. She would never pay two hundred forty-five dollars for knives.

Aubrey? Not likely. He'd been inside the painter's kerosene and oil smelling pig pen. Even Lizard Little was neater. Aubrey lived on Krispy Kremes and pizza, always with lots of mushrooms. "Every mushroom bears in it's flesh-aping body the seeds of Blakean vision." No gourmet knives for him. No, but there was a place where, on a Saturday night, you could buy a T bone steak after you'd put away a six pack or a filet mignon after you'd tanked up on tequila, a place where expensive steak knives would not only come in handy, they'd be downright essential.

* * * *

Roxanne's dishwasher called him around 10:00 PM Saturday night just as he and Rosie were about to get into bed. A fight between two kaolin workers, spilled out into the parking lot, cleared the bar.

Roxanne was hurt.

He got dressed and headed down.

When he arrived, two men, standing but swaying, were drunk-slugging inside a circle of their beer-holding buddies, still swinging but long past the point of doing damage.

He was watching the dance of time-tamed warriors, middle-aged, blubbery, still clinging to a movie-made image they could only pay homage to when their conscious, salary-earning selves were dismissed by Anheuser and Busch.

"One more, Robbie! C'mon, you got one more in you!"

Robbie blinked, hair hanging down over his eyes.

"You losin' your Dickies!" his buddy said, pointing and giggling.

While Robbie struggled to get his Dickies up, the other guy raised his index finger:

"You fat tub of guts!" he shouted.

"One Eyed Jack!" Robbie's buddy shouted. "But . . . that ain't what Brando said, is it?"

He rubbed his unshaven chin, thoughtfully. "What the hell did Brando say?"

HB grabbed Robbie's arm. "I don't know what Brando said, but Rob bie's wife said if he's not home in ten minutes he's sleeping in the truck for two weeks."

Robbie threw his arms around HB. "Chief! I'm glad to see ya.." He pounded the lawman's chest with his finger. "Hey, I'm pullin' for you ol' buddy. Ol' Robbie's got your back. They can't throw my old buddy out like the dishwater, no siree!"

Against a background of cat-calls and beer born obscenities, HB loaded him into the truck.

Within minutes he was back, but this time the parking lot was empty.

He found her inside, perched atop a high bar stool, one elbow on the bar, the other hand pressing an ice pack to her bruised face. Against the wall her juke box played as her blond head bobbed in time with the music.

She wore blue velvet, bluer than velvet were her eyes

The image of loneliness: a woman sitting in the dark listening to a heart-tugging tune for the lost. She had caused so much discord in his family, but it was hard not to feel sorry for her.

He slipped onto the stool behind her. "You interrupt a punch?"

Her head stopped bobbing.

"Who called you?" she said, turning back towards him.

"Your dishwasher."

"He shouldn't have done that."

He surveyed the room. Tables were overturned; Bar-B-Que was smeared over the concrete floor like roadkill; and the buxom brunette on the beer lamp that hung from the ceiling was missing teeth.

"Those two idiots need to pay for this."

Keeping her back to him, she said: "Go home."

She slipped off her stool and passed into the kitchen where she sat down and opened her laptop. Her screen saver leapt up: a black weightlifter, glistening with grease, arms and legs laced with veins like vines, flexing his biceps and leering out at the viewer between long, dangling dreads.

"So, you don't want to press charges?" he said.

Without once looking at him, she yelled: "I said go home! Can't you understand English!"

The next day, Sunday, he waited until the afternoon before he drove his truck around to the side of her place and parked behind a massive clump of plum bushes. Her two story building housed the bar in brown brick on the bottom, her apartment in white clapboard on top.

Across the entrance, R-O-X-A-N-N-E-S in neon. By the side entrance two cars, a rusty Toyota and Roxanne's yellow Corvette. Beside the front door a breeze stirred the beer-stained rebel flag hanging off a pole.

With his binoculars, he could see into a large eight by ten window in her apartment.

He waited an hour, the knife beside him in a croker sack. Nothing stirred except the rebel flag.

He didn't have a warrant. First, he wanted to find the case with the other knives, then, return with a warrant on Wednesday, her slowest night, and search the place. He'd know exactly where to look.

A cloud no bigger than a child appeared above the bar.

Fear like a wind gust passed over him. Was the cloud an admonition? A misty mannikin sky-born? Sent to ward him away?

Shake it off, he told himself. Mind tricks, par for the course.

She often boasted she slept all day on Sundays, but he wanted to be sure, so he waited one more hour.

Still no movement.

Carrying a backpack with tools wrapped in cotton, he approached the downstairs window, covered with an iron grill. She had removed the jagged shards of glass around the frame, so it stood open for the stench of beer, fries and cigarette smoke to air out. Inside, tables were righted, the bar b que cleaned up, but the brunette was still missing teeth.

He unscrewed the grill, laid it on the ground and slipped in.

After he removed his boots and left them by the window, he searched the kitchen. The ice maker released a rumbling chunk; he startled. He opened all the cabinets, searched the refrigerator, high shelves, low shelves, big cartons of napkins, straws, stirrers, liquor, beer, and wine.

In the storage room, stashed behind a box of hot dog buns, crammed down so deep he was sweating by the time he cleared a path, he found it, a five knife cedar case with only four knives in it, two on each side of the missing middle. The name embossed on the cover: Yarenh Best Chef. He pulled the knife from the croker sack. When he slid it in, it snapped with the precision of a Starbucks lid.

In Ocopeeco gossip spread like kudzu in July, but Big Rig and Roxanne? He'd never seen them together. Usually, rumors got back to him, but he had heard nothing, ever. She grew up in Florida and didn't know the trucker in school. She'd been in town for what? Ten years? He lost himself in speculation, motives, connections, histories.

The light switched on.

"Had to keep picking, didn't you?"she said, a pistol aimed at him, her face a flank steak pounded by the edge of a saucer. She stood squared under the single light bulb in the door, a booze-peddling angel of judgement.

"Put the gun down, Roxanne. It's over."

He set the knife case down. "Ocopeeco is my home, Roxanne. I don't just do a job. If something's wrong, I want to make it right."

"Oh, something's wrong all right. But you don't have a clue."

She pulled off her wig, revealing a bald head. Then she unsnapped her fake breasts. They dangled from their adhesive tape like limp-headed, shotgun-blasted ducks.

HB put his hand over his eyes, half-chuckling, "Well, I'll be double-d-damned!"

"Oh, c'mon, chief, that all you got? Some good old boy cliché?"

"Roxanne . . . wait, what's your real name?"

"Bobby Gene Farnsworth. Chief, your train runs on the straight line, 24/7. You see goodness every-damned-where. You would never have clocked me. For ten years in Miami I headlined at Cock Hudson's. Guys hit on me every time I went to the grocery store. That's how good I was. Now, some of the old regulars here, they have their suspicions, late at night, they mutter stuff, but Big Rig Scruggs, ooooh, he flat clocked me. I mean it was weird. I'd heard tell at Cock's about certain men you could never fool. It was like a legend. I'd never seen one, but Big Rig was it. And the whole cross dress thing revved his troglodyte engines. You know he batted on both sides of the plate, right?"

"I have recently learned that."

"Well, I see a black woman over in Macon, a computer programmer every Friday night. Big Rig knew I was straight. I told him I didn't want to hook up, but he told me he'd pay me $1,000, provided I would dress like Roxanne. But when I realized how violent he would be, I tried to get away, but he raped me, Oct. 25, 2014. After that, he found out about that little malfeasance charge hanging over me from Cock's and he had me over a barrel. I became his little ATM/sex machine. So last year I had enough and gutted that over-sexed gorilla at the shack like the bottom feeder he was. Had to tie his body to my 'Vette to get him to the river."

"I'm sorry about the violation."

"It don't bother me," Bobby Gene said.

"I'd have to disagree with you on that."

"What?"

"Trauma infects you, a mental sepsis sets in, poisons every smile till all smiles cease."

When the cross dresser sneered, the grease on his upper lip resembled the glissando of a green snake, darting away.

"Like you give a damn."

"A jury in Jeffersonville might understand. Heck, Lurleen might even testify on your behalf. The man was evil. I imagine once you tell the whole story they will show you some leniency."

Bobby Gene raised the pistol to eye level, supported it with his other hand and took aim.

"No, they won't," he said, "cause I'll be long gone, and you'll be dead."

Then he fired.

HB spun, dervished by pain and fell back, sending boxes flying and for a few seconds the room went black.

When his head cleared, his left shoulder ice pick throbbed, and his blood pressure and heart rate had dropped. He was sprawled over a box of straws, blood in his mouth where he bit his tongue, the visible world slantdicular and his mind an anthill panic.

Someone pounded a flat head screwdriver into an ignition, sparks sputtered, and the engine revved to a high-pitch scream in the old Toyota.

But he was fading again. He fumbled for his phone and called Rosie.

"It's Roxanne," he said. His consciousness was laddering down, so he talked fast. "She killed Big Rig."

"What! Are you hurt?"

"Not bad. Call the Bibb County Sheriff. Tell him to head to the bus station in Macon. I'm Okay. I'll call Grace to drive me to the ER. I'm fine. But you have to call the sheriff—he needs to get to the bus station, now Rosie!!"

Rosie whipped the wheel off to the side of the two lane. Kudzu plunged down the banks on both side of the road. Her heart surged in quick thrusts.

The woman uncoils a sleazy come-on to him in the middle of a funeral; then she lures him up the water tower every Christmas; now she shoots him!

She switched off her phone. He'd call her back, she knew it. To make sure.

Lying on the boxes, tossing and re-tossing in the breaking waves of consciousness, he jerked up.

He forgot to tell her: Roxanne wasn't Roxanne! And she wouldn't be driving the 'Vette.

He tried her cell again, but she'd cut it off.

Rosie pulled her pistol out from under the dash. What was running through her mind might cost her husband his job. After all, this was a nation of laws. But she had noticed over the years that the laws in her adopted country were applied selectively according to education, wealth and class. And pity the poor sheriff's deputy, who'll have no idea the woman he's facing's a cop shooter and a killer. Probably an innocent green recruit, wife, new baby, freshly shaved and oozing hope, who'll walk into a deadly situation thinking how hard can it be to arrest an old lady who dyes her hair bar room gold.

* * * *

The antique lamps atop the concrete rails reminded her of the ones across the Rhine just below Cologne. In her Uni days she crossed daily in an ancient Peugeot so decrepit she could see the pavement passing under her feet.

She slowed down to turn into the bus station parking lot. Three times she drove through.

No yellow Corvette, Roxanne's car.

She pulled into an empty slot and switched off the ignition.

He said the bus station. She toyed with contacting him. But she wanted to do this, alone. She wanted revenge; she wanted to punish that gold glittery she-wolf for all the pain she'd caused her family.

Her father's voice barked: "Don't do this!"

But the violent history of her adopted country had opened a door. She wasn't about to refuse it.

Finally, she had to pee.

The brightly lit waiting room was filled with well-slid church pews, grape leaves carved on the arm rests, an homage to the Baptist church on the site before the station was built. The smell of cigarette smoke and chewing gum. Clumps of passengers slumped in the pews, bedraggled moms with squirming toddlers and a chatty skin head at the ticket counter, yukking it up with the clerk.

In the restroom mirror she told herself the woman was probably halfway to Atlanta by now, or if she headed south, halfway to Tallahassee. She applied gloss, ran her index finger around her lips and stepped back into the waiting room.

The skin head turned her way and for a second, stared at her.

A fleshy face, large, oily lips and what? The residue of eyeliner?

Instinct told her to sit, so she scrolled through her phone, aping invisibility, even as she glanced up and back at him, her legs crossed and bouncing.

"Bus Three," the skin head said, turning away from the clerk. "Ten minutes."

"Yessir," the clerk said, "this time of day, Sunday afternoon, Atlanta traffic is not too bad."

"Great!"

Carrying a backpack, the skin head passed in front of her on his way to the exit. He paused, stooped down. "Ma'am, you sure look mighty lost."

She slipped her phone into her purse, assumed a forced smile, and even though her stomach was knotted like a rock, she looked up.

"What makes you say that?" Rosie said.

He leaned back and folded his arms. "Now, honey, I know me a broken heart when I see one."

When he sat down beside her, he thrust a gun in her ribs.

"We've all been there, sweetheart. Lord, I'm old as Methuselah, but I remember every single one. Why don't you and me step outside so you can have you a good cry?"

He jammed the gun deeper.

On the sidewalk outside he put his gun in his jeans pocket and grabbed her elbow. "What the hell are you doing here?" he hissed.

Her chin trembled. "I'm . . . I'm helping my husband . . . "

His lips to her ear. "Honey, your husband is dead. Dead and done."

A deep voice spoke from behind him: "Not dead and not nearly done."

HB, arm in a sling and a black Bibb County sheriff's deputy 6' 5" with sinewy arms and huge, long-fingered hands. He slipped the gun out of Bobby Gene's pants.

"Gimme your hands," the deputy said and grabbed the back of the assailant's neck whose mouth opened. "Argh-gh-gh!"

When he resisted, the deputy squeezed his trapezius, and a girlish squeal came out. He dropped to his knees.

"Jesus, you big ape, that's excessive force!"

HB leaned down and whispered. " I've seen Deputy Wells' excessive force. That was a love tap."

He put his arm around his wife. "Rosie, I want you to meet Bobby Gene Farnsworth, alias Roxanne Sapp. The cross-dressing killer of Big Rig Scruggs."

She backed away, shaking her head, looking back and forth at the killer and HB. "I knew I'd seen him before!"

As he was dragged to the car, Bobby Gene sneered and yelled over his shoulder: "You fat Nazi cunt!"

Deputy Wells shoved him in."Shut yo' filthy mouth, boy!"

"Ouch!" HB whispered into her ear.

As the car pulled away, HB took her in his arms.

"I'm an idiot!" she said, "Ein überausgebildeter Scheisskopf!"

"I'll buy that," he said, kissing her forehead.

"How do you do it?"

"Do what?"

"Keep from going to pieces when the guns come out! I've never been so terrified."

He put his arms around her shoulder. "Iggy says it's a charism, a Holy Spirit gift."

"I was saying Hail, Mary's, the Lord's Prayer and Psalms and losing my mind. I'm so sorry. I just didn't know what it takes to do what you do."

"For nearly getting yourself killed and violating a slew of state laws, I know how you can make amends."

"I'll do anything."

"One of your Oma's Kirschtorte."

"Absolutely."

As they approached his truck, he paused and looked at her. "I don't do what I do on my own. Truly, it's a gift. Sometimes I'd like to give it back. But duty doesn't work like that. Steel and stone."

"Steel and stone?"

"Like Maximus. They told him what they would do to him if he continued to preach and teach the truth and what did he do? He spit in their eye. Steel and stone."

"Maximus," she said, as she snuggled against him.

"He was a man."

"I wonder if he and Hildegard have met in heaven."

"Sorry, sweetheart. In heaven there is no marriage."

* * * *

After their third visit, Pain finally absorbed the news, sat up and ate an entire bowl of chicken noodle soup. Gradually, his brain's acceptance of what happened Oct. 25, 2014 informed his body, and his limbs began to stir.

"So, it was Roxanne's or . . . what was his name?"

"Bobby Gene," HB said, slicing a fork into Rosie's Kirschtorte.

"Bobby Gene," the old Creek repeated, nodding his head as a way to insure his memory would retain the name. "It was his pain I felt?"

"And by the time you arrived that afternoon, Big Rig had driven him to a more remote spot."

"And this Bobby Gene killed Big Rig?"

"He did," HB said, sipping coffee.

His Dad sat upright against the oak wood back board of his bed, the empty soup bowl on the lap tray. His single gray bound tail came down his shoulder and lay spread out over an old, tattered quilt blanket.

HB grinned and squeezed Rosie's knee: "Just like Jimmy Buffett says: "It's just a Cuban crime of passion, messy and old fashioned."

Mico looked up from his Kirschtorte. "I didn't know Big Rig was Cuban."

Rosie kissed the top of her son's head.

HB chuckled. "He's not."

"What?" Mico asked, looking around at the adults.

The old Creek's eyes twinkled as he considered his grandson. "Your Dad is making a comparison between two dissimilar situations. He's taking a line from a pop song about a piano player from Miami who killed his girlfriend's lover in Cuba. We'll call that Scenario 1. Your Dad's erroneously applying that line to what he thinks is a similar situation involving Big Rig Scruggs. We'll call that scenario 2. In Scenario 1 there are three people. In Scenario 2 there are only two. In Scenario 1, a man was killed because of heterosexual love. In Scenario 2 a man was killed because of homosexual love. So, the two scenario's aren't even remotely the same, but

Buffett really nailed that line. It's a seven foot line that old Arthur Golding used so well in his translation of Ovid back in the 1600's, not a four feet, three feet, as Buffett would have it."

"And I was worried about you," HB said.

Rosie stood and gave her father-in-law a hug.

"But was this really about Roxanne and Big Rig?" Pain went on.

"What do you mean?" HB said.

For the first time in months, Pain grinned.

"I see a town that was tested. It was tested and it failed. But the town was lucky: there was a make-up, and this time it passed. And it's possible the town may have learned something."

"What?" Rosie asked.

"To value its own."

HB rolled his eyes. "Oh, I don't know about that . . . "

Rosie punched her husband's knee. "Did you tell him?"

"Tell me what?" Pain said.

"The council doubled his salary and, here's the big one: they bought him a fingerprint scanner."

Pain raised his arms. "Hallelujah!"

Finis

www.ingramcontent.com/pod-product-compliance
Lightning Source LLC
Chambersburg PA
CBHW051819020726
47502CB00005B/1528